THE PULPIT LADIES

Shelia Writes Books

Perfect Stories About Imperfect People Like You...and Me!

Book 14
"My Son's Wife" series

"Perfect Stories About Imperfect People
Like You...and Me"

THE PULPIT LADIES

Shelia Writes Books

Perfect Stories About Imperfect People Like You...and Me!

Book 14
"My Son's Wife" series

NATIONAL BESTSELLING AUTHOR
Shelia E. Bell

Acknowledgments

Thank you for reading my work! Plain and simple. No elaborate words. No rambling. Just a simple and humble "Thank You."

Thank you to every reader, beta reader, editor, friend, critic, book club, social media person(s), and those who help me to live my literary dreams!

I love what I have been assigned to do. I thank God for His continued grace, unmerited favor, and mercy. I thank Him for His continued blessing of mental, physical, emotional, and financial health and wealth. Most of all, I am thankful He isn't through with me yet!

SHE IS MORE

precious

THAN JEWELS

• PROVERBS 31:10 •

Chapter 1

Don't Look Back

"Don't ruin a new day by thinking about yesterday." Unknown

"Look, sweetheart, I keep telling you not to stress about things out of your control. When you do that, it means you're not putting your total trust and faith in God," Christian Black told his wife.

Luna looked at him like she didn't know him. How could he tell her not to worry or stress when she was walking around every day, not knowing who had sexually assaulted her and if they would come for her again? The one thing that came out of that horrifying time sixteen months ago was Little Laiyah Rose. She looked at her sweet baby girl asleep on their bed and smiled before her face turned back into a frown.

"Seems like we're no closer to finding that...that monster."

Christian stepped behind her before wrapping his arms around her waist and pulling her into a gentle embrace. He pressed a soft kiss to the side of her neck. "Didn't I promise we'd do everything to find him? I meant that. We won't give up, and we won't let the police give up, either."

Luna nodded and leaned her head against his chest. The past months had been stressful.

Having a seven-month-old, a two-year-old, and a husband was rewarding, but it was a new level of *different* for Luna. She was used to the corporate, big-time senior executive lifestyle that reaped bountiful rewards for her professionally, financially, and emotionally. She and Christian had lucrative careers that allowed them to take luxury vacations if they chose or travel at a whim. But living that lifestyle was nothing compared to motherhood.

She enjoyed taking care of Laiyah Rose and Dax. Her love for her children was unexplainable. Yet, when it came to her baby girl, every time she looked at her, it was a constant reminder of how the child was conceived. The nightmares were far less, but they were still a part of her life. She was mentally tormented even more because she didn't know who the man was. But she believed it had to be someone who knew her and that she wasn't some random person he had abducted off the street. After hearing the man's strange voice and smelling that distinct scent at Pastor's repast a few months prior, she believed he was someone who traveled in their circles. He must have known Stiles or Pastor. What other reason would he be at the repast?

She felt Christian's embrace and soft kiss pulling her from her tormenting thoughts.

"Come on," he said tenderly, "let's finish getting ready."

"You're right," she said, turning toward him and smiling. "I wouldn't want my favorite, newly appointed deacon to be late." She kissed him on his lips, turned, and walked past.

He playfully swatted her backside.

Upon arriving at New Holy Rock, Luna went to her usual pew after taking both kids to the nursery. Taking them to the church nursery was something she'd recently started doing. She was leery about leaving them in the past, not because she didn't think they would be watched after, but simply because she was a doting mother who trusted no one with her kids. But she had come to know and befriend many of the people at New Holy Rock. She also volunteered once a month to work in the nursery, providing her with an extra sense of mental comfort.

As the service started, she scanned many familiar faces in the pews. With pride, she watched Christian fulfill his role. Today was what New Holy Rock called "Sacrament Sunday," and Christian was excited to assist with the Lord's Supper. Christian had been a deacon at the church he and Luna were members of when they lived in New York, so he was equally grateful when Stiles appointed him to serve at New Holy Rock.

At the end of the service, Stiles announced, "We are presenting before God and committing their lives to the one and only Savior, these little ones whose parents and guardians are bringing to the altar. Pastor McCoy," Stiles said, "will you please come forward and give the blessing over these little ones."

As the congregation began singing, the parents, with their little ones, walked toward the front of the sanctuary, stopping at the altar.

As one of the men passed her row, Luna inhaled the almost medicinal scent she would never forget. Her palms grew clammy, and the edges of her vision blurred. This was the first time she could see his face because she never saw his face during the assault, but his voice and that scent were seared into her memory. Every instinct screamed to get up and run, but her legs felt anchored to the carpeted floor.

"When I come to you," Hezekiah said to the parents, "please introduce yourselves and your child to the congregation. The word of God says to train up a child in the way he should go, and when he is old, he will not depart from it. Today, you are standing here, making the first crucial step toward these little ones' eternal futures. You are presenting them back to the one and only God."

Hezekiah soon stood before the man Luna believed could be her abductor. The man stood next to a short, narrow-hipped Asian woman with flowing, coarse black hair, which Luna assumed was his wife.

"My name is Maria Torres. This is my baby...our baby, Carmen Valentina Torres," she said, looking at her baby and then up at the man who towered over her.

"We are committing her life back to God," the man said, picking up where the mother left off. "My wife and I have much to be grateful for as she has struggled to conceive for many years. God has heard our prayers," he said in broken English. His voice was deep and demanding.

Luna suddenly felt sick. The baby looked like a replica of Laiyah Rose. She had the same thick black hair, oddly shaped eyes, and olive complexion as Laiyah Rose. *Could this be the monster that ruined my life?* But now, listening

4

to him, his voice sounded different from what she remembered. And that scent may not have been exactly how her abductor smelled. Or was it? She was confused, with a thousand doubts running through her mind.

Luna and the man seemed to lock gazes for a split second, causing her heart to race like she was in the Indy 500. *That's not him,* she told herself. No way could someone as evil as the man who assaulted her be standing at the front of the church, professing to have a relationship with God. But if this *was* him, then he deserved to be roasting in hell, not in a church dedicating his kid.

For the first time in her life, the church's familiar safety now felt like a trap, and she was once again a prisoner. She stiffened as memories of her assault and kidnapping surfaced in vivid flashes. At the same time, Hezekiah effortlessly continued the christening while Christian gloried in his newly appointed position, oblivious that his wife was falling apart on the inside.

She struggled to contain her emotions on the drive from New Holy Rock to their suburban home.

"You good?" he asked, briefly looking away from the road at her.

"Yes, I'm good. We'll talk at home," she whispered.

She didn't want their kids to see her emotionally upset, so she put in her earbuds and turned on her playlist.

Arriving home thirty-five minutes later, Luna put the kids in their highchairs, and she and Christian prepared lunch.

Afterward, with a tray of sandwiches, chips, and sodas, Luna and Christian went into the family room while the kids ate. Their home's open-style layout gave them a clear view of them at all times. Laiyah Rose already had a face full of mac and cheese, and the rest was spread across her highchair like she was designing a masterpiece. Christian and Luna laughed, seeing the mess she made as she ventured into the excitement of feeding herself.

Dax was a two-year-old with a gigantic appetite. He had already devoured his serving of mac and cheese and had started eating his second of three fish sticks.

"It was him," Luna insisted, putting a handful of chips into her mouth.

"I don't know, sweetheart. I think it's someone you *think* may be him. I'm not trying to downplay your feelings or what you believe you saw, but I want you to be realistic. How likely would it be for the person who abducted you to show up at New Holy Rock with his wife and kid? What would be the sense in that?" Christian said.

"I don't know, and maybe it doesn't make sense, but I'm telling you, he looked at me like he was letting me know it was him. I'm scared, Christian," Luna began crying.

Christian moved next to her and held her in his arms, hoping to comfort her and bring her some sense of ease to replace the fear attacking her. He loved his wife. He wanted nothing more than to have whoever was responsible for the assault to be arrested and put behind bars for life.

6

It was because of this monster that Christian still found it hard to love his daughter the way she deserved. He was still aloof with her at times, especially during times like this when Luna was having a moment, and all Christian could relive was knowing another man had gotten his wife pregnant. It wasn't Laiyah Rose's fault; he understood that, but he was human and beyond perfect. He could only pray that God would soften his heart and show him how to love and fully accept Laiyah Rose as his daughter, just as he loved and accepted Dax.

Chapter 2

Skeletons

"Let today be the day you learn the grace of letting go and the power of moving on." S. Maraboli

After the Monday morning briefing, Christian went into his office and called Stiles.

"Hey, what's up, Black," Stiles answered, nursing a cup of lukewarm coffee while leaning back in his office chair.

"I need your help." Christian went on to tell him about the couple at yesterday's christening and what Luna's thoughts were.

"Man, that's crazy. But to answer your question, they joined New Holy Rock a few weeks ago at midweek service. You and Luna weren't there. I think one of the kids had a fever or something. But, yeah, anyway, he and his wife joined. If I remember, they migrated here from Venezuela. They arrived in the States a few months before the pandemic. I can't believe you haven't seen him around. He's part of New Holy Rock's housekeeping staff. We hired him a few months ago," Stiles told him.

"Hmmm. He legal?" Christian inquired.

"Hah, what you trying to do? Get me in some immigration trouble?"

"You know me betta than that," replied Christian. "I'm just trying to find out as much as possible about this guy. I told you, Luna thinks he could be the kidnapper. If he is, I won't rest until I make him pay."

"I don't know much about him. I rarely see him, but I've heard no complaints from the staff. I've talked to him briefly, but his English is quite limited, and it's the same for me when it comes to Spanish—I understand very little. But I didn't get any weird vibes. He seemed straight."

"I heard that. Well, I'm going to look into his background a little deeper. See what I can find out. I want Luna to feel safe and secure when coming to church or going anywhere for that matter."

"I want that for her, too," said Stiles. "I want whoever did this to her to pay for his crimes. Hey, why don't you check with Hezekiah too? See if he knows anything more than I do. He's more in touch and hands-on with the daily going on of the staff."

"Okay, I'll do that. Well, thanks for your time."

"No problem, my friend. God bless you and Sista Luna. Have a good one. Talk to you later."

After the call with Stiles, Christian followed up by calling Hezekiah.

"You've reached Hezekiah McCoy's voicemail. Please leave a message...."

"Hezekiah, it's Christian. Hit me back up at your convenience. I want to talk to you about one of the employees at New Holy Rock—Nicolas Torres."

While waiting for Hezekiah to call him back, Christian began researching Torres. He was surprised to discover that Torres previously worked as a custodian in the building where

Luna worked. Christian found it even more odd that Torres now worked at New Holy Rock. Was this a coincidence, or could Torres be tracking Luna? He grabbed his phone and keys, checked his back pocket for his wallet, and dashed to his garage. This was one of those times he was glad Luna hadn't returned to work because he was going to go to her office building and ask some questions, and he didn't want her anywhere around when he did.

†

Luna fed Dax a snack and breastfed Laiyah Rose, and now they were down for the first of two naps they took during the day. She moseyed into the kitchen and poured a glass of sugar-free root beer before going into the family room and propping her feet on the ottoman.

She sighed heavily. She was already tired, and it was only a little past noon, but she'd been up since the crack of dawn. Between spending most of the morning feeding, dressing, and playing with the kids, she had washed a load of clothes, put in another load, folded a load from the day before, ran the vacuum, mopped the hardwoods, and dusted the house. Christian had suggested on more than one occasion that they bring on a housekeeper to take some of the load and pressure off Luna.

Christian would help, but that was usually on the weekends and focused more on the kids. Coming home late in the evening after a long day at the office and, most times, in and out of court was draining. Being an executive with heavy responsibilities, Luna understood the demands of his job. Whenever she returned to work, she told herself she wouldn't think twice about hiring a housekeeper. Until then, she would continue to do it herself. She used it as a form of exercise. It was working, too, because Luna had recently lost seven pounds.

She reached for the glass and took a gulp of the refreshing beverage.

Ding.

"Hey, sis. What's up this morning?"

"laid back with my feet propped up."

"L O L. Already? What time is it there? Eleven?"

"No, noon, but I have to take a break when the kids take a break."

"They must be napping?" **Lorie texted.**

"Yeah, but you better believe it won't be for long. What's going on?"

"Not a whole lot."

Luna picked up the phone and FaceTimed her sister. "Hey, I didn't feel like texting back and forth. So what's going on?"

"I was checking to see how everything was with you and the kids," she paused, "and that husband of yours, too."

"We're good. Other than I think I'm beginning to get on hubby's nerves."

"What?" Lorie tilted her head, her brows knitting together. "Why do you say that?"

"You and I haven't talked, other than through text, in a couple of weeks, but since then, I think I saw the man who assaulted me, Lorie. Christian thinks I'm being overly paranoid, but I know what I saw."

"The last time you mentioned anything to me about him was when you said you saw someone who sounded like him or something at that preacher's repast."

"Yes, at Pastor Graham's repast. But that was months ago. But yesterday, at the end of service, we had a baby christening. This couple was one of about five couples that came up to have their babies christened. That's when I saw him."

"Are you serious?" said Lorie after hearing the full recount of the incident.

"Yes. And that baby, Lorie. Lorie, I swear that baby looked like Laiyah Rose. I'm telling you."

"Come on, now, Luna. Like Laiyah Rose? That sounds a little weird," Lorie said.

"It's the truth. I'm serious, Lorie."

"Do you really think that could have been him? And if it *was*, why would he be at your church? Have you seen him there before yesterday?"

"No, but I asked Christian if he knew anything about him. He said he and his wife were new members, and get this, he's the church's new janitor. I'm going to find out more about him. I have to know if it's him or not."

"I don't know, sis. You need to be careful. If it turns out that this *is* the guy, then you know he's dangerous. Please don't do anything foolish."

"I won't. I have my kids to think of. But if that *is* him, I don't want that monster walking around free to hurt me or anyone else ever again. You know what I mean?"

"Yeah, I do. But enough of the creepy talk. On a lighter note, I thought you'd like to know that I met a guy."

"O M G! Lorie, that's great. Tell me all about him."

The sisters chatted for half an hour when Dax woke up, calling for his daddy and for food.

"Eat. Nuggets," he said. "Eat. Nuggets."

Dax rarely called for Luna, but she'd learned to get past her feelings of insecurity about it. She often told Christian that God blessed them with two children, one for him and one for her. They would laugh over that.

"Look, I gotta go, Lorie. Dax is awake, and of course, he's screaming to eat like he's starving."

Lorie laughed. "I hear him. That little boy is so funny. Love you, sis. Buh-bye. Oh, and kiss them for me."

At the end of the call, Lorie held her phone while sitting at her office desk, wondering just who the man was who attacked her sister. Could it be someone from Luna's past? It had been years since the sisters had seen each other or been in each other's lives until six months ago. Before then, Lorie had no idea what kind of lifestyle her sister and Christian lived. Then again, they didn't know her lifestyle either. Yes, she was a successful businesswoman in the real estate arena, but her personal love life was in a shambles.

Lorie was looking for love, the kind of love Luna and Christian appeared to have. She couldn't help but smile when she relived those stolen nights she'd spent with Christian Black.

"Ummm, all things happen for a reason," Lorie mouthed, twirling in her chair and tapping the desk with her long, polished fingernail. "But I'm here to tell you, big sis, you better keep your man full because if you don't, he might get fed somewhere else." Lorie laughed, shook her head, and then turned to face her computer. "Time to get back to making this money."

Chapter 3

Second Chances

"Moving on is easy." Shelia E. Bell

"Fancy, this is the job of a lifetime! Think about it. In two weeks, I will officially start my new position as senior account executive at one of the top ad agencies in the South. Oh, did I mention they're starting me at seventy-five K!" Victoria squealed with excitement.

"O M G! God is good, girl. I'm telling you. It couldn't happen to a better person, Vicky. You deserve it. You've worked hard, and you've earned it."

"Thanks, bestie. I know this position will be one of the best jobs I've ever had. I mean, the salary alone is enough to change my life. No more struggling or having to rob Peter to pay Paul. You know what I mean?"

"Yes, that is amazing. When God opens doors, I tell you, he opens them wide!"

"Yes, he does. So when I receive my first check, you and I are going to hit this city running," Victoria exclaimed. "We'll do lunch at one of the fanciest restaurants in town. Then we'll do some retail therapy and whatever else our little ol' hearts desire."

Both ladies laughed.

"I can't wait," said Fancy. "Now, tell me what's up with you and your new boo."

"I like him. We have fun together and good conversations, and did I mention he's a great lover."

"I don't get it then, so what's your hangup?"

Victoria shrugged. "I don't know. I'm fifty years old, Fancy. I don't have time for all the drama. My life is easy now, and it's about to get even easier. At least, I hope so with this new job. But still, I don't want to deal with someone underfoot all day and night. I used to think I wanted a man, you know, someone to spend the rest of my life with."

"What happened, Vicky? What changed?"

"I've been married and been divorced. Dated around. Ran into some bums. Met some possibles. I even witnessed the downfall of *your* relationship. I saw how much Hezekiah and Winston hurt you. Then you meet a good man, Micah Daniels, who thought the sun rose and shined on you, and look what happened to him. Some crazy, jealous B takes his life," Victoria said, her words filled with rage.

Fancy's face reddened at the thought of her lost love, Micah Daniels. He was such a good man. She was falling in love with him, but for some reason or other, she felt like God said that was another no-no, and He allowed him to be taken.

"Vicky, I'm so sorry; God knows I am. I had no idea my problems affected you like that."

"It's not just your problems, Fancy. That's not what I'm saying. I'm talking about relationships. Period. Look at my daughter. Pepper is gobbling anxiety pills like Skittles because she blames herself for Xavier's suicide. Look, I'm sorry for bringing up bad memories."

"It's okay. With God's help, I'm learning to cope with his death. I feel sorry for Pepper, though. I hate she feels the way she does."

"Me too, Fancy," Vicky sighed.

"As for you, it's perfectly fine to want someone in your life, Vicky."

"Am I wrong for wanting to be content dating and having a nice male companion without all the other baggage?"

"No, you're not wrong, but let me ask you this. What about Stiles? He was a good guy. And yes, I've heard your story a thousand times about you not wanting to be a first lady. But did you really give that relationship a chance, Vicky?" Fancy questioned.

"Yes, I gave it a chance. I stayed in it longer than I should have, and not because of anything bad happening. It was me. I've told you that and told Stiles, too, when I broke up with him. But you're right; Stiles is a good guy. And Mya is the perfect person for him. I couldn't be happier for them. This guy I'm seeing now is cool so far. He's a few years older. He goes with the flow. My flow, I should say. Which means I like things just the way they are. If I want him to spend the night occasionally, or he wants me to spend the night with him occasionally, that's fine. He travels a lot with his job, so that's an added plus. I believe he understands that I mean it when I say I only want a casual relationship. Then again, I told him I also don't want someone who sleeps around or still wants to be a player. I know you may say I can't have it both ways, but this guy,

I think he's pretty much on the same page as me. He's around Hezekiah's age. He's originally from Butte. His family still lives there."

"Wait, did you say Butte? As in Butte, Montana?"

Vicky nodded.

"Are there any Black folks in Butte?" Fancy asked, looking wide-eyed in surprise and chuckling.

"Uh," Vicky smiled and replied, "I never said he was Black, did I?"

"Well, excuse me. You mean you went and got yourself a white boy?"

"Yep. I told you, at my age, all I'm looking for is good companionship. Someone who treats me nice. Who has his own and doesn't have a lot of drama. If he meets that criteria, who cares what color he is."

Fancy nodded in agreement. "I heard that. Tell me about him."

"He's been married twice and divorced twice."

Fancy frowned.

Vicky continued, ignoring Fancy's scowl. "Hey, it is what it is. I can deal with that. I've had a ton of relationships. Thank God I only married once. He has grown kids with his second wife and three grandchildren."

"What's he do for a living and why is he in Memphis?"

"He's an executive at FedEx. His main office is headquartered here, but because of his position, he gets to travel free, so he sees his family often. They live in Montana, except for his oldest son. He lives on the East Coast. Anyway, that's the full rundown on my secret lover." Victoria laughed out loud.

"Does this secret lover have a name?" Fancy's expression changed from a scowl to a pleasant look.

"Uh, do you have to know ev-e-ry-thing?" Victoria asked.

"I sure do," Fancy replied, "so what is it?"

"Wyatt."

"Wyatt—hmmm, Wyatt," Fancy said, smiling.

"Good. Now, enough about Wyatt and me. What's going on with you and the man living in your backyard who just happens to be your ex-husband?"

"He just signed another six-month lease," Fancy quickly said, almost mumbling.

"Uhh, will you repeat that?" Victoria asked, pretending she didn't understand her.

"You heard me. His lease was up last month. He only signed a six-month lease initially. We talked the other day, and I mean, since things are going well, we don't see any reason to change the setup we have. He said he's in no rush to move anywhere, and honestly, I'm in no rush for him to move either. He likes the casita. He likes the privacy of Lion's Gate. I mean, think about it. If Hezekiah wasn't renting it, I'd be listing it again as an Airbnb with God knows who staying in the back of me. Like you told me at the beginning, he's someone I know. He pays his rent on time. He loves to help when I have the grandkids. He even does a little handiwork around the place. I mean, it's a win-win for both of us. And, before you even ask, I've told you once, if not a thousand times, that we have not messed around. Not one time. It's the farthest thing from my mind," Fancy said.

"You don't have to explain anything to me. You certainly don't have to try to convince me about whether the two of you are sharing the sheets. You're both grown. Whatever works for you and Hezekiah works for me. I don't want you walking around here fooling yourself."

"What do you mean, fooling myself?" Fancy said, adjusting herself on the FaceTime screen.

"Please, you know what I mean. You still have feelings for the man. I don't care what he's put you through; you still love him. I'm your bestie. I know these things. And it's obvious he still has feelings for you, too."

"Vicky," Fancy sighed, "let's not go there. Not today."

"Hey, lucky you. You just got off the hook. This is Pepper trying to call me. We'll pick this conversation back up another time. Talk to you later."

"Okay, see ya, Vicky."

Fancy went into the kitchen and began washing dishes. She rarely left dirty dishes, but earlier, she had rushed out of the house to avoid being late for a meeting at Holy Rock. She usually prided herself on being prompt, but waking up to rain and thunderstorms put her behind schedule. First, she overslept. She knew she shouldn't have taken that Tylenol, but the fierce storm caused her head to hurt, and the caplet put her out like a light. The flip side was that when it was time to wake up, she hit the snooze button twice before realizing she would definitely be late if she didn't get up when she did. The rain was already going to slow her down.

She managed to make it just in time for the meeting, which lasted a little less than two hours. After that, she talked to Khalil and Sista Mavis and then headed home to work on some designs for a client. She didn't get much done because that's when Victoria FaceTimed her, and they ended up talking for almost two hours.

With the kitchen tidied up, she looked at her Apple watch; it was 3:57 p.m. She went to her office and worked on designs for a newlywed couple from Holy Rock who had purchased a fixer-upper and hired Fancy as their interior designer. God was definitely making room for her to use her gifts.

Another huge blast of thunder followed by lightning seemed to shake the house. Fancy jumped. At the same time, the doorbell rang.

"Who is this? The guard gate didn't call me," she said, feeling a little nervous.

She opened the door quickly, just as another round of thunder and lightning darted across the sky.

"Get in here," she barked, stepping aside to a dripping-wet Hezekiah. "What happened?"

"That rain is coming down like it's about to be a tornado. When I got to the casita, I couldn't find my keys. I must have left them on my office desk. Of course, it didn't take but a few seconds for me to get drenched. That storm ain't playing. It's not even five o'clock, and it looks like it's ten o'clock at night," he complained.

"I know," Fancy said, "But stay right there. No, wait, step over into the mudroom," she said, pointing to her left.

Hezekiah did as he was instructed.

"Get out of those wet clothes. There are clean towels on the shelf."

"Hol' up, there's no need for all that. I just came to get the extra key. I'll dry off when I get home," Hezekiah insisted.

"Right, but you can still dry off a little. I don't want you dripping water and mud all over my hardwoods," she scolded, but not in a harsh manner.

"I know how you are. You don't want a drop of water on your floors." Hezekiah laughed, grabbed a hand towel off the mudroom shelf, and wiped his head and face.

"Let me get it. Oh yeah, don't forget to take off your shoes. I'll be right back. You can go through the kitchen so you won't get as wet, " Fancy said.

"Thanks, have a good night," Hezekiah said when she returned. He reached down and petted Sebastian gently while he sat in the kitchen corner, eating his evening meal.

"Good night," she said, "I mean good afternoon."

Fancy watched as Hezekiah walked out the back door and along the covered, paved steps to his casita. She closed the door as another lightning bolt streaked across the darkening sky.

Sighing heavily, almost as if she were heartbroken, Fancy retreated to her bedroom again, all alone.

22

Chapter 4

We Can Work It Out

"Just because you miss someone doesn't mean you
need them back in your life." Unknown

Tornado warnings and relentless thunderstorms
battered the mid-south throughout the evening
and into the night.

Fancy never was one to fully embrace rain,
let alone a storm like this. As a child, she was
taught that whenever it stormed, God was
speaking, trying to warn his children. The
storms often scared her as a child, and now, as
a woman about to turn fifty-two in a few
months, part of her was still frightened,
especially when they were fierce like they were
now.

She lay in her bed, her nightstand lamp on,
trying to read since she couldn't sleep. A loud
boom caused her to jump, and immediately, she
was surrounded by darkness. She huddled in
the bed, pulling the covers around her. Her
phone rang, and she jumped when it lit up.

"Hey, Hezekiah," she whispered, almost like
a frightened kid.

"Did I wake you?"

"No, you know better than that."

"I do, but I also know things change. I didn't
know if you still had that fear. But you good up
there?" he asked.

"Not really. The lights are out. I guess you could say I should be able to sleep, but now I'm as wide awake as ever." She screamed slightly when another round of thunder boomed.

"I'll be up there in a second. You think you can find your way through the dark to the back door to let me in?"

"I can use the flashlight on my phone," she said. "But are you sure you want to come and babysit a grown woman afraid of a storm?"

"Open the door. I'm on my way."

Minutes later, Hezekiah dashed into the back door and removed his jacket and shoes.

"I can't offer you anything with the power out," she lamented. "Oh, I have bottled water, an open bottle of wine, and some diet root beer."

"I don't think so. It's almost one o'clock in the morning. I'm not that kind of drinker of anything anymore, or else I'll be. Never mind." He smiled, removing his jacket and stepping out of his shoes.

The light from the phone illuminated his handsome face, and suddenly, she imagined him pulling her into his arms and taking advantage of her.

"Come on, let's get out of this kitchen," he said.

"Of course."

They walked through the house until they reached her bedroom.

"I'll sit in the chair," he said, using the light from his phone to lead him to it.

"You get some sleep," he told her, propping his feet on the matching ottoman. "I'll be right here."

"Wait, let me get you some cover." With the flashlight still on, she went to the linen closet and returned with a colorful oversized throw. She grabbed one of her pillows from off her bed.

"Here you go."

"Thanks."

"I appreciate you doing this. It's been a long time since we've had a storm like this. Sebastian won't even come out. He's hiding around here somewhere."

"Look, I don't mind, Fancy. Now, go to sleep."

"Yes, sir," she said, giggling and turning over onto her side. She mouthed a quick prayer and closed her eyes. Almost as soon as she did, she felt a weight on the bed behind her.

It was Sebastian. He rubbed against her and meowed until she cuddled him in her arms.

†

The following morning, Fancy yawned, stretched, and sat up in bed. The nightstand light was on, indicating the power was back on. She'd forgotten that Hezekiah had come over during the night but quickly remembered when she looked toward her chair and saw Sebastian lying on top of folded covers instead of Hezekiah.

Taking a moment to fully awaken, she sat on the side of her bed. Sunrays peeped through the wooden plantation blinds. She exhaled deeply, relieved that the storm had passed.

Suddenly, the aroma of coffee attacked her nostrils, and like a magnet, it drew her toward the kitchen. She stopped in the hallway, turned around, and dashed to the bathroom to brush her teeth and wash her face.

"Good morning," Hezekiah said just as she entered.

"Good morning," Fancy said, stifling a yawn by placing a hand over her mouth.

"Here's your coffee," he said. "You'll have to add whatever you want to it."

"Thank you. And thanks again for staying with me last night. I told you I couldn't sleep, yet I don't remember a thing. I think Sebastian got in the bed, and that's it."

"Yep, you were out like a light. You snored a little, then a lot." He laughed.

She playfully tapped him on his back. "Liar," she said.

"Ask Sebastian. Why do you think he was in the chair and not your bed?" Hezekiah laughed.

She placed her cup on the counter, opened the pantry, and removed a bin. "The least I can do to pay you back for your kindness is make your favorite breakfast." She did not wait for a response. She started gathering utensils and bowls, followed by bacon and eggs from the fridge.

"I will not refuse your offer, my dear Fancy. Do you know how long I've dreamed about having breakfast by Fancy the Creator?" He laughed and grabbed her around her waist, kissing her on the cheek. She looked over her shoulder at him.

He met her glare by kissing her fully on the lips.

Stop, tell him to stop, but the words didn't come out. She took in his caffeine-laced breath and moaned as his lips devoured hers.

As if suddenly stuck with a prod, he backed up. "I'm...I'm sorry. I didn't mean to do that."

"Right. We...that shouldn't have happened," she said softly but with little protest. "We can't do this, Hezekiah."

"I know," he stumbled, "you're right. I'm sorry, Fancy. Look, why don't I do a raincheck on that breakfast? I have a full day and need to get started."

"No, don't go. I'm alright," she said, feeling a familiar tingle in her belly like she almost always did when he was close in her presence. She quickly recovered and joked, "Just don't let it happen again."

They laughed together, but both of them were hiding the war going on inside.

Chapter 5

Kiss Lonely Goodbye

"Life moves forward." Shelia E. Bell

"Remember, *The Pulpit Ladies* meeting starts at two. You need me to get you?" Eliana texted.

Pepper looked at the date on her phone. "Dang, I forgot about it just that quick," she chastised herself. She picked up her phone and called Eliana.

"Hey, girl, I just saw your text. I forgot all about the meeting. My mind has been swamped, and my plate is beyond full. I think I'll pass this one up."

"Really?" questioned Eliana.

"Yeah, I know. Anyway, I'm not a first lady *or* a pulpit lady," Pepper said dryly. "Especially now that Xavier is gone. He was a vital part of New Holy Rock, but that's in the past now."

"It is not about being a pulpit lady, per se, Pepper. I explained that to you already. Maybe I initially envisioned *The Pulpit Ladies* being only for first ladies, but God quickly changed that and told me not to limit it to just first ladies. And first lady or not, you are an essential part of the ministry, Pepper. You know that. You and Luna have been my right hands in getting this ministry off the ground. You have been with me

28

since I told you about it. I couldn't have done it without you. "

"I understand, but Eliana, I have too much going on right now. I'll catch next month's meeting. I promise. Don't be mad," Pepper pleaded.

"I'm not mad. I just wish you'd get out more. You've always been a lively, silly, funny person, a joy to be around. But I don't know where that person is anymore. Now, you always find an excuse not to do things. We provide childcare, so you don't have to worry about the boys. They'll be taken care of. That'll give you a break for at least a couple of hours. You can fellowship with other women and just relax your mind."

"Alright, stop it already, I'll come."

"Yay," Eliana squealed.

"But I don't need you to pick me up. I'll drive. I'll see you later."

†

"The meeting... everything was perfect," Eliana beamed.

"I think we did a pretty good job," Luna said, standing beside Eliana.

"Me too," said Pepper.

"And to think, out of the fifty-three ladies who signed up this month, thirty-seven attended. That's a success, I'll say!" exclaimed Eliana.

"I agree," said Luna.

"I appreciate you two so much." Eliana hugged Luna and then Pepper. "Pepper, I'm so glad you decided to come. I hope you see how much you were needed."

Pepper cracked a slight smile.

"Not to mention, I saw you laughing a time or two. You were interacting like the old Pepper." Her voice trailed off, "You know..., before Xavier."

"I'm going to help you clean up a little, but then I need to go," Pepper said and suddenly rose. "When Khalil returns with the boys, I'm heading home. I know they'll probably be worn out, so hopefully, they'll be ready for a nice long nap. I already know they're going to fall asleep in the car; I guarantee it," Pepper smiled.

The ladies laughed. "Well, come on, let's do this. It shouldn't take us too long to clean up. No one made a big mess or anything. By the time we're done, Khalil will probably be back."

While cleaning, the friends talked.

"Thanks again. Both of you. God is blessing this ministry so quickly." Eliana's eyes sparkled as a smile spread across her face.

"Amen, speak it into existence, First Lady," Luna added.

"Luna, how are things going with you? If you want to share, that is," said Eliana.

Pepper stacked the pile of dirty table linen into an oversized dirty clothes bin on wheels.

"I'm good," Luna said. "I'm actually beginning to enjoy the kids. I feel more confident every day," she said while putting the last of the clean dishes away inside the industrial-size cabinets.

"That's good," Pepper said. "Having two little ones at one time can be rough."

"You are right about that," Luna replied.

"Who has them today? I told you we were having childcare on site," said Eliana.

"I know, but Christian didn't have court today. He came home early, so he's with them."

"You're talking about having two being rough? I have one, and she's a handful. Khaliyah keeps me running," added Eliana.

The ladies laughed.

"And how is Christian doing with Laiyah Rose? Is he becoming a real girl dad yet?" Pepper asked.

Luna put the last of the clean dishes away and leaned against the counter.

"It's no secret that things are still tough for him. I can't thank both of you enough for giving me a place to share my feelings without feeling ashamed and to have friends I trust who won't spread my business. You guys are real friends," Luna said, tears forming.

Eliana and Pepper walked up and gathered their arms around her. "That's what friends are for," said Pepper.

"It's what women of God do for one another," Eliana said.

Luna continued, "All I can say for Christian is that he's trying. I see the effort he makes to hold her, to feed her. But I can clearly see the difference in his relationship with Dax and the one with her," Luna said sadly, looking toward the ground. "It comes easy with Dax. It doesn't seem forced. I can't explain it."

"Maybe Dax being a boy makes it easier, too," said Pepper. "Laiyah Rose is a little girl, so he may just be extra cautious about how he handles her."

"Either way, I believe God is going to work it out. You'll see," Eliana told her and hugged her briefly again.

"At least you know he's trying," said Pepper.

"Right, and I'm grateful," Luna said. "To add to what he's going through, here I am, always talking about the man who did this to me. If I could forget all about him. If I could stop imagining seeing him everywhere I go, like a crazy woman, things could probably return to normal for me and Christian. But I can't do it. I feel like he's always somewhere watching. Who knows? He's probably wondering if my little girl is his. What if he comes for Laiyah Rose? Oh, God," Luna cried.

"Stop it, Luna. He's not going to come for Laiyah Rose or for you. He's going to be found. Sooner or later. But until that happens, please try to live your life and not let him consume your every thought. Rely on your faith," Eliana ministered. "God's your protector. He has angels encamped around you and your family."

"She's right, Luna. And you better believe Christian won't let anyone get close to his family if he suspects they could bring harm to you or those babies," Pepper said.

"Let me say a prayer for you. Come on," Eliana said, reaching out and embracing Pepper and Luna in a circle. After a short but powerful prayer, Khalil appeared in the doorway.

"I'm here to deliver a couple of packages," he said jokingly, entering with Zavion and Davion at his feet and holding his daughter.

When the boys saw Pepper, they ran to her. She kneeled and gave them tight hugs and sloppy kisses.

"Did y'all have a good time with Uncle K?"

"Yes, yes, yes," the boys squealed.

Khaliyah clapped her hands, her daddy still holding her.

"Now that you're here, I can be on my way. Did they eat?" Pepper asked as she took hold of each of the boys' hands.

"They sure did. I took them to that pizza place with all the rides and games. We had a ton of fun."

"Thanks for watching them," Pepper said, walking up to Khalil and hugging him.

"It's not a problem. They're my nephews. I made a promise to you….and to my brother. I'm going to look out for them, Pepper. You can trust me on that. Anytime you need me, give me or Eliana a call."

"I will," Pepper answered.

Khalil then acknowledged Luna. "Hello, Sista, uh, Black, right?"

"Yes," Luna smiled and nodded. "Hello."

"Well, look, I've gotta run. Baby," he said, looking at Eliana, "I'll see you before I leave tonight." He put Khaliyah down. "Daddy will see you later, okay?"

"Okay, Daddy."

He kissed Khaliyah's cheek, then leaned in to kiss Eliana on the lips, but she subtly turned her head, guiding his kiss to her cheek instead. She promised to act a certain way in public, to give the church folk the look of them being a happily married couple, but this was different.

She was with her friends. She didn't have to pretend that everything was peachy and perfect. Khalil knew that, but of course, in Khalil fashion, he acted otherwise.

"What time did you say you were leaving?" she asked.

"Eight-thirty. But I'll be home way before then. So, uh, I'll see you later," he said, his face swollen with disappointment. His shoulders slumped. "Good evening, ladies. God bless." He turned and walked out of the hall.

Eliana grabbed hold of Khaliyah's hand and turned the lights out as they exited the fellowship hall. "Have a good evening, and thanks again for your help. *The Pulpit Ladies* would not thrive without your help. That's for real."

"Girl, please. You know we got you," Pepper said, not mentioning Eliana and Khalil's awkwardness.

"Yep, Pulpit Ladies or not, we sure do," Luna added.

†

On her way home, Pepper stopped at Chick-fil-A and ordered a sandwich and a garden salad for dinner. Her initial intention was to make a plate of leftovers from today's meeting, but the Kitchen Ministry took the remaining food and made individual plates. The Sick and Shut-In Ministry came and dispersed it to the church's homebound.

The boys fell asleep on the drive, just like Pepper predicted.

Arriving home, she got them out of the car, placing one on each hip. Their heads dropped against her shoulder, and she carried the two heavy boys inside. Of course, almost as soon as she walked into the house, their heads popped up like they'd been stuck with a pin.

"Mommy," Davion said. "I want to play with my trucks."

"Me too," Zavion pleaded as she put them down. They took off toward their rooms.

"Only for a few minutes. It's almost bathtime," Pepper said, following behind them as she threw her purse and phone on the foyer table. "Dang, I forgot my food," she fussed, turned, and ran back into the garage.

When she reentered the house, she heard the boys screaming and hollering. She knew them all too well, and that sound meant they were fighting. She raced into their bedroom.

"Stop it, stop that fighting!" she yelled, pulled them apart, and popped each of them on the back of their hands. "I told you never to fight each other. Do you hear me?"

Both boys started crying.

"Hush. You hush right now!" But they cried even louder.

"If your daddy were here, you wouldn't be acting like this," she continued screaming. They cried harder. "But he isn't here, is he? You wanna know why?" She cried and huffed. "Because he would rather die than to be with me, to be with us! But you think it's my fault your daddy isn't here. Don't you," she continued yelling.

She stumbled out of the room, leaving them crying.

"I'm so sorry," she said, dragging herself up the hall.

Angry and frustrated, she went into her bathroom. Opening the medicine cabinet, she removed the bottle of medication. Instead of taking the prescribed dose of one pill, she took two, followed by another one.

She went back to the boys' bathroom and started running their bath water before returning to their bedroom and making them get undressed. They were still crying but not as loud.

"Stop crying, or I'll pop you again!" she threatened.

The little boys stopped crying but kept jerking from the aftermath of having cried so hard.

By the time she bathed them, fed them a snack, and put them to bed, she was feeling the effects of the medication.

She took a quick warm shower, jumped into a nightie, and lay on the couch for a much-needed rest. It had been a long and exhausting day, and she was drained physically and mentally.

As she closed her eyes in sleep, she thought she heard the boys. When she opened her eyes, she thought she saw an image of Xavier standing in front of her.

"Xavier? Xavier, sweetheart, is that you? I knew you weren't dead. I knew you'd come back." A faint and hopeful smile filtered across her face. She eased up on the couch to get a better look, but the apparition was gone as quickly as it had appeared. She scanned the room but saw nothing. Tears formed as a heaviness washed over her. Slowly, she got up.

Almost stumbling and with tears flowing, she returned to the bathroom. She took two more pills, or was it three? She didn't know. She'd lost count. What she did know was that she wanted peace. The kind of peace they talked about in the Bible. But since Xavier's death, peace seemed to elude her at every turn.

Chapter 6

The Masquerade Is Over

"If we are strong, our strength will speak for itself.
If we are weak, words will be of no help."
John F. Kennedy

Later that evening, across town, several people gathered at a local restaurant to commemorate Josie's 87th birthday. They laughed, talked, and reminisced.

"This past year was marred by death, grief, and heartache. But, we still have so much to be grateful for because we've also experienced some good times this past year as well," Stiles shared. "And Sista Josie, stay encouraged. God's got you."

"Yes, he sure does," Josie added. "I know that growing old is a privilege not given to everyone. So I appreciate and thank God every single day that He sees fit to wake me up."

Stiles reached across the table and gently squeezed her wrinkled hand. "I love you, Josie."

"I love you. You're like a son to me," her voice soft and trembling. "You too," she added, looking at Hezekiah and laying her wrinkled hand on his. "Y'all have richly blessed my life. You didn't have to accept me into your family. I had no idea my life would be as blessed and favored as it has been. I miss Pastor every day.

He was a good man and husband, and he loved the Lord."

"Yes, he did," said Stiles, "and we love you, Josie. Thank you for making him a happy man."

"Everything is so nice, Stiles. And I know you helped him put this together." She smiled and looked at Fancy and Mya.

"Thank you, Josie," Stiles said, smiling.

"Sista Josie's right. You did good, honey," Mya leaned in and whispered while squeezing her fiancé's hand.

Stiles kissed her briefly.

"Hol' up, none of that mushy stuff while we're eating," Hezekiah said, chuckling and placing a huge piece of mouthwatering ribeye into his mouth.

"Josie, you have a lot of gifts. I don't know how we'll get all of them in the car." Mya laughed.

The friendly banter continued.

"Hey, Fancy, what happened to our son? I was expecting to see him and Eliana," Hezekiah said, wiping his mouth with the cloth napkin.

"Khalil left last night for a pastor's retreat," Fancy answered.

"Oh, yeah, that's right--in Austin, right?"

"Yes," Fancy said.

"Yeah, he did mention something about that the other day," Stiles said.

"On top of that, Eliana didn't want to bring Khaliyah back out this evening. She had her Pulpit Ladies luncheon today. It was nice. Next time, I'll bring you along, Josie, if you'd like," Fancy offered.

"Yes, baby, that would be real nice," Josie said, nodding.

"But yeah, after they got home Eliana said Khaliyah started whining and pulling at her ear. She thinks she might have an ear infection. She had a slight fever, so she gave her some medication." Fancy looked at her phone and read her incoming text.

"CALL ASAP!"

"Excuse me a sec."

Fancy rose from her chair and left the table. In the ladies' room, she returned Victoria's call. "Hey, what's going on? I had my phone on VIBRATE," she explained after seeing several calls from her best friend she missed.

"Fancy!" Victoria screamed into the phone. "They think Pepper may have overdosed. We're at Baptist Desoto," she cried. "I'm, I'm...." she continued uncontrollably.

"Don't say anything else. I'm on my way."

She returned to the table and hurriedly explained what had happened.

Hezekiah got up quickly. "I'll come with you."

"No, I'll be fine. But I'll call and let you know if I need you to come to pick up the boys," she explained. "I'm not sure if they're with Victoria or not. She didn't say, and I didn't ask after hearing how upset she was." She grabbed her purse and dashed toward the front door.

Hezekiah followed. He opened her car door, allowing her to get inside easily. "Call or text me if I need to come get the boys."

"Don't worry, I will," she said as Hezekiah closed the door.

Fancy drove away, leaving Hezekiah in the parking lot. After a few seconds of watching her drive off, he turned and walked back toward the restaurant.

Fifteen or so minutes after leaving the restaurant, Fancy dashed into the hospital ER. Within minutes, she spotted Victoria.

Victoria jumped up from her seat and rushed toward Fancy. The friends embraced as Victoria burst into tears.

"What happened?" Fancy asked, leading Victoria back to her seat and sitting beside her.

"I don't know. I mean, you know she's been dealing with Xavier's death. I know it's been a year, but she still has a hard time accepting his suicide."

"You know I understand. There's not a day that passes that I don't grieve for him," Fancy sadly stated. "I just hate to see her go through this, and then the babies. My poor grandsons," Fancy cried.

"Pepper blames herself for his death. I hate that the doctor prescribed her those pills. Instead of helping her, it's destroying her. She's abusing those things," Victoria cried.

"*Shhh*, it's going to be fine. Have they told you anything?" Fancy asked as they pulled apart, swiping their tears.

"Only that they're still running tests. I came out here so I would see you when you came."

"What about the boys? Where are they?" Fancy asked.

"Thank God Pepper's neighbor volunteered to take them to her house."

"That's good. So tell me what happened."

41

"I was going to spend the night at her house because she said she wasn't feeling well. She had been at Holy Rock earlier for *The Pulpit Ladies*' lunch meeting."

"Right, I was there. We talked," Fancy said. "She seemed fine. Maybe she looked a little thin, but having two wild little boys can do that. I didn't think anything of it."

"Well, when I got there, she didn't answer the door. I could hear the boys inside, but she didn't answer. I let myself in. She was lying on the couch, out of it. The boys were running around the house like wild animals. I woke her and asked her what was wrong. She just said in a real lethargic voice that she was tired and sleepy. When I heard her words slurring, I knew it was more than her being tired and sleepy. Her eyes almost rolled in her head, and her skin was all clammy. Fancy, she was barely conscious!" Victoria cried, placing her head into her hands. "Think what the boys could have gotten into."

"Oh, Lord!" Fancy exclaimed.

"I knew she had taken too many pills. I just knew it. I asked her how many she had taken, but she kept nodding. I called the ambulance when she seemed to slip into unconsciousness. And here we are! Oh, God, please take care of my baby," Victoria cried out. "Please, Lord."

Fancy held her and let her cry. After she was composed enough, Fancy told her, "Look, we're probably going to be here for some long hours."

"No, don't you stay, Fancy. I'll be fine. I just wanted you to know what was happening. I needed my bestie, but I'm good now," she said, smiling. "But you go home. I'll keep you updated," Victoria assured her.

"You must be crazy. I'm not leaving you here by yourself. I'm going to call Hezekiah. He said he would be on standby in case we needed him to pick up the boys.

"Good," Victoria said. "I won't have to worry about them as long as they're with family."

"Right, and they love Grandpa Hezekiah," Fancy said, chuckling.

"Yeah, they do. I'll be right back. I have to pee," she whispered and went toward the bathroom.

Fancy called Hezekiah. "Hey, we need you to go get the boys. They still have Pepper in the back, and it looks like we're not going anywhere anytime soon."

"I'm on my way. They're at the hospital with you guys, right?" he asked.

"Oh, no, that's right. I'm glad you remembered to ask. They're at Pepper's next-door neighbor's. She's going to call them and let them know you're coming. When you get there, give me a call."

"How is Pepper?" he asked.

"We don't know yet. They told Vicky they would call her when they're done running tests."

"Okay. I'll let you know when I have the boys," Hezekiah said.

"Thanks," Fancy replied.

"Would the family of Pepper McCoy come through the double doors? Only one family member," the person on the intercom announced.

Just as the person began to repeat the announcement, Victoria came out of the bathroom. She started toward the double doors but briefly looked over her shoulder. "They just called me. I'll text or call you," she said to Fancy and pressed the button on the automatic door.

"Okay," Fancy replied just as the doors swung open. "I'll be here."

Fancy paced the polished tiled floors of the ER. After waiting over an hour without Vicky reappearing or texting to let her know what was happening, she went outside to the covered sitting area. She looked at her phone and decided to text Hezekiah. Just as she started texting, her notifier dinged.

"Pepper is going to be ok. accidental overdose. Keeping her here. go home. check on the boys. Will call u when they get her to a room."

"R u sure?"

"Yes. They won't let but one person back here. I am fine now that I know she is," Vicky texted back.

"Ok. Love you. Call me later."

Chapter 7

Beyond Hard Times

"Being heartbroken doesn't mean you stop feeling.
Just the opposite—it means you feel it all more."
Julie Johnson

Hezekiah silently prayed, driving through the city while his grandsons were content in the back seat. He hoped with everything in him that Pepper hadn't taken those pills on purpose, that she wasn't trying to end her own life. He could understand the depth of her grief, as he was in the midst of experiencing it as well. Losing his son, especially to suicide, had ripped him apart, and it hurt like hell every day. He prayed that his daughter-in-law would find the strength to pull through for the boys' sake. The family couldn't withstand another tragedy of that magnitude. Not now. Not ever. But this Pepper he'd seen lately reminded him of the Pepper, the psychologically impaired Pepper, who had to be committed and looked after when she gave birth to the triplets. She suffered from a severe case of postpartum psychosis back then, and losing one of them was hard on her, too, especially when she was told it was a little girl. It took some time, but Pepper became stronger mentally and physically and was able to be a mother to Zavion and Davion.

45

Hezekiah's phone rang. "Hey there," he said, smiling over the phone.

"Hey," Fancy said. "How are the boys?"

Hezekiah looked over his shoulder. "They're good. Y'all straight back there?" He asked the boys who were watching a movie on their tablets.

"Yes!" each kid said.

"You hear that?" Hezekiah said, entering the fast food drive-thru and pulling behind a line of cars.

"Yes," Fancy laughed, "I heard that. I'm glad you were able to get them. I'm about to head home, so I'll be there to relieve you in a bit."

"No need to hurry. We're not home yet. I just pulled up at the Coffee House. I thought I might need an extra shot of caffeine. I want to be prepared." Hezekiah chuckled. "See you when you get to the house."

"Okay, I'll be there soon."

She ended the call and smiled. Hezekiah? A grandpa? It made her heart glad to think about him and that he seemed genuinely changing— in a good way. Maybe him turning fifty-five did it—perhaps that and being given another chance to live as a free man.

Moments after arriving home, Hezekiah's Mercedes pulled in and claimed its parking space. He opened his car door at the same time Fancy's garage door opened. When she got out, he put a hand up to his lips, silencing her.

She saw the reason why when he lifted the two sleeping boys out of the SUV.

"Go open the door," he whispered.

Fancy hurried up the walkway to her front door. Inside the house, they got the boys in bed without either waking up.

"Thanks, Hezekiah," Fancy said, closing the door to the boys' bedroom.

Hezekiah walked ahead and stopped in front of the family room. "I'm G-Pa," he said, chuckling.

"What? G-Pa?" Fancy laughed. "Is that what you want them to call you?"

"Yep, I already told them, and they were all for it."

"Well, G-Pa, I hope you have a good night."

"Yeah, you too. I'm going to go hit the sack. Do you think Pepper will be alright?" he asked as he proceeded up the hall toward the kitchen.

"Physically? Yes. I don't know about mentally. I'll have to wait and talk to Vicky. She's been abusing those anxiety pills for a while; at least, that's what Vicky believes. I think she's right. This incident tonight was the tip of the iceberg. I think she needs to seek professional help."

"I agree," Hezekiah said, reaching out and turning the knob on the back door. "Get some sleep. Call me if you need anything."

"I will. Thanks again," she said.

He kissed her cheek before closing the door.

Fancy clicked off the kitchen light, smiled, and walked toward her bedroom.

Early the following morning, she woke up to a FaceTime call from Victoria. "Thank God we are finally in a room," Vicky said, yawning.

"I know that's right, after spending all night in the ER," Fancy said. "How is she?" Fancy asked, turning over in her bed and stretching.

"She's still sluggish and groggy and still sleeping a lot. They gave her some activated charcoal."

"Charcoal?"

"Yes," said Vicky. "The doctor said it absorbs the drugs. They also have her on intravenous fluids to help speed up the body's removal of the drugs. Now, we have to concentrate on her mental health. She says she didn't mean to take too many pills. She said she was tired, wasn't feeling well, and the boys were getting on her nerves. She took a pill, but she says she doesn't remember taking any more after that. I don't know if she's telling the truth about that. But I honestly think she's addicted to those pills. I blame the doctor for even prescribing them in the first place," Vicky cried.

"Why don't you let me come out there? You come home, take a shower, and get some sleep. I'll be there, and you won't have to worry. Hezekiah, or should I say G-Pa—"

"Wait, hold up." Vicky chuckled. "Did you say G-Pa?"

"Yes, that's what Hezekiah says he wants the grandkids to call him. He said he told the boys about it, and they love it." Fancy laughed along. "So anyway, I'm sure he'll be glad to watch them while I'm gone. You don't have to worry about a thing."

"Why did this happen now? I'm supposed to start my new job next week. Dang, Fancy. What's going on?"

"Look, all I know is that God is in control. He's allowed all of this to happen for a reason. We don't know and don't understand why most of the time. But I do know that He wants us to trust Him and not try to figure stuff out on our own."

"I'm trying, Fancy. God knows I am. I just want my baby to get her life together so she can raise her boys and, hopefully, one day, find love again. She's young, she's beautiful, and she's a good person. She deserves someone who will love her completely."

"Yes, she does," Fancy agreed. "And all that will happen in God's time—not ours."

Chapter 8

It's All Over

"You've got to make a conscious choice every day to
shed the old – whatever "the old" means for you."
Sarah Ban Breathnach

After spending two nights in the hospital,
Pepper was transferred to a behavioral health
facility for further evaluation. She initially
pushed against going, but after much talking
with Victoria and the hospital psychiatrist, she
admitted she needed help, but to be in a mental
hospital was something she was nervous about.
It made her anxiety go through the roof, and she
didn't say anything to her mother or her friends,
but she wanted—no—she *needed* her anxiety
meds.

"Hey, what's going on? Are you on your way
to pick up the boys?" Luna asked Eliana.

"No, Miss Victoria called right before you did.
She's going to drop them off on her way to see
Pepper."

"That makes sense since Stateside is not that
far from you," said Luna while breastfeeding
Laiyah Rose.

"Yeah, but what do you think about her
going to a place like Stateside?"

"I think inpatient treatment might be good
for her. At least, I hope it is." Luna put a
contented little Laiyah Rose in her pack-and-

play and gave her a teething cookie and her favorite stuffed bear.

"I pray it is, too," said Eliana.

"Anyway, what's the latest on you and Khalil?"

"He says he wants things to work out between us."

"And you? How do you feel about that?"

Eliana twisted her head slightly and shrugged. "I still love him, if that's what you mean. But I don't know if I can take being married to a cheater. Khalil says he's changed, but I still can't trust him."

Almost as soon as she spoke those words, she received a text from a number she didn't recognize.

`"and my man, thank you, thank you for my man. L O L."`

A picture of a man who appeared to be asleep and lying half-naked in a bed was attached to the text. The picture didn't show his face, but it didn't matter. Eliana knew it was Khalil for sure when she caught a glimpse of a scar on his upper calf that he said he'd gotten when he was a wild boy in Chicago going around stealing and robbing.

Eliana screamed into the phone like she'd been stabbed with a jagged knife.

"What is it? What's going on?" Luna screamed back.

"Oh my gosh, Luna. Oh, my, Lord," Eliana cried. "I just got a text from her talking about *'thank you for my man.'*"

"A text from who? Who are you talking about?"

"Who else? Nobody but Khalil's skank mistress." She read the text to Luna. "You see, that's what I'm talking about. How could I ever think this could work when he's still lying and cheating? I can't believe he has her at the retreat. That is if he's really at a retreat! Oh, God," she cried. "That's it, Luna! I'm done with Khalil and his mess!"

"I am *so* sorry, Eliana. I can't believe this," Luna said.

"This chick has some nerve texting me. But you know what, he can kiss my black behind. I'm done. *Lemme* call you back, Luna."

"Okay, but promise you'll call back. Don't forget."

"I won't." Eliana ended the call and reread the text. Then she called Khalil.

Surprisingly, he answered on the third ring. She was expecting to get his voicemail.

"Hey, what's up?"

"You tell me!" Eliana snapped.

"Huh? Tell you what?"

"Where are you, Khalil?"

"What do you mean, where am I?" his voice suddenly had an edge to it. "You know where I am. Is everything okay? Is Khaliyah okay?"

"I just got a text, Khalil," Eliana fumed.

"Uh, a text from who? Not me. I was heading to the next workshop. You caught me on my way there. What's wrong?"

"Your bitch just texted me. She says you're with her in New Mexico."

"My B? What? Look, Eliana, I don't know what or who you're talking about. I'm in Austin at this pastor's retreat. I do not have time for this foolishness."

"*Khalil...come on, baby,*" she thought she heard a female whisper.

"Foolishness? Are you serious? I just heard her, Khalil. She sent me a picture of you in her bed! I'm nobody's fool. You're with that B. I know it. But that's alright. You say you don't have time? Well, neither do I, Khalil McCoy. I'm sick of you. Wherever you are, you can stay!" she abruptly ended the call.

In tears, she rushed to her bathroom, dipped her face in some cold water, and stood before the lighted mirror.

"No more acting like some weak little girl," she fussed at her reflection. With fresh tears appearing, she kept talking aloud. "You will not break. You will not crumble, Eliana McCoy. Let him go. Move on," she said as if trying to convince herself. "He's not worth it."

She ignored her phone ringing. Whatever he had to say, it was too late. She'd had enough. But suddenly, she remembered she was supposed to watch Pepper's boys while Victoria went to visit her. She rushed out of the bathroom and looked at her phone. The missed call was from Victoria.

A text message popped up. "about ten minutes away. see u in a bit."

"Ok, see you soon," Eliana texted back.

"Mommy," she heard Khaliyah. She was up from her nap. The little girl was headed toward her.

"Go potty," she reminded her. "Davion and Zavion are coming to play. I want you to treat them nicely." Sometimes Khaliyah, I guess the result of being an only child, could behave selfishly and not want to play or share with other kids.

Khaliyah smiled and ran off to do as she was told.

Eliana went to her bedroom, washed her face, and tried to regain her composure. Soon after, the doorbell rang, and mother and daughter raced to the front door.

Eliana pushed aside the sting of betrayal and greeted Victoria happily as if everything was perfect in her messed-up, miserable, unhappy world.

Khalil called and texted long after Victoria returned to pick up the boys. Her notifier chimed every few minutes until she decided to temporarily block him.

The following day, with her eyes swollen almost shut from crying most of the night and with a splitting headache to top it off, Eliana dragged herself into the kitchen, made a strong cup of black coffee, something she hardly ever drank, and then called her next-door neighbor to see if she could watch Khaliyah for a couple of hours. Her neighbor had been a lifesaver ever since they moved next door. The grandmotherly woman would often watch Khaliyah without prior notice. Today was one of those days. She needed some time to clear her head and decide what her next move would be. One thing was certain, and two things were for sure—Khalil's despicable actions had irretrievably shattered

54

their marriage. Only God could restore it, and she believed it was highly doubtful He would.

After she returned home from taking Khaliyah to the neighbor, she flung herself across the bed like a chick on a movie screen and bawled her eyes out.

Chapter 9

Seek, And You Shall Find

"Don't let anyone who hasn't been in your shoes
tell you how to tie your laces." Unknown

Luna felt sorry for her friend. She knew how much Eliana loved Khalil, and for him to behave in the manner he did was unacceptable, especially coming from a popular pastor like him.

She pushed aside the thought of Eliana and her marriage and started researching Torres. She had been looking for information on him almost daily since seeing him at church two weeks ago. She would not sit back and wait for Christian to look into his background. He had enough already on his plate, and she didn't want him to know she was doing what she could to find her attacker on her own. If it was Torres, she had to know as soon as possible.

Until she could rest easy knowing if he was the one, there was no way she could comfortably attend New Holy Rock—not as long as Torres was there. Now that he worked at the church, she was even more frightened about going.

She called her friend and co-worker Trisha. They used to talk all the time, but with Luna on extended leave, the friends went from talking almost every day to sending each other random texts now and again.

"Hey, Luna. How are you? How are the babies?" Trisha asked, her voice resonating with excitement.

"They're fine, Trisha. They're getting bigger every day. Quite a handful."

"Tell me about it. I'm sure you've learned that motherhood is definitely not for the faint of heart. I'm just glad mine are all school-age." Trisha laughed.

"I know that's right. Look, I need you to look into something for me, Trisha."

"Sure, what's up."

Luna proceeded to tell Trisha about her suspicions of Torres.

"Let me see what I can find out. I can have my admin pull up his HR file if he worked for Global Pharmaceuticals. I don't know how much it will help, but I'll do what I can," Trisha reassured Luna.

"Thanks, Trisha. I'm not sure if he worked for our company, but Christian clearly said he used to work in our building. I might be barking up the wrong tree, but I don't want to leave a stone unturned, especially if it leads to who did this to me."

"No problem, I'll see what I can find out and get back to you as soon as I know something. Give me a day or two."

The next afternoon, Trisha called. "Hey," she said, "Torres did not work for our company, but he did work for the janitorial service this building has a contract with. I talked to his former supervisor. He told me Torres was a quiet but thorough employee. He did an excellent job until one day Torres told him he had an offer he couldn't refuse, and he had to start right away, or the offer would be rescinded."

"When was that?" asked Luna.

"About a year ago, from what he remembers."

"So if Torres is the monster who did this, why me? I don't know him. I don't even recall seeing him ever in our office building. Why would he do what he did to me?"

"I hate to say this, but you were probably just a convenient target. He saw you downtown, probably recognized you from coming and going in and out of our office building, and he just, well, his sicko behind, did what he did. You can never know what goes on in the mind of a person like that."

"That's true, but it still stands to reason I would have run into him or something at some point."

"Not necessarily; that building is huge. You can't possibly see or know everyone who works there. Not to mention the hundreds, if not thousands of people who go in and out of that building a day."

"True," responded Luna. "Look, thanks again, Trisha, for looking into that for me. I'm about to get the kids fed and ready for our daily outside adventure," she laughed.

"Okay, call me if there's anything else I can do."

"I will. Oh, Trisha, remember, we still have to get together for lunch soon," Luna reminded her work friend.

"Great, sounds good."

Luna dried and fed the kids and then packed their bags for their park outing. Having a park within mere walking distance from their home was one of the perks of living in their upscale neighborhood.

Majestic maple trees stretched along the winding trails, offering shade and a peaceful escape for park visitors. Joggers and bikers seemed to enjoy what could easily mimic a hidden paradise. Scattered throughout the park were charming park benches, lively play areas for children, and a spacious dog park, creating a perfect haven for families to relax and enjoy.

In the heart of the sprawling 25-acre park was a pristine man-made lake with glistening waters that looked like sparkling diamonds when the sun was at its brightest. It was like being in another world.

Luna parked the double stroller beside the park bench and settled into the shade of a nearby tree, relaxing as she gazed at the peaceful lake. To her right was a playground.

She pulled back the stroller top and eyed Laiyah Rose, who had fallen asleep. A summer breeze gently whisked the little girl's curly hair from side to side.

Dax stretched and reached for Luna. "Out," he cried, trying to climb out of the stroller alone.

"Wait, Dax," Luna told him. "Let me get you unbuckled." She reached over, unfastened the seat belt, and gave him a hand.

He popped out of the stroller and ran straight to the climbing bars.

"Be careful, sweetie," she cautioned. Taking no chances, Luna got up and followed him, pushing a still-sleeping Laiyah Rose. She was pleasantly surprised that no other children and parents were on the playground. Then again, she recalled that this was just one of three play areas. She smiled as she watched two-year-old Dax. He was growing into such a confident little boy. She gave Christian all the credit. He was exceptionally good with Dax.

Doctors told her and Christian that Dax would probably advance slower than most kids his age because of the trauma he experienced as a baby. His mental faculties would likely be impacted due to the state of malnutrition and neglect he had suffered starting when he was in his teen mother's womb. So far, he was defying those odds because, looking at him today, one wouldn't know that he had suffered such abuse. As for advancing slower, he seemed to be on track with most other two-year-olds, except his speech was slightly jumbled, and he said very few words. They planned to enroll him in speech classes when he turned three. It had been a mere two months since they had finally gotten him weaned off the bottle, a feat in and of itself, but he still insisted on his binkie, and although he wasn't potty trained, he had graduated from wearing pampers to pull-ups.

He still clung to Christian and preferred him over Luna, but he was turning into an outgoing, determined, and happy boy. He loved giving his sister little kisses and hugs. Sometimes, Luna had to stop him because he could be a little aggressive. It was cute, though, how their bond was evolving.

Luna could tell already that Laiyah Rose loved her big brother just as much. When he came around, she would often giggle and reach for him.

Laiyah Rose woke when Dax toddled over and kissed her chubby red cheeks.

"Dax, honey," Luna said. "Don't—" She stopped mid-sentence when she saw a man approaching who reminded her of her abductor. He wore a burgundy hoody with the words "NOPE: NOT TODAY" scrawled across the front. His jeans were tattered at the knee, and it looked like he had earbuds in his ears. He held a phone in his right hand. His sneakers were Jordan's. Her heart went into a frenzy of fear at seeing him. His walk. His height. Her mind began flashing back, seeing herself pinned inside that awful place with him doing vile things to her.

Quickly, she grabbed hold of Dax, scooped him up, and almost threw him into his side of the stroller, barely missing Laiyah Rose's head.

"Nooo! Nooo!" The little boy screamed and kicked.

"Stop it, Dax!" Luna said under her breath, keeping an eye on the man still approaching them.

While he kicked and clamored, she pushed the stroller away as fast as possible. When she finally stopped and briefly looked over her shoulder, she saw the man embracing a woman who had appeared. The two of them looked like they were an average couple in love. They kissed and held hands as they walked in the opposite direction.

Luna breathed a sigh of relief, placing one hand over her heart. *You've got to get it together. You're behaving like a crazy person. Every man you see is not the man who raped you. Get it together.*

Dax kept crying, waking Laiyah Rose, and she started crying.

"I'm sorry, baby. Don't cry. Mommy got a little—oh, God, why am I talking to a two-year-old like he would understand," she said, her heart racing. She took another look over her shoulder. The couple was almost out of her view. She kept walking. Dax was still in the throes of a tantrum.

"Laiyah Rose, sweetheart. Your brother is just a little upset. You don't have to be," Luna cooed, removing the little girl from her side of the stroller and bouncing her in her arms.

Dax continued crying and kicking until she approached the next bench. She sat down, reached into the stroller's storage compartment, and gave Laiyah Rose a teething cookie, Dax one of her homemade butter cookies, and a box of apple juice. Of course, the little boy was happy once again.

She sat quietly, her mind whirling with one thought after another until Dax and Laiyah Rose started whining and pulling at her for more snacks.

"No more cookies," she said. "And Dax, you better calm down. Mommy's going to take you home, and we'll have lunch." She gave him his binkie, which satisfied him.

Once home, Luna prepared lunch for herself and the kids and decided what she would make for dinner. Then her doorbell rang, startling her.

She wiped her hands and went to the front door. Looking through the peephole, she didn't recognize the person. Cautious, she asked, "Who is it?"

"Excuse me, ma'am, uh, Mrs. Black."

"Yes, who are you? How do you know my name?"

"I'm with the HOA committee. I don't mean to bother you, but I'd like to know if you would be willing to take a short survey about what we could do to improve our community."

She stood on her toes to get a better look at the man. He appeared of average height, with a protruding belly and a bald spot in the center of his head. The remaining thinning hair was black or maybe dark brown. She guessed him to be in his late fifties or early sixties.

"Uh, I'm sorry. What did you say your name was again?"

"Harry, Harry Goldberg. I'm the new HOA secretary."

"Oh," she said, partially opening the door. "I wish I could, but I can't right now. I'm busy. Can you come back another time, or can I give you my email, and you can email it to me?"

"Of course. I should have that information in your and your husband's file. I'll email it. Today, since it was such a nice day, I thought I'd get out of the office and canvas our neighborhood. Some of us prefer face-to-face interaction, and others, like yourself, prefer online interaction. It's a way for me to get to know the members of our community better. I'll leave the information on your porch. I hope to see you at the HOA meeting at the end of the month. Good day, Mrs. Black."

"Thanks," she abruptly replied, watching until he disappeared up the sidewalk before closing the door.

Returning to finish her work, she glanced at the TV screen above the fireplace in the family room.

She paused, turned up the volume, and watched when she saw a headline about the capture of a suspected serial rapist.

"This is your mid-south reporter, Jeremy Parker, with breaking news: *Local business executive and philanthropist Rex Sanchez, 59, pleaded not guilty Friday to first-degree and second-degree aggravated rape and kidnapping in the abduction of five women in the mid-south area over a span of three years.*

When she saw the lone figure, flanked by two police officers, she once again thought he could be the person responsible for her abduction and assault. Only this time, she was even more certain than she was with Torres. When she saw his face and they stated the name of his company, she realized she had seen him before in the parking garage of the building where she worked. His company shared the same garage. She felt a chill come over her at the possibility, the real possibility, that this was him this time. If it *was* him, he was not only her rapist and kidnapper—he was Laiyah Rose's father.

Chapter 10

Happy Being Lonely

"There comes a time when you must choose to turn the page, write another book, or simply close it."
Unknown

Pepper looked around the small, private hospital room. In addition to a single steel bed, the room had a bedside table and a well-worn olive green upholstered armchair in a corner next to the window—a window with a view but one that did not open. It didn't even look like real glass, more like Plexiglas. Pepper figured it was made to keep people like her from throwing themselves out of it!

She positioned herself on the side of the bed, legs dangling, her mind clearer than it had been since Xavier's death nineteen months prior. If she admitted it, the pain was becoming easier to bear the more she talked to the therapist about him and their marriage.

Initially, therapy was something she hadn't looked forward to. After that terrible bout with postpartum psychosis, she didn't want to sit before another therapist ever again. Yet, here she was—a different diagnosis but the same amount of crazy. That's what she told herself about herself.

"Mrs. McCoy, time for group therapy," a male orderly said when he opened and peeped inside her room, dragging her to the reality of where she was—a psych hospital with a bunch of other mixed up, messed up folks.

Pepper looked up like she had been yanked from space back to earth. "Oh, sure. I'm on my way." This would be her first group session, and she was nervous and not looking forward to it.

The orderly nodded and pulled the door shut.

Pepper went to the bathroom, looked in the mirror, and studied her pale-skinned face. She frowned at her reflection. She looked like death warmed over—like a vampire had sucked all the blood out of her. Her hair was scraggly and uncombed, and bits of crust were nestled in the corners of her eyes. Despite looking haggard and worn out, she shook it off, splashed cold water on her face, pushed her hair away, and left her room.

Entering a room labeled "Group Therapy" at the far end of the long corridor, she hesitated when she saw through the small window seven individuals seated in steel chairs forming a circle.

Don't go in here and start talking and sharing your life's woes with a roomful of crazies. Stop it, Pepper! If they're a bunch of crazies, then what does that make you? She shook off the thoughts, took a deep breath, and sauntered into the room.

As she entered, a thin, white guy with a thick Mario Luigi mustache beckoned, "Come in, Pepper. We're glad you could join us," he said, pointing to an empty chair in the circle. "Please, have a seat."

Pepper, eyes cast downward, shoulders drooped, hands clasped, ambled to the empty chair and slowly took a seat.

"Group, let's welcome Pepper to today's session." The doctor did not give Pepper's last name.

"Welcome, Pepper," they said collectively.

"You may introduce yourselves if you'd like."

Each person stated their first name.

Pepper's eyes lingered on the man sitting across from her. When the man said nothing but only stared, the therapist told him, "If you don't want to share with the group right now, it's fine."

Pepper was somehow drawn to the man as if she could sense his feelings. He sat quietly, almost lifeless. His head was full of thick, black hair, which looked like it hadn't been cut or trimmed in some time, and he wore an even thicker, unkempt beard. Stylish black glasses framed his deep brown eyes. She never thought she would see someone whose eyes looked sadder than hers, but there he was, sitting across from her like all the life had been sucked out of him. She quickly looked away when his stare met hers.

Focusing back on the therapist and the questions he posed to the group, Pepper listened to the responses from most of the patients.

"Do you have anything you'd like to share, Pepper?" the doctor asked.

"Uh, no," she said, nervously shaking her head and looking away.

For the remainder of the session, the group, minus Pepper and the man in glasses, shared their feelings about various events that ultimately led them to treatment.

After group therapy, she had just enough time to use the bathroom and grab a bag of chips and a bottled tea from the vending machine before it was time for her individual therapy session. Today, her mother was going to attend at the therapist's request. She hoped she remembered to bring her more change for the vending machines.

Pepper didn't fully grasp why the therapist felt it was necessary to talk to her mother. Victoria wasn't responsible for the stupid decision she made to marry a guy she knew was gay. It wasn't her mother who went into postpartum psychosis after giving birth to three babies, one of whom she never grieved because of her stupid mental illness. When she *did* make a recovery, she had to give her time and attention to getting to know her two remaining babies. Then there was Xavier's suicide. She would forever blame herself for forcing him into a life he never wanted. There was so much anger she held against herself.

Victoria's attendance turned out to be enlightening. She opened up about the impact the divorce from Pepper's father had on Pepper. Especially when Victoria took a job that relocated her from Texas to Memphis. Pepper hardly saw her father after that.

It wasn't all Victoria's fault, but sometimes Pepper felt like her mother was to blame for her father meeting someone else, falling in love, having a whole other family, and moving on without Pepper. It was hard, but she'd managed, at least she thought she had. When she met Xavier, they clicked. They could talk and relate to so many of the same things. They accepted each other for who they were. How could their marriage not work? How could two people with so much in common be so far apart? Yet, the inevitable happened, and here she was—locked up in a psych hospital with a dead husband and two kids who still, to this day, wanted to know when Daddy was coming home.

After therapy, the mother and daughter ate their cafeteria lunch in Pepper's room.

"Look at this," Victoria said, laughing as she showed Pepper one of the many entertaining videos of the boys.

Pepper enjoyed watching her boys laugh and play. They were so precious to her. She was grateful for her mother, her mother-in-law Fancy, and her friends and family for stepping up and taking care of them while she was in this phase of her life.

"You'll be home soon," Victoria said as they finished lunch and she prepared to leave. "Another couple of weeks or so."

Pepper nodded. "I know. I can't wait. I never should have agreed to this. I mean, don't get me wrong, I'm feeling better. But it's because I needed rest, Momma. I haven't been able to shut down since Xavier's death. But that doesn't mean I needed to be in this place."

"But that's exactly why being here is good for you," Victoria reassured her. "You're feeling better because you've been able to talk things out. You've been able to work on yourself without having to be responsible for two rambunctious little boys. You've never given yourself time to grieve fully. That's why you're here, sweetheart."

Victoria approached Pepper and lovingly embraced her daughter.

"It took courage to admit you needed professional help, Pepper. The road you were going down could easily have led to the same road as Xavier. God knows no one wanted that to happen. Where would that leave the boys? Where would it leave me? I couldn't stand the thought of losing my child." Tears trickled down Victoria's cheeks. She stood back and looked at her only daughter. Tears were running down Pepper's face, too.

Victoria wiped Pepper's tears away, kissed her on her face, and embraced her again. "Call me tomorrow," she said, turning toward the door. "I love you, sweetheart."

"I love you, too, Momma. Remember to show the boys the video I made for them."

Pepper walked up the hall to the community showers. Her room had only a toilet and sink, reminding her of a prison cell. She showered quickly, knowing the hot water would soon run cold, as it always did after just a few minutes.

Returning to her room, she closed the blinds and sat in her chair. Her countenance changed from a sullen look to a half smile when she turned the television to one of her favorite sitcoms.

For the next couple of hours, she watched television, nodded on and off, and flipped through some of the books her mother had brought. She fiddle-faddled with one of the word search books, something she usually didn't indulge in, but being in this place left her few options for entertainment.

The door opened. Pepper looked up.

"Time for your medication," the portly older white lady with shocking purple hair said. If the woman thought purple hair made her look younger or more in the present, Pepper wanted to tell her that she was living in a fantasy world because the ol' girl looked....well, Pepper stopped her thoughts. She was not one to talk badly about anyone, not if she could help it. After all, when she looked at herself in the mirror, she saw someone she did not like. That person was miserable and sad and had almost lost her own identity.

Unlike Xavier, she didn't want to die. She wanted to live. She didn't want to be sad anymore. She was tired of crying, tired of grieving, and tired of her old life. It was time to make a change—time to get her life together, time to take care of her boys and move on. Xavier hadn't seen the need to stay in their lives, so it was time to release him, to let him go. For the first time, she gave his death some thought, but in a different way, because although Xavier was dead, maybe he was finally free.

Pepper climbed into bed, her eyes fixated on the TV screen. Within fifteen minutes of taking the little blue pill, she felt her body relaxing. She pulled the covers to her chin. The familiar faint scent of disinfectant lingered in the air as her eyelids grew heavier.

She began to pray aloud. "God, grant me peace. Heal my mind. Make me better all over. Make me whole again so I can be the best mother to my sons," she prayed, tears forming and running down the side of her face, dissolving into the pillowcase.

Chapter 11

For Once In My Life

"Life doesn't get easier or more forgiving; we get stronger and more resilient." S. Marshall

Fancy laid out a number of paint swatches and sample tiles across the eight-foot table. "I think this color will go perfectly as a backsplash against white quartz countertops. But, frankly, any of these colors will make this kitchen pop," she eagerly shared with her new client.

Thanks to Victoria, she'd snagged a high-level client who wanted a designer for a home he recently purchased in Memphis. Like Victoria's new beau, he was an executive at FedEx.

"I don't know. I never thought about incorporating more color, but I think I like where you're going with this," he said, studying the tiles like he was examining the pieces of signature art lining the walls of his luxurious home.

He stood tall, with a sorta dark complexion and strikingly handsome features, framed by a salt-and-pepper beard that highlighted his chiseled jawline. And, according to Victoria, he was single.

He seemed to glance at her for a sign of objection as her eyes took in his powerful presence. Without warning, she suddenly felt a tingling in her belly. A bout of nerves attacked her as his enigmatic voice and confident assurance made her weak in the knees.

He must have noticed something was awry because he asked, "Are you alright?"

"Yes, I'm fine. But...well, it *has* been a long day. I guess I am a little tired. May I have some water, please?"

"Sure," he said, walking to the double-wide refrigerator on the other end of the expansive kitchen. He returned with bottled water. "Here you go," he offered. "Oh, wait. Let me get you a glass for that."

"No, this is good, thank you."

She pulled herself together and tried for the remainder of their meeting to avoid looking and sounding like a silly schoolgirl who had crushed on a cute guy.

As their meeting progressed, Fancy offered suggestions about the interior design of the kitchen and other areas of the home, including his ginormous regal primary suite, with a sitting area and twin French doors opening to a private covered balcony.

"And, here is where I suggest carrying the same color scheme," she said as they stood in the middle of the master bath. "It will give your home an even flow while adding character."

"I like how you think," Noah said as they continued through the 6,700-square-foot space.

Noah walked her to the door at the end of the almost two-hour meeting. "Let me carry that."

"Oh, that's not necessary," Fancy said, placing the materials underneath her arms. "I'm used to this." She smiled and continued to the door.

"Nope, I've got it," he insisted, removing the items from her hands and walking her to her car.

"After you've had a chance to go over the samples, let me know what you decide. If you have questions, shoot me a text or an email. Or if you want to see more. We'll meet again after you've made your decisions. Once your choices are finalized, I'll call in my contractors, and we can start turning an already beautiful home into one with your very own personal style and touch." She openly smiled and looked briefly over her shoulder at the three-story coastal design structure before looking at him.

She was slightly caught off guard, but pleasantly so, when he met her smile with a captivating one of his own.

On the drive home, she called Victoria.

"Girl, why didn't you tell me Mr. Alexander was such a hunk," she said, laughing into the phone over her Bluetooth.

"Uh, I thought I'd let you find out for yourself. So tell me, how did it go?"

"Great. But you know he and I had already talked on the phone so that I could get an idea of what he was looking for. But meeting him in person was, girl, like I said, a good meeting. He's going to go over some of the samples I left, and we'll meet again when he's ready."

"Good for you. And who knows where this might lead."

"The only thing I hope it leads to is more clients like him," said Fancy. "The ones with big bucks to spend."

"Uh, you know that's not what I'm talking about."

"Well, if you're thinking of anything other than a professional relationship, then forget it, sista girl. You know I am not having it."

"Don't play with me, Fancy McCoy. This is your bestie you're talking to. I know you like I know the back of my hand. And I knew when you saw him, you would go goo-goo gah-gah."

"I almost did, but I kept it professional. I told you I am *not* looking for a man. I do not *want* a man. I am fine, just the way I am. I've had my share of heartbreak. I don't want to experience another one. Hezekiah scarred me for life."

"Don't let Hezekiah ruin it for everyone else, Fancy. You may not want to hear this, but the truth is you're not getting younger. And I know you don't want to be sitting in a rocking chair on the porch all alone one day, now, do you?" Victoria burst into laughter.

"Rocking chair? Girl, you got me messed up. I don't plan to be sitting in anybody's rocking chair any time soon."

"All I'm saying is you deserve to be happy, Fancy."

"And who says I'm not, Vicky? You? Well, in your own words, just because I don't have a man does not mean I am not happy. Anyway, my precious grandbabies keep my life full. I have good friends like you. God has blessed my design business. I have a little money in the bank. I'm in good health. So, you see, I'm good."

"Yeah, yeah, yeah. I know all that, but having a good man next to you every now and then won't hurt. Will it?"

76

Fancy's shoulders lifted in what could have been mistaken for a careless shrug. "Okay, I confess. I do sorta miss the comfort of being held by a man sometimes."

"And you should. We're not dead, Fancy!"

The besties laughed and continued talking.

"How did it go with Pepper the other day?"

"It was good, actually. I think Pepper got a lot out of it. I was able to share some things I was feeling about how I thought my divorce affected her. It's not like she was a kid when her father and I decided we needed to go our separate ways before we started hating each other. She was almost eighteen, and she could have remained with him in Texas, but she was the one who decided not to."

"But that decision was probably tough. You said she was close to him at one time. So I'm sure it wasn't easy for her to leave," added Fancy.

"No, it wasn't, and when he got remarried and started a whole other family, it shook her to the core. Then to come here and, well, you know how things worked out. Anyway, the child has gone through a lot."

"Tell me about it," lamented Fancy. "There's not a day that passes when I don't think of my Xavier. I miss that boy so much. And when I see Zavion and Davion, all I see is their father's face. It tears me apart sometimes, so I can only imagine what it does to Pepper."

"I'm just praying and hoping this hospital stay does her some good."

"I thought you said she was getting better," Fancy responded.

"She is, from what I can tell. She's talking more upbeat, and I even saw a smile on her face instead of tears when I showed her pictures and videos of the boys. Fancy, I just want her to be happy again. I want my child to heal."

"I know you do, Vicky. I know you do."

Chapter 12

You Met Your Match

"Someone I once loved gave me a box full of darkness. It took me years to understand that this, too, was a gift." Mary Oliver

Fancy turned onto her street. From a distance, she saw Hezekiah getting out of his car. She watched closely as the passenger door opened and Hezekiah's son, Jude, appeared. He was chattering away about something as he made his way around to the other side, where Hezekiah was standing.

Her first inclination was to wait until they disappeared inside the back gate before she pulled in. She had never met this kid, and she had no desire to meet him or get to know him. Her baby was dead, and here Hezekiah had the chance to do it all over again and, possibly through this kid, make up for his shortcomings with Khalil and Xavier. It wasn't fair. After all the low-down, dirty things he'd done, he was still given a chance at redemption. She didn't like it. Not one bit. Why him? Why was God giving him chance after chance, but her baby was gone? She knew all about the scripture that said not to lean to her own understanding but to trust God. But Fancy was having a hard time trusting, especially when situations like this were thrown in her face.

When she pushed the garage remote, she saw Hezekiah stop and look over his shoulder in her direction. He stood stationary with Jude standing next to him.

Fancy pulled into the garage, and it slowly closed.

Moments later, after going inside, she heard her doorbell chiming.

She went to the front door and opened it, seeing Hezekiah and the boy standing there.

Hezekiah shifted uncomfortably before speaking. "Hi," he said.

"Hi," Fancy said dryly, not acknowledging the boy. She stared at Hezekiah, arms folded and not a smile on her face. "How can I help you?"

"Uh, I saw you pull in, and uh, well, I thought this might be as good a time as any for you to meet my, uh, son Jude."

"Oh, well, I'm busy, Hezekiah. As you see, I'm just getting in, and I have a ton of stuff I need to get done."

"I just wanted to introduce you. Jude, this is, this is uh, Miss Fancy. My uh, my landlord. Remember, I told you about her."

Jude looked at her like she had a piece of raw meat plastered on the side of her face.

Miss Fancy? No, he did not introduce me as Miss Fancy. Like I'm the help or somebody. And who the heck did he tell this kid I am? The landlord? Yeah, buddy, if only you knew! "Hi, Jude." Fancy half smiled, halting her thoughts. "It's nice to meet you."

80

Looking back at Hezekiah, rolling her eyes, she said, "I really need to go, Hezekiah. Enjoy your son," and closed the door.

Rushing to the kitchen, she poured herself a glass of iced tea before she stormed off to her bedroom while cussing under her breath. "Lord, forgive me, but this fool has pushed one too many buttons on me today! How dare he introduce that kid to me. And then to tell him I'm *Miss* Fancy, the landlord? He has some nerves!"

While she was FaceTiming Vicky, she paced the floor, waiting for her to answer. Meanwhile, Sebastian jumped on the bed, looking at her as if she had lost her mind. At that moment, that's what she felt like. Absolutely insane! She didn't even notice when Victoria came on the screen.

"Hey, hey there, what's wrong with you?" she heard Victoria say and then looked at her phone.

"Girl, I'm so mad I can hurt somebody!"

"What's going on? You were straight when we talked earlier. What changed?"

"I'll tell you what changed. Can you believe Hezekiah had the nerve to introduce me to his bastard kid?"

"Jude? When?"

"Yes, Jude, and just a few minutes ago. He was pulling up when I was pulling up. I couldn't avoid it, although I tried. I even went inside the house, and this idiot rang my doorbell."

"I mean, you knew that was bound to happen sooner or later. Frankly, the boy needs to know he has siblings other than his mother's kids. It's a shame he didn't get to meet Xavier before his death. He needs to know Khalil. And to be honest, I think it's a good thing for him to know who you are, too."

"Vicky, I'm sorry, but I cannot agree with you on this one. I don't want to know that boy. I don't want anything to do with him. If Khalil wants to meet him, then that's on him."

"I just don't understand what's got you so upset."

"I just am," retorted Fancy. "Seeing that kid reminds me of Hezekiah's cheating ways. He ruined everything, Vicky. Everything! And to think, I didn't even learn about that boy until he was five years old! And now, he looks like, well, he looks like he could be ten or eleven. I don't know."

"I know, but getting yourself worked up like this will not do you any good. So now you've met him. All the formalities are out of the way. If Hezekiah chooses to introduce him to Khalil, then that's on him. But as for you, let...it...go."

Slowly, Fancy's anger subsided as she began listening to Vicky. All the time, she called herself a Christian, but here she was, taking out her frustration and disappointment in Hezekiah on a little boy. Yes, he may have been the result of Hezekiah's infidelity, but it was not the boy's fault.

"You're right, Vicky. I shouldn't take it out on him. But just seeing him reminds me of Xavier. He looks just like him when he was that age."

"Really?"

"Yes, and it makes me even madder!"

"Look, it's time you stop wearing that jacket of bitterness. That's the same thing I've been telling Pepper. Let the past go. I don't know much about the Bible like you do, but I do know that somewhere in those pages, it says to forget the past or what happened in the past. Something like that," Victoria said.

"Close enough," Fancy said and chuckled lightly. "I was taken off guard, that's all. I wasn't expecting Hezekiah to do that."

"Seems like Hezekiah is proving a little bit more each time that he's changed, or at least trying to," Victoria said.

"Yeah, I guess. Come to think about it, he has been more grandfatherly," Fancy said, laughing. "More mellow and less out there."

Victoria laughed, too. "Yeah, the Hezekiah before prison was a booger bear. So give the man a little credit for trying to be a better person, that is, until he gives you a reason not to."

"I think I can do that."

"Good for you. So, what do you say we get together for dinner this week? I don't know how much time I'm going to have after the next couple of weeks pass. Pepper will be coming home soon, I hope. And when she does, I know she's going to need my help with the boys. And I'll be on my new job."

"Right, so I'm good for tomorrow night. Let's go to Sage downtown."

"Oh, Sage sounds good. I haven't been there in a while. I love their food."

"Me too. Especially their soul food egg rolls. They are the bomb!" exclaimed Fancy.

"I want one of their salmon burgers," Vicky said, "and their fried green tomatoes are to die for. So, tomorrow night it is. I'll meet you there. What time?"

"What about six?"

"Six sounds good. Bye, I'll see you tomorrow."

Fancy pushed aside the earlier surprise with Hezekiah and Jude. After a relaxing hot bubble bath with a glass of white wine, she sat in her family room, scrolling from one channel to the next until she found a DIY show. She liked watching HGTV because it gave her many ideas she could incorporate with her clients.

Her phone rang. She quickly eyed the time. It was almost seven-thirty.

"Hello," she said when she saw the name of the caller appear.

"Did I catch you at a bad time?" the baritone voice asked.

"No, I was just about to shut it down for the evening, but of course, I always have time for my clients," she stated, thankful Noah Alexander couldn't see her blushing through the phone.

"In that case, I have a couple of questions about some of your suggestions. You said I should call if I had questions. Correct?"

"Yes, I said that, and I meant it. So, Mr. Alexander."

"Noah," he corrected.

"Uh, Noah. Tell me, how can I help you?"

Noah told her the questions he had, and she readily answered them to his satisfaction.

"Thank you," he said at the end of their conversation.

"You are quite welcome."

"Well, now that you've addressed my concerns, I think we can finalize the designs. The only thing is I have to fly out first thing tomorrow morning on business. I won't be back for two weeks."

"That's fine. We'll finalize everything together when you return to the city."

"I'll look forward to it," Noah said.

When the call ended, Fancy placed a hand over her heart and smiled as she exhaled. "Wow, be still my heart," she said aloud before rising and heading to the kitchen to pour a second glass of wine. Taking a sip, she went to her office and started reviewing some of the swatches and sample tiles she'd shown Noah previously. She decided she would choose a few more to take with her whenever they met again, just in case he had a change of heart.

For some reason, she was excited about seeing Noah again. So far, he was easy to talk to and be around. She couldn't quite explain the reason, but he made her feel alive without flirting. Just being in his environment, listening to his thoughts and ideas, and hearing his likes and dislikes made her feel present, not just talked at. Being around a man like him, a man other than Hezekiah, was possibly the change she needed. It was good to hang out with her bestie. She and Vicky always had fun together. But unlike Vicky, who had a man in her life, Fancy was alone.

Consumed by her thoughts, she looked around her bedroom. The only male in her bed was Sebastian. She smiled, stroked his fur, and listened as he began purring. There was no one to talk to, no one to ease the bouts of loneliness that visited her from time to time. The grandchildren filled some of the void, but male companionship was far different. She longed for affection and attention from a man.

Immediately, her mind went to Hezekiah. She returned to her bedroom and walked over to her window. Peeping through the blinds, she saw the lights on in his place.

Just as she turned to leave the window, his front door opened, and he and the boy appeared.

She eased back so he wouldn't see her. Father and son walked up the path and disappeared. Shortly after, she heard his car. She rushed to the front of the house just in time to see him backing out of his parking space and heading up the street.

With folded arms, she slowly turned and walked back to her bedroom.

"Forget about that man, will you," she scolded herself. "I don't know why you let him get you all frustrated." She tried to switch her thoughts to Noah, but she somehow ended up thinking about Hezekiah.

"Dang, you, Hezekiah McCoy! Get out of my head!" she yelled and retreated to her bed.

Chapter 13

I'd Be A Fool Right Now

"Giving up doesn't always mean you are weak;
sometimes it means that you are strong enough to
let go." Unknown

Eliana booked a one-way flight to Atlanta after she spoke to Ian. He assured her that there would be room for both her and his niece and that they could stay for as long as they needed.

Later that night, Khalil returned home from his so-called retreat. For the performance he put on, he could have been awarded an Oscar. On his knees, with crocodile tears and a snotty nose, he begged and pleaded and then begged and pleaded some more.

This time, however, Eliana wasn't moved by his theatrics. He would have to come out of a whole new bag if he wanted things to work between them. As much as she loved him, she was not going to put up with his infidelity anymore. She didn't want her daughter to not be around her father, but she realized that if that situation happened, it wouldn't be her fault—it would be Khalil's. His actions, decisions, and empty promises destroyed everything they were building or should have been building together.

"Don't leave me, Eliana. Please, baby!"

Eliana packed two suitcases for her and Khaliyah while Khalil followed her through the house like a sick puppy dog.

During his performance, she received a text notifying her that her driver had arrived. She grabbed Khaliyah's hand, picked up their bags, and headed toward the door.

"Don't, Eliana," he said again, tears pouring from his red eyes.

"It's too little too late. Tell Daddy you'll see him later," she said, looking at their daughter.

"Bye, Daddy," Khaliyah said, looking sad.

Khalil kneeled to his daughter's level, scooped her in his arms, and squeezed her tightly.

"Daddy, you're squeezing me too tight."

"Daddy's sorry. Come on," he said, turning to Eliana. "I'm going to walk you to the car. At least tell me where you're going."

Eliana walked past without acknowledging what he'd said. She arrived at the UBER.

The driver opened the trunk and placed her bags inside.

"Tell me, where are you going?" Khalil asked again.

"Why is that important now, Khalil?" Eliana bit back.

"I need to know where you and my daughter are going to be," he said, his voice becoming elevated.

"Uh, I know you're not catching an attitude," she said, pulling back and giving him a look that made it clear she couldn't believe his nerve. "Not after you've been *retreating* all week at your so-called pastor's getaway. Well, you did what you wanted with who you wanted, so don't worry about me or your daughter. Just know this—wherever we go, we'll be just fine."

She reached for Khaliyah. "Come on, Khaliyah," she said.

Khaliyah pushed against her father's arms, and he let her down.

Taking hold of her hand, Eliana helped her get inside the car. When Khaliyah was seated, and before Eliana got inside, she looked at Khalil. "Remember, you did this. I didn't want this. I loved you, Khalil," she said, tears flooding her eyes and rolling down her face. "I loved you so much. All I wanted was for you to love me back."

"But I do, baby. I love you and Khaliyah so much."

"Listen to what you're saying. It's always me and Khaliyah in the equation. And don't get me wrong, because I understand that you love your daughter, as you should. I'm grateful for that. You're a good father, but what about me? Do you see me, Khalil? I'm your wife, but you don't treat me like that. Heck, you give your sidepiece more attention than you ever give me." She paused, looked over her shoulder, and looked inside the car to see what Khaliyah was doing. The little girl was already nodding, her head slung to the side and her eyes closed.

"I've got to go. Goodbye, Khalil."

She got inside the car and closed the door. As the driver drove off, she did not look back.

†

'You've made it already?" Luna asked.

"Yes, a nonstop flight here takes less than an hour and a half. I've been here long enough to get Khaliyah fed and bathed. She's asleep."

"Good. Have you talked to Khalil?"

"Girl, he's been calling and texting like a madman, and you already know I haven't answered. I can't listen to Khalil right now, Luna. I need some time to clear my mind so I can make a rational decision about the future of my marriage."

"I understand."

"No, I don't think you do. I love Khalil, but I will not tolerate his cheating. I can't do it, Luna. I can't," she cried.

"Look, you're there with your twin brother. Enjoy him and do fun things while you're in the ATL. Keep your mind on something else."

"That's the same thing Ian said. It's been a long time since he and I have hung out. I didn't realize how much I missed my brother until I saw him standing at the gate waiting on me and Khaliyah."

"Good for you. Please take care of yourself. I'm going to be praying for you. I know God is going to lead you to do the right thing. I believe that with all of my heart."

"So do I," Eliana agreed. "And Luna, thank you."

"I love you, girl," Luna said. "You and Pepper have become like sisters."

"I feel the same. By the way, have you talked to your sister?" Eliana asked.

"Yes, we talked a few days ago. Having my little sister back in my life feels better than I can put into words."

"I'm sure it does. Nothing can replace family, real family," said Eliana. "But look, I've been so consumed with what's going on with me that I haven't asked how things are with you. I hate to bring it up, but have you heard anything else about that guy you think might be your abductor?"

"Not a lot, but I know he didn't work for my company. He worked in janitorial services in our building, but only briefly. But I saw this executive guy on the news the other day. They say he could be responsible for several rapes and abductions in the city over the past three years."

"Oh my gosh! That's awful," Eliana replied.

"I know. I'm looking into his background but I also haven't stopped looking at Torres. The thing about this new guy is, guess what, Eliana?"

"What?" Eliana said, her voice rising in anticipation.

"Unlike Torres, I've seen this guy before."

"You have? Where?"

"In our building. In the parking garage, too. He may have been the fellow at the repast, but I can't be sure. I thought it was Torres I saw at Pastor's repast. Now, I don't know what I saw or who I saw. I know I sound crazy, but it's just all so confusing, Eliana. God knows I'm scared. I want whoever did this to me to get caught and locked away for life. I don't want him ever to have a chance to be near my daughter."

"He won't," Eliana reassured Luna. "Let's stop talking about that anyway. We need to talk about more pleasant things. Pepper's mom said she was doing a whole lot better. She said Pepper might be coming home."

"That will be good," said Luna. "I hope when she gets out, she has a whole new outlook on her life. She's such a sweet person."

"Yeah, she is. But sometimes being good and sweet still isn't enough," Eliana said, her voice melancholy. "I'm going to let you go. I was just calling to let you know we made it. I'll call or text you sometime tomorrow."

"Goodnight, Eliana."

"Nite, Luna."

Later the same evening, Eliana and Ian sat outside, taking in the downtown Atlanta skyline from the eleventh-floor balcony of his two-bedroom apartment.

"It feels so peaceful," Eliana said, resting in the lounge chair and sipping a freshly squeezed lemonade with strawberries. It was one of Ian's favorite refreshers to make.

"Yes, it is peaceful. I like sitting out here, especially after coming home from work. It levels me. I can't explain it."

"I know what you're saying. It's beautiful." Clusters of stars pierced areas of darkness. "I like this apartment better than the one you had in the suburbs. Aren't you glad you moved downtown?"

"Yes, I love it. I like the nightlife. I like that I can walk outside my apartment to restaurants and bars. I can meet my friends along the strip. Then I can come home to this," he said, looking briefly over his shoulder and back at the views. "You know, sis, it took a minute for me to get over Xavier. That breakup was hard on me, and when he died, it was even harder. No one really knew the extent of my pain."

"I think I knew," said Eliana. "I mean, I know you loved him, but I also knew you were hurt when he went back to Pepper."

"I guess as long as he was alive, I thought I could deal with us not being together, but his death made me hurt in a whole new way. I still can't believe he did it."

"I'm glad to see you're doing well. It looks like you're moving on with life."

"I am," Ian agreed. "I recently started seeing someone. It's nothing serious, at least not yet. And that's fine with me. I can't say how I'll feel tomorrow. Know what I mean?"

"Yes, I know," Eliana said.

"What about you, twin? What are your plans?" Ian asked.

"I don't know. That's why I'm here. I hope I can sort out things. I'm so confused, Ian."

"All I know is you don't deserve to be mistreated, sis. I don't care if he's a big-shot pastor known in the community as a servant of God; the man is a cheater and a liar. He doesn't deserve a good person like you."

"You're prejudiced because I'm your twin," Eliana said, smiling at her brother.

"I admit I might be slightly prejudiced, but I'm still stating facts. Khalil McCoy is a man whore."

"Did you say a man whore?" Eliana laughed.

"It's the only way I can describe him. You might say Xavier was a cheater when he and I were together, but I wouldn't exactly agree. Pepper was sick then, and they were going through a divorce, too. If I had known he would go back to her, I never would have allowed myself to fall in love with him," Ian confessed.

"I know, and I agree, you and Xavier's relationship was not the same. For one thing, Pepper knew he was gay when they got married, but she thought she could change him. It wasn't an excuse for him to cheat, but at least he admitted the marriage wasn't going to work. I know they ended up getting back together, but even with that, Xavier didn't go behind your back. He told you he wanted to give his marriage another shot, and that's what he did."

"Yeah, and look where it led him?"

"Let's not do this tonight, Ian, or we'll both end up sad and depressed."

"Right, so what do you say we go watch *Living Single* reruns," Ian said, chuckling.

"I say, the last one inside has to pop the popcorn and make the drinks," Eliana challenged.

They jumped up from their chairs, laughing as they raced inside.

Chapter 14

More Than A Dream

"Sick of crying, tired of trying. Yes, I'm smiling, but inside, I'm dying." Prestus Hood

"Christian, it's him," Luna insisted.

"You think so?" Christian asked.

"Yes, and before you say it, I know what I said before, and that's because, at the time, I really did believe it was Torres, but honey, it's not. I've seen this Sanchez fellow several times. I think we've even spoken a few times."

"I've heard of him," Christian said. "He's known for giving large monetary gifts to HBCUs like LeMoyne Owen and Jackson State. I never would have pegged him as a rapist. Geez, that's crazy."

"I don't care how crazy it is; if he's the one responsible for assaulting me, then I want to know! What can I do to be sure if it's him, Christian?" Luna was growing upset; her voice rose, and her eyes glistened.

Christian walked over to his wife and embraced her. "I'll find out, sweetheart. Please, don't get angry with me. I'm doing all I can to get justice for you and Laiyah Rose."

She swallowed hard as his gentle touch calmed her. "I know you are. I'm sorry. It's just that I want that monster found and locked up,

Christian. I never want him to be in Laiyah Rose's life."

Christian bristled and let out a heavy sigh. "That will never happen. I put my life on that."

Her chin dropped on his chest, and she began to relax. "I love you," she cried.

Christian tilted her chin toward him, tenderly moving his mouth over hers.

She breathed lightly between parted lips as his hands traced a path along her body.

"I'll always be here," he whispered. "No one will ever hurt you again. No one. I promise." His lips searched hers again as if sealing his words with a kiss.

"The kids are asleep. Why don't I make us a cocktail, and we sit outside on the lanai?" she suggested as her anxiousness subsided.

"I have an even better suggestion," Christian commented.

"What?" she asked, smiling mischievously.

"I think you know." He kissed the palm of her hand before leading her to their bedroom.

Luna welcomed her husband's tender lovemaking until thoughts of Rex Sanchez overtook her mind. Was it him? Was he the man who raped her and made her life a living hell? From what she'd learned about him, this man had a family and grown children. From what his employees described, he lived an exemplary lifestyle, had no prior criminal record, and was a no-holds-barred but considerate employer. How could such a person like that possibly be a monster?

She tried to focus back on her husband as he continued to make love to her, but her mind just wasn't in it. Times like this was when she resorted to other measures, meaning she faked the good feelings until she heard his moan of satisfaction.

When he rolled over to his side, she exhaled and turned on her side so she could let the tears flow. If Sanchez was Laiyah Rose's father, what would that mean for them? Would his children want to meet Laiyah Rose? Would this sick man want to be part of Laiyah Rose's life? It wasn't a farfetched thought; it was very real. It could indeed happen, but where would that leave her? She didn't want any part of this man's sick, demented world, and definitely not her daughter. It was bad enough that Christian hadn't fully warmed up to their almost one-year-old, but this could put an even bigger gap in their relationship.

She heard Christian's light snore and eased out of their bed. Going into Laiyah Rose's room, she opened the door and stopped, standing from a distance and watching her sweet little girl sleeping. She was so innocent, so pure, yet she had been conceived in the most vile of circumstances.

Luna walked into the room and stood over Laiyah Rose's crib. Looking down at her baby girl, she felt overwhelmed with sadness, and tears fell. She lightly caressed her tiny locks of hair.

"God, please protect my daughter. Take care of her all the days of her life," she prayed and cried. "Don't let any harm, hurt, or danger come near her."

She remained looking at her daughter for several more minutes before returning to bed.

Laying on her side, she tucked herself in and closed her eyes only to open them when she heard her phone vibrating on the night table.

Who is this calling me? she questioned. *It's almost midnight.*

She picked up her phone and flipped it over.

"Hello? Hello, Lorie. Is that you? What's going on?" she asked when she heard Lorie crying.

"Oh, God, Luna. I need you. I need to get away. Please say I can come there. I promise I won't cause trouble. I need to get away!" Lorie screamed.

"Sure, but what's wrong?" she rose from the bed and went into the master bath so as not to wake Christian.

"I'm in trouble. I can't go into detail right now, but I might be dead if I don't get out of Virginia."

"Oh my God," Luna cried. "Where are you? How soon will you be here?"

"I'm on the way now. I'm on the bus. I was too afraid to take the plane or even drive. I'll tell you everything when I get there. And Luna, please don't tell Christian that I'm in trouble. Please, just let him think I came for a visit or that I had a conference or something nearby. Anything but the truth. Promise me!"

"I promise, but I don't like keeping things from Christian, Lorie."

"Listen, just promise me this one time. Can you do that?" she pleaded.

"I said I would," Luna replied, unsure what was happening.

The call ended, and Luna sat on the toilet, thinking about what Lorie could have gotten herself into. She remembered when they were teens that Lorie had gotten on drugs and tried to kill her. She hoped her sister was not mixed up in anything like that again. Surely not. But who or what was she running from? What kind of trouble was Lorie in, and how much of it was she dragging along with her? Had she messed over a real estate deal? Had she run off with somebody's earnest money?

"Oh, God, whatever it is, keep my sister and this family safe from harm," Luna prayed.

She eased back into the bed. Christian was still asleep and snoring. When she nestled beside him, he turned toward her and draped his arm across her, pulling her into him as he slept.

Luna lay staring at the ceiling until sleep conquered her sometime over in the night.

The following morning, the Black household was chaotic as usual. She enjoyed a routine of getting the kids up, dressed, and fed with Christian. Mornings like this made her adore her husband even more, as he stayed around long enough to help her before he left for the office. It was part of their bonding time.

She also took moments like this to strengthen the bond between Christian and Laiyah Rose. Of course, she still breastfed her daughter, but Christian spoon-fed her oatmeal or rice cereal, which Laiyah Rose loved.

"Honey, I meant to tell you I got a call last night from Lorie. You were asleep."

Christian immediately stiffened. "Is that so?" he said, momentarily stopping to feed Laiyah Rose.

"Ah, ah," Laiyah Rose whined from her high chair, reaching.

"Sorry," he said, putting a spoonful of cereal into her mouth. The little girl showed her satisfaction by beating her hands on her high chair. He placed another spoonful into her mouth. "What did she want?"

"She, she's on her way here."

Christian stopped feeding Laiyah Rose and looked at his wife. "On her way where?"

"Here, honey. Some conference or other. Anyway, she said it was a spur-of-the-moment decision." Luna hated lying to her husband, but in this instance, she would keep things a secret until she found out what was happening.

"I don't like the idea of her popping up last minute," Christian barked. "We have enough going on in our lives without Lorie and her problems or whatever she's up to. I don't trust her. Something sounds suspicious, is all I'm saying."

"Honey, stop. Show a little empathy. Before Laiyah Rose was born, I hadn't seen or heard from my sister in years. She begged me and my parents to forgive her, and we did. Now, she needs me; I can't turn her away. That wouldn't be right. That's what family is all about."

"Yeah, yeah, yeah," Christian said, unconvinced, "but I'm telling you, I don't buy what she's telling you, Luna. But, we'll see."

Chapter 15

Seems So Long

"Time flies, people change." Shelia E. Bell

These past six weeks, though challenging, proved beneficial for Pepper's mental health. Tomorrow, she was scheduled to be released. Looking back on her stay, she would admit that talking, sharing, and listening to others had done her a world of good. For once, she felt like she was among people who understood her pain and identified with it in some small way, the same as she could see theirs. A prime example was Ryan, the man she met at her first group therapy session. She picked up on his emotions without knowing who he was, his name, or anything about him.

When he started opening up more at each session, she wished she could be as vulnerable as him and some of the others, but she hardly ever talked. When she did share, she came from those sessions exhausted, like she'd worked a full nine to five.

Ryan stopped her in the corridor after the fourth, maybe fifth, group session.

"Uh, hey, Pepper," he said as she walked toward her room.

"Yes," she answered, feeling funny on the inside and nervous because she didn't know why he chose to talk to her. She wasn't against it; she just didn't understand the reasoning behind it. The last time she had actually talked and interacted with a man was, well, it hadn't been since before Xavier died. Of course, she talked to Stiles, Khalil, and Hezekiah. They were family. They were the ones who checked on her and helped look after her boys.

Ryan was more like she was—grief-stricken and heartbroken. He lost his wife and their three young children—ages one, three, and five—in a tragic head-on collision caused by a driver who lost control of his vehicle. Ryan was the lone survivor. He was emotionally crushed, and understandably so.

In Pepper's eyes, he was the epitome of strength in dealing with such a horrendous accident.

"I was just wondering how you like group therapy."

"I didn't like it at first," Pepper told him, standing in place but hardly looking at his dark eyes and handsome face. "I looked at it as an invasion of my privacy. I didn't want other people to know what I was dealing with. I didn't think anyone would understand. But the more I attend, the more I feel at ease—like I am part of something. It's like finally being among people who aren't trying to get me to mask my pain. Instead, I'm learning how to say what I feel. Sometimes, those feelings are not so good, but other times, I can cope with them. I hope that makes sense," she said.

"It makes a whole lot of sense. When I was forced to come here, I didn't see how this place, or therapy, or any of this mental health stuff could benefit me, not after what happened, but it's helped me. Helped me a lot. So, today is your last day here, huh?"

"Yeah," Pepper said. "And your last day is coming up in a few days."

"Yes, Monday," he answered.

"Do you live in Memphis?" she asked, not knowing why.

"No, I actually live in Jackson."

"Mississippi or Tennessee?" Pepper asked.

"Tennessee," Ryan answered.

"Oh, I'm familiar with Jackson, Tennessee. Well, I used to be. A lot of folks go there to eat at that restaurant, Casey Jones. I've been a few times, but it's been a minute since I've been there."

"Well, maybe you'll come back," he said, almost under his breath.

"Uh, yeah, maybe I will."

"Look, I really just wanted to have a chance to tell you it was nice meeting you, even if it was in a setting like this." Ryan looked briefly around the cold, sterile hallways of the hospital.

"Thanks, Ryan."

"Uh, well, good luck." He started walking off but then stopped. "Hey, Pepper," he called, "would you like to exchange numbers? And please don't read anything into it. I mean no disrespect. I just thought since we were able to talk in Group, maybe we could stay in touch once we get out of here."

"I'd like that, but I don't get my phone back until tomorrow," she replied.

"And I won't get mine until I leave on Monday. We can write 'em down on something."

"Okay. Come on, there has to be pen and paper in the Reading Room," Pepper suggested.

They exchanged numbers, and before parting ways, Ryan said, "Take it easy. I wish you nothing but success. It's a cruel world out there, you know."

"Yeah, I know. Ryan. I know..."

The next afternoon, Pepper said farewell to the staff and some of the patients, including Ryan.

Victoria was waiting in the car outside the hospital with Zavion and Davion.

Pepper took off running toward the car when she saw the handsome little faces of her sons.

"Mommy, Mommy," they cried when Victoria opened the front car door.

"No, I'm getting in the back with my boys, Momma," Pepper said.

"Sure," Victoria said, smiling.

Pepper sat in the middle of the boys, put an arm around each of them, and kept it like that all the way home.

Victoria planned on spending at least the first week with Pepper to make sure the boys didn't wear her down too quickly. She wanted Pepper to be stable-minded and not feel pressured to return to the hustle and bustle of life as a single mother. The last thing she wanted was for her daughter to become overwhelmed. She talked to Fancy about Pepper's release. Fancy, Eliana, and Luna all agreed to be present for Pepper in any way they could. Hezekiah vowed to help as well. The village was coming together and with God and the village around her, Pepper could not fail.

She made a commitment to herself, her therapist, and her family not to abuse her anti-anxiety medications or any other drugs. To prove how serious she was, she purchased a pill lockbox that, when programmed, would only open at set pre-chosen times and dispense the appropriate dosage. The device reminded her of an automatic pet feeder. She laughed a bit at her dilemma, but she was grateful to get another chance to be the woman and mother she needed and wanted to be to herself and for her boys.

"Do you want to order delivery?" Victoria asked after arriving home.

"We should have stopped somewhere on the way home," Pepper said, "I didn't think about that."

"I did, and honestly, I didn't suggest it because I thought you probably wanted to get home. And the boys are already excited to see you, so stopping somewhere would only keep them on edge," she said, laughing at them as Pepper started tickling them.

"You're right," Pepper agreed. "Hey, what would you guys like to eat?" she asked.

"Pizza," said Zavion.

"Macheese nuggets," Davion said.

"Okay, pizza, mac and cheese, and chicken nuggets it is," she announced.

"Yay," the boys chimed and dashed to their mother, hugging her legs.

While Victoria ordered the food, Pepper walked around the house like it was the first time she'd seen it. It was an eerie feeling but not a feeling of sadness. But she did feel like what once was now was no more. Xavier was gone. The boys were four years old. Not babies anymore. She was a single mom who had no idea how to raise boys to be men. But here she was. God had assigned this responsibility to her. She realized that now. She didn't want to fail God. She didn't want to fail Xavier, and she didn't want to fail her boys.

When it was bedtime, she was impressed when Zavion and Davion prayed "The Lord's Prayer" without stumbling. Before she went into the hospital, she had tried for months on end to teach them "The Lord's Prayer," but with little success. She looked over her shoulder at her mother standing in the boys' doorway, smiled, and mouthed, "Thank you."

Chapter 16

Don't You Worry 'Bout A Thing

"Sometimes it's tough to explain what's going on in your head when you don't understand it yourself."
Karen Salmeron

Fancy didn't speak publicly often, not as much as she did when she held the title of First Lady of Holy Rock, but whenever she did share a message, people were attentive and inspired. Today was no different.

"Without God, we cannot be successful. We cannot weather the storms of life. Without God, we will fail every time. It may not seem like it at first, but in due season, you will see the fruit of your labor, whether that fruit is good or bad. It's your decision. What life will you lead? What choices will you make? What example will you set? Who will you rely on?"

Fancy received a standing ovation when she took her seat.

Eliana, Pepper, and Luna exited Holy Rock after *The Pulpit Ladies* meeting. The less time Eliana spent at Holy Rock, the stronger she felt. Khalil was not making their separation easy, not that she had expected him to. But sometimes, he could go a little too far.

"I was surprised when I saw Fancy was today's speaker," said Pepper.

107

"I thought I told y'all she was our speaker for today. I guess I forgot."

"Yeah, you did," said Luna. "I didn't know she could speak like that. She was good."

"Yeah, she sure was. But honestly, I didn't think she would continue participating in *The Pulpit Ladies* after she learned that you and Khalil were separated," Pepper said.

"Girl, please. One thing I'll say about Fancy is that she knows her son. She's been trying to get him to do right since the beginning. That's one thing I love about her; she's going to call a spade a spade even if that spade happens to be her son."

"She wasn't like that when it came to me and Xavier," said Pepper. "After we got married, she changed, and suddenly, she wasn't for our marriage. But in the beginning, she was all for us being together. I guess she thought him marrying a woman would scare the gay away." Pepper cracked a fake smile. "Boy, was she wrong," she said, shaking her head.

"Well, she was good today. I'd like to hear her again," Luna said. "Come on, let's go eat," Luna said.

"Are we going in one car or taking separate cars?" Eliana asked, looking at Luna. Pepper had ridden with her. "Luna, after we leave the restaurant, I can bring you back to pick up your car."

"No, I'll drive. Where did we decide we're going?"

"Uh, what about that new bistro in Whitehaven? I heard their food is delicious,"

Luna said. "I haven't had the chance to go because I'm hardly ever on this side of town."

"Let's try them. What kind of food do they serve?" asked Pepper.

"Plant-based, mostly, from what I've heard, and some African dishes."

"Sounds good," Eliana said.

"I'm hungry, so I'm willing to try just about anything," Pepper agreed.

At the restaurant, the ladies laughed and enjoyed each other's company. "I can't believe we just left *The Pulpit Ladies* meeting where there was a ton of food, and here we are eating somewhere else."

"It's not going to waste. Those who wanted to take home an extra plate did, and everything else that was left, we did like we always do," Eliana said.

"Took it to the shelter?" said Pepper.

"It's not going to waste. Those who wanted to take home an extra plate did, and everything else that was left, we did like we always do," Eliana said.

"Took it to the shelter?" said Pepper.

"Actually, our Homeless Ministry picks the food up and distributes it."

"That's good. Thank God for the Homeless Ministry and for our ministry, too," said Pepper. "*The Pulpit Ladies* is growing and is beginning to inspire first ladies all over the city."

"Not just first ladies," said Eliana, "*The Pulpit Ladies* is *us*. We are the women who reach out to our sisters to help them navigate life as women of God with pride, respect, and reverence to Him." Eliana pointed a finger toward the sky and looked up.

The server brought their dishes to the table, and the ladies became quiet as they tasted the delightful cuisine.

"Girl, this stuff is so good," said Luna. "I am so glad we came." Luna loved food and found it hard to resist, especially when she tasted food like this. "And this is plant-based? Who would have thought?"

"I know, right," said Eliana. "We'll have to see if they cater. Maybe we can have them cater the next *Pulpit Ladies* meeting."

"That's a good idea," said Pepper, putting a forkful of her African dish into her mouth, followed by a swallow of iced tea.

"So, where do things stand with you and Khalil?" Luna asked.

"Well, I'm still staying with Ian. I'm only here because of *The Pulpit Ladies*. I started the ministry, and I don't want to be the one to let it go down the drain. I believe God called me to do this, so that's what I'm going to do."

"Not to get all up in your business, but can't flying back and forth be a little expensive?" asked Pepper.

"This is my first time coming home. I've only been gone two weeks. And not really. I spent less than a hundred dollars round trip. Ian has a friend who works for the airlines. He gets deep discounts."

"Wow, that's great," said Luna.

"Yeah, that's a huge saving," said Pepper. "And Khalil has Khaliyah?"

"Yep, I told him I would be in town for the meeting and was dropping her off with him. He had no problem with that, but you know he hates that I'm in Atlanta. At first, I didn't tell him where we were going, but I realized that would be wrong. I'm not going to be one of those vindictive baby mamas. Know what I mean?"

"I do," said Luna. "Matter of fact, I think it's very first lady-like of you."

They burst into laughter and then took time to enjoy their food.

"I want a DNA test," Luna blurted after taking a gulp of her diet soda.

Eliana almost choked on her food when Luna said that.

"A what?" Pepper asked. "Who and what are you talking about? What did I miss while I was in the looney bin?" she snickered.

"Stop doing that, Pepper," Eliana said, her tone serious. "You were in a facility that treats people with mental issues the same as a hospital that treats physical diseases and ailments. Stop making fun of yourself, please. It's no joke."

"I know, and you're right. That's one of the things the therapist told us not to do, to make light of our situation thinking we're making others feel comfortable."

"You're doing just the opposite," Eliana said.

"I'm sorry. Luna, what are you talking about?"

"The man who they arrested for abducting and sexually assaulting those women. I think he could be the person who assaulted me," Luna whispered, looking around the restaurant like she suspected someone was eavesdropping on her. "I told Eliana that I've seen him in my building and in the company parking garage on more than one occasion. But why would I ever suspect a man of his caliber to do something like that?"

"But what about the other guy you told us about before I went for treatment?"

"His name was Torres. I've scratched him off my list. Yes, he worked temporarily in my building, and his cologne, well, I can't be certain it was the scent I smelled. I told y'all it was more of a musky smell, and the man had an accent."

"And you're saying Torres doesn't?" asked Eliana.

"He has a Spanish accent. And I did say Laiyah Rose looked just like his baby, but I think I was trying to make it true. I want so badly to find this guy and have him put away forever. But I don't want to put the wrong man behind bars. I just don't think it's Torres. But this Rex Sanchez man, I'm telling y'all, I think it's him. I heard his voice too, and it gave me the chills."

"What did Christian say?" asked Eliana.

"Yeah, what is he saying about all of this?" asked Pepper.

"You know Christian; he's very supportive and attentive to my needs. He's doing everything he can to understand my feelings and how much I need to get this resolved. I haven't told him about wanting to have a DNA test done, but I don't see why he would be against it."

"But suppose he doesn't want to know who Laiyah Rose's biological father is. You said it's already hard enough for the man to accept her. I mean, maybe you should leave it alone," Pepper suggested.

"Did you say I should leave it alone? Are you serious? How can you, Christian, or anyone think I'm supposed to forget about a person who nearly killed me? A man that raped me and tortured me for days. A monster who abused me and left me with memories of him forever because he left a baby in my belly." Luna began to cry.

"I'm sorry, Luna." Pepper reached across the table and squeezed Luna's free hand. "I didn't mean it like that. It's just that I don't want you carrying this around like a noose around your neck for the rest of your life."

"But that's it, Pepper," she said, clenching her teeth, "I *am* going to carry this with me for the rest of my life. Or did you forget that I have a child by this monster!"

"Calm down," said Eliana. "It's going to work out. You'll see, and maybe taking a DNA test would be the thing to do. That way, you can know for sure if this is the man or not. If it is him, he'll go away for a very long time. I can almost guarantee that. And if it isn't, then we'll have to keep searching until this creep is revealed."

The ladies nodded and continued dining.

"Who's up for dessert?" Luna asked after they were done with their entrees. "No time like the present if I'm going to indulge my appetite."

Chapter 17

Joy Inside My Tears

"Don't let yesterday take up too much of today."
Will Rogers

Pepper had been home for nine days. Having her mother staying with her made her transition much smoother. Today, Victoria returned to her own home, and Pepper had mixed feelings about it.

Victoria was so helpful with the boys, but Pepper told herself it was time to resume her motherhood role without Victoria.

So far, the day had been uneventful. She took them to the park and also checked on their applications for admittance to Pre-K in the fall. She couldn't believe how fast time was flying. In a blink, her sons would be in kindergarten! Unbelievable.

She had been thinking about what she would do when they started pre-K. Would she remain at home or volunteer somewhere, perhaps at Holy Rock's school? Or she could go back into the workforce. Thanks to the substantial life insurance policy Xavier had taken out, she didn't need the money. It was more than enough for her and the boys to live comfortably for quite some time. Yet, the thought of going to work, mingling with coworkers, and doing something outside the home sounded like a possibility.

Her text dinged. She stopped sorting laundry and picked up her phone.

"Hmmm," she said, smiling.

`"Hi, Pepper. It's Ryan. From uh stateside."`

`"I remember. Hi, Ryan. HRU?"` She hadn't heard from him since they exchanged numbers the day of her discharge. She thought about him a time or two, but the normality of life kept her mind occupied with other things, mainly her boys.

`"Good. How are you?"`

`"I'm good."`

They texted back and forth until Ryan asked, `"Would you like to have lunch sometime?"`

Pepper studied the text like it was an exam. *Lunch? She was taken off guard with that question. Lunch with another man other than her husband?* Xavier was dead, but that didn't change the way she felt. She looked at her hand. She had never taken off her wedding ring. In her mind, just because she was considered a widow didn't mean she wasn't married.

`"I have to go. My boys are calling me."` She did not wait for Ryan's response. She put the phone down, sighed, and returned to sorting and folding laundry. She refused to entertain anyone or anything that would make it look like she had forgotten about Xavier.

In therapy, she was told that she should move on with her life. "That includes being open to meeting new people, dating, and entering into a relationship," her therapist said. Pepper

Shelia E. Bell

couldn't see that happening anytime soon. Ryan was handsome, seemed nice enough, and was widowed, the same as her. She felt like they understood each other's pain—something a lot of people would not understand unless they had experienced it the same way as she and Ryan.

She picked up the phone and looked at the text exchange again. "I brushed him off. He probably never wants to hear from me again," she mumbled. "I could have been upfront and just said I'm not ready. But not ready for what? Girl, you are one crazy chick," she said, folding the last few towels.

The boys had been asleep for the past hour, which allowed her to do some things around the house. She planned and prepared their lunch and had it in the fridge for when they woke from their naps.

"Mommy," Zavion called from his bedroom.

"I'm in the laundry room," she said, picking up the last stack of folded laundry to put away.

Zavion appeared, walked up to her, and hugged her around her hips. She hugged him back and kissed the top of his head.

"You ready for lunch?"

He nodded. "Yes, ma'am."

"Come on, let's go to the kitchen."

Davion woke up shortly after.

While they were eating, she called Eliana. "Are you back in Atlanta?" she asked.

"Yes, why? What's going on?"

"Oh, nothing much. I thought you left, but I wasn't sure. You said you might hang around since Khalil wanted to keep Khaliyah a few extra days."

"I decided not to. I just left her with him, which meant I had no reason to stay. All I would have been doing was incurring unnecessary expenses by paying for an extra night in a hotel."

"I don't know why you stayed in a hotel anyway. I told you, and I know Luna did too, that you could stay with us. And I know Fancy would have let you stay in her house. Like you told me and Luna, Fancy knows her son. She knows he's a real piece of work."

Eliana chuckled. "Yeah, that he is. And of course, I know that I can stay with one of you. But I don't want to drag y'all into me and Khalil's mess. Plus, I charged it to his account, so it's all good. Anyway, guess what I'm doing?"

"Uh, what?" Pepper asked.

"Girl, I'm kicked back on Ian's balcony. He's at work so I have the place to myself. It's like the perfect getaway."

"Good for you."

"I think I've made up my mind about two things."

"What? Tell me," Pepper urged.

"Number one. I'm going to file for divorce."

"What?" Are you serious, Eliana? Are you sure this is what you want?"

"Yes. I mean, I love him, but I can't do it anymore. I've tried to make it work over and over, but it hasn't, and now I can't make sense of it, Pepper. I will not be the kind of woman who lays up every night wondering where her husband is and who he's with. I won't do it. I deserve more."

"I hate that it's come to this, but I understand you. I'm still sorry," said Pepper.

"Thanks, Pepper."

"Do I want to know the second thing?" Pepper asked.

"The second decision I made is I'm going to start looking for a job now that Khaliyah is old enough to go to Holy Rock Academy's daycare. And I don't want to ask anything of Khalil except for him to take care of his daughter. I have no doubt he will do that."

"That's funny that you would say you're thinking about looking for a job," Pepper replied.

"Why is that?"

"Well, because I've been thinking the same thing. The boys will be starting Holy Rock Academy in the fall, too. I want something to do, even if it's just something part-time."

"Right," said Eliana. "I want to work at a church again. I enjoyed working at Holy Rock. I like church administration."

"I'm going to look for something in customer service. That's my background experience. I'll even entertain working from home. I figure I can do that while the boys are at school."

"Oh, yeah, that would be a good idea unless you want to get out of the house. I mean, working from home sort of defeats the purpose of getting out and meeting and interacting with people."

"That's true. I didn't think about that, and you know I do want to start socializing more. Speaking of meeting people, remember I told you and Luna about that guy I met when I was at Stateside?"

"Oh, yeah. What about him?"

"He texted me."

"He did?" Eliana laughed. "What'd he say?"

"Not a whole lot. Asked how I was doing. He said he's returned to work."

"Do you know what he does?"

"Yes, he's an intake specialist at Jackson Utility."

"Oh, cool."

"He asked if we could have lunch sometime."

"Oh, that sounds cool, Pepper. I'm excited for you. When are you going?"

"Girl, I know you're going to flip out, but I didn't give him an answer. I told him the boys were calling for me, and I had to talk to him later. I haven't heard from him after that."

"Why would you not go out with him? From what you told me and Luna, he sounds like he might be a cool guy. Y'all can relate to some of the same things, and you said you got good vibes. So what's the problem?"

Pepper sighed into the phone. "I don't know. I guess I'm not ready. I don't think it's been enough time. Xavier hasn't been gone for quite two years, and I don't think I can; well, I don't feel it would be right."

"I don't want to sound insensitive, Pepper, but don't you think it's time to move on? Xavier is dead. He's not coming back. You're young, not even thirty yet. You need to get out and meet people. Have fun. You have plenty of help with the boys. You don't have to worry about finances. You can live life with no regrets. You can even fall in love again one day," exclaimed Eliana.

"Hold up, girl. Fall in love? I don't think so. We're trying to get me to have lunch first."

Pepper and Eliana laughed.

"Look, just think about what I said. Text him back. Tell him you're sorry about cutting him off and that getting together for lunch sounds good."

"Uh, I don't know. I'll have to think about it some more," Pepper said.

"Momma, I want more juice," Davion said.

"Look, Eliana—let me."

"I hear them," Eliana interrupted. "You go on and see about them. We'll talk later. But think about what I said. For real, Pepper."

"I will. I'll talk to you later."

Chapter 18

Ordinary Pain

"A divorce is like an amputation: you survive it, but there's less of you." Margaret Atwood

Eliana sat at her computer and updated her resume. It had been four years since she last worked at Holy Rock. She hoped her job skills and degree would give her an edge when she started actively looking.

After she finished, she posted it online. Next, she called Stiles to let him know about her interest in returning to work, preferably for a church. He knew many ministers, so if anybody could give her a lead about a job, it was Stiles. Khalil could do the same, too, but she was not about to ask him to help her find anything, especially a job. She had to make sure she had more than enough money in case he gave her a hard time when he found out she filed. Speaking of filing, she FaceTimed Luna.

"Luna," she said when Luna's round face appeared on the screen, holding Laiyah Rose.

"Is she crawling yet?" Eliana asked.

"Yes, all over the place," Luna said as she put Laiyah Rose down on a pallet she'd made on the floor. The little girl had plenty of room to crawl around and play with the toys Luna had lined on the pallet.

"She is so cute. Where's Dax?"

"Oh, Christian took him to the barbershop. They're having their Boys Day Out, that's what Christian calls it."

Eliana laughed. "Good for them. Hey, I need you to ask Christian something for me when he gets back."

"What is it?"

"I'm looking for a good divorce attorney."

"What did you say?"

"You heard me. I've made up my mind, Luna. I'm divorcing Khalil."

"Oh my gosh, I know you said you were going to do it, but I thought you would change your mind. I was hoping the two of you could work things out, but I understand that you can't live with someone you can't trust, especially when he breaks that trust by sleeping with another woman over and over again."

"Yeah, tell me about it. So, I'd appreciate your asking him for some recommendations."

"Sure thing. Have you told Khalil?"

"Nope, and I'm not going to until I talk to a lawyer. I want to have my ducks in a row when I tell him. He can be manipulative and slick, and I don't want to get caught up listening to him trying to justify our staying together. I just want to move on, or else I won't be able to go through with it."

"If you don't think you can go through with it, then why do it? Maybe God is showing you that you need to fight for your marriage. It's not easy, but you say you love Khalil, so isn't it worth a shot?"

"Love on a one-way street just won't work, Luna. I love him, but he obviously doesn't feel the same toward me. I don't see how he could if he can keep cheating. And with the same person! He must have some really deep feelings for her for him to keep going to her bed, Luna. I mean, it is what it is. I've accepted it."

"I'm so sorry. I hate it for you and Khalil."

"I know, but I don't know what else to do. I also wanted to tell you that I updated my resume."

"Really, aren't we just full of surprises today?" Luna said, sitting on the couch while Laiyah Rose played on the pallet. She was such a happy baby. Luna smiled at her daughter.

"Look at her," she said to Eliana, focusing the screen on Laiyah Rose.

"She is such a cutie pie, Luna. And just as chubby as she can be. That breast milk is keeping her good and healthy."

"Yep, it sure is."

"But getting back to you, how do you think he's going to take it when you tell him you want a divorce?" Luna asked.

"I'm sure he's going to be pissed," Eliana went into the kitchen and put on the tea kettle."

"What are you making? Coffee or tea?"

"Tea. But yeah, I can hear him now. First, he's going to say he doesn't understand why I'm doing this; then he's going to start begging and pleading, telling me he's sorry, and he promises he is not cheating anymore. Whatever he says, I've heard it all before."

"Well, sounds like you've really made up your mind this time. You're really done, huh?" said Luna.

"Yes, I think I can truly say that I'm done. Now, what about you?"

"If you're talking about the DNA test, I was going to FaceTime you and Pepper later today and tell you that Christian is supposed to meet with the DA and see when we can do it."

"How do you feel about it?" she asked Luna.

"Anxious but scared at the same time. I can't keep going on like this. It's too much on me mentally. It puts a strain on my marriage."

"If it turns out that this *is* the guy, how do you think Christian will react?"

"I hope he'll be just as relieved as me. But if you're asking me how it will impact his relationship with Laiyah Rose, then I can't answer that. The man tries his best to show love for her. And I have no doubt that he loves her, but I don't know if it's unconditional like Dax. He loves that boy, and I tell myself he loves him because he is a boy. They have a unique bond, and I'm so grateful for that, but I would like him to have that father/daughter bond with Laiyah Rose, too. You know, like Khalil has with Khaliyah."

"Give him time, but like you said, Dax is a boy. Their bond is different. So don't look at it as he's intentionally making a difference between them. I don't think it's like that."

When the tea kettle started whistling, Eliana laid the phone on the counter and poured the hot liquid into her mug.

"I hope you're right," Luna said, "but anyway, I was going to tell you, too, that Lorie is here for a few days, so I might be out of pocket for a minute."

"That's cool. I know you're glad to see her. You didn't tell us she was coming."

"Yeah, I know, and that's what Christian got bent out of shape about. She just called out of the blue and said she was coming."

"Some people don't roll like that. Christian seems to be one of them. He likes everything planned out, or so it seems."

"Yeah, he does. Sometimes. But, hey, she's here now, so I'm going to enjoy her."

"Is she there now?"

"Yes, she's still asleep. She got in before day this morning.

"Well, before she leaves, maybe me, you, and Pepper can take her to lunch or dinner," Eliana suggested.

"Yeah, that would be nice. I'll let her know."

"Okay, well, I'll talk to you later."

When they ended the call, Eliana resumed her search for a lawyer. "If only Trevor Price was still alive," she spoke aloud. "He was one of the best. God rest his soul."

Chapter 19

I Wish

"If you spend your time hoping someone will suffer the consequences for what they did to your heart, then you're allowing them to hurt you a second time in your mind." S. L. Alder

Lorie had shown up at their door at two-thirty in the morning, looking haggard and wide-eyed like she was scared or high. Luna couldn't be exactly sure which it was. She prayed it was not the latter.

Lorie was addicted to drugs for years, but from what she told Luna and their parents, she had been clean and sober for the past eleven years.

Luna went into the guest bedroom to check on her sister. Since she arrived, she had been in a deep, almost comatose sleep on and off, only getting up to use the bathroom.

"Knock, knock," Luna said, tapping lightly on the half-open door. She peeped inside and saw Lorie on her side, asleep.

"Lorie…Lorie?" she called, sticking her head inside the room. Instead of leaving, she walked inside and over to her sister's bed.

"Lorie, wake up," she said again, going so far as to shake her.

Lorie stirred, and slowly, her eyes opened. "What time is it?" she asked, groggy.

"It's after four—in the afternoon."

Lorie rubbed her eyes and pulled herself up in the bed. "I'm so tired."

"Tired? You've been asleep since you arrived. What's wrong with you, Lorie? Talk to me. Christian already suspects you're lying about coming here for a conference."

"He doesn't know anything about me or what I have going on," Lorie suddenly snapped.

"Wait a minute. Don't get mad at Christian. He's right. And I hate lying to him. You don't have a conference. What kind of trouble are you in? Who or what are you running from, Lorie?"

"I messed up, Luna," she said, and tears suddenly appeared, making her eyes look glossed over.

"Messed up? How? What are you talking about?"

"I'm in real bad financial trouble. I stole from my own company, and then I had to take out huge loans to save it. My three rental properties are in the process of being foreclosed on if I don't come up with the two hundred and fifty thousand to stop it. Now, I'm in trouble with the real estate commission. I could even go to prison for real estate fraud," she cried. "I might lose my condo, my business, everything."

Luna reached out and grabbed her sister, pulling her against her chest. "It's going to be all right, Lorie. There has to be something you can do. And if you have to start from scratch, then so be it, but you've got to come clean and try to work this whole thing out. You can do it. With God's help, you can do it, sis."

127

Luna stroked her sister's hair before pushing Lorie back and looking at her. "You're going to be just fine. You hear me?"

Lorie nodded, but more tears fell. "I'm over a million dollars in debt. "

"All of this didn't just happen overnight, Lorie. Why now? Why haven't you told me any of this before now? Do Mom and Dad know?"

"No, and I don't want them to know!" she bellowed. "For once, let them believe that I turned my life around and that I'm doing just as good as you, no, that I'm doing better. Better than you!" Lorie screamed.

"My God, Lorie, is this what this is about?" Luna fumed. "And here I thought you had changed. But you still hate me, don't you, Lorie? You never liked me. That's why you tried to kill me, your own sister! I should have known you were still jealous. Why? I never understood, but you are."

Lorie threw the covers back and jumped out of bed, almost knocking Luna to the floor.

"You think you're so perfect, so right about everything," Lorie yelled. "Jealous? Jealous of a nothing like you? No way. You were always in my shadow, Luna. Always!"

"*Your* shadow? You must be on drugs like you were back then. You always were such a pushover who did any and everything to be part of the in-crowd," Luna accused. "I wanted my sister back so badly, but I should have known you would never change. How could I ever want you around my kids? I didn't know what was wrong with you back then, and I sure as heck don't know what's wrong with you now. But I'm sick of being the one who always thought I did something wrong for you not to like me when all I wanted was a sister. You were selfish then, and you're selfish now."

"You think you're all of that. You always acted like you were the perfect one. Well, you haven't changed one bit, either, Luna! You run around wanting everybody to think you have the perfect life with the perfect little family, but you're a bigger fake than me! You parade around like you have it all together. Well, let me straighten your tie a bit, madam!" Lorie snarled.

"What's going on?" Christian asked, suddenly appearing in the doorway, holding a whimpering Laiyah Rose. "Didn't you hear Laiyah Rose in there balling her eyes out? Dax and I walked in, and you've scared him as well! What the hell is happening?" he demanded.

"You were right, Christian," Luna cried out. "You said I should be careful. You said I should take things slow, but *noooo*, I wanted a relationship with my one and only sister! I wanted to believe what she said. But I should have known. She hasn't changed. She's the same old Lorie. Just like she was when we were teenagers, she hated me all those years ago, and she still hates me," Luna said.

"Look, I don't know what this is about, but I do know that I cannot have you coming into my home and upsetting my wife," Christian said, a deep frown appearing on his wrinkled face. "Dax, go to your room, son, and play. I'll be in there before you know it."

The little boy did as he was told and left the room.

"Ohhh, so now you, Mr. Hot Shot Christian Black Esquire, you want to be Mr. Big and Bad. Well, let me tell you about your big and bad husband, Luna."

Christian stood in front of Lorie, his eyes blazing with anger. "Don't do this," he said, gritting his teeth and giving her a brutal stare. "I'm warning you. You do not want to do this."

Luna looked at Christian and then at Lorie. "Do what? What's he talking about, Lorie? You don't want to do what?"

"Oh, I couldn't imagine, sis. Hmmm, then again, could it be he doesn't want me to tell you that he and I, uh, used to be...no, I better not. That would be naughty of me." Lorie giggled.

"For chrissakes," Luna snapped. Her eyes darted back and forth like a tennis match between her husband and her sister. "Just say it already," she demanded, holding a squirming Laiyah Rose.

"Alright, since you insist. Did you know your oh-so-perfect husband Christian and I used to...do the nasty," she laughed. "No, but seriously, could that be what he's talking about? Or should I say what he's NOT talking about? Yep, we slept together. Not once," she began laughing, "not twice, not three times, but a whole *buncha* times," she laughed louder. "Right, Christian?"

Luna's eyes widened, her face crumpling as if the weight of Lorie's words had physically struck her. Her mouth opened, but no sound came out at first, only a silent gasp of disbelief. The color drained from her cheeks, leaving her pale as she stared at Lorie. "No... no, please," she finally whispered, her voice trembling. "Tell me you didn't... not with Christian... please." Her eyes filled with tears.

"Uh, I wish I could say it ain't so, but I can't say it ain't so," Lorie kept taunting.

"Tell me it's not true, Christian. Tell me," Luna screamed, and Laiyah Rose started crying, too. "Please, Christian. Please tell me she's making all of this up."

"Baby...I'm so sorry, Luna, it was a long time ago. I promise it was. I didn't know she was your sister. It was years ago. It meant nothing. She meant nothing."

"This happened when we were married?" she asked, her tears uncontrollable. "You actually cheated on me? Oh, God."

"Baby, I'm telling you, it meant nothing."

"And that's supposed to make it better, Christian? That it meant nothing? Oh, God," Luna said, throwing a hand to her face. She walked up to Christian and slapped him with all of her might while Laiyah Rose continued crying.

Christian rubbed his face. "Luna, baby, it was so long ago. When I found out she was your sister, it was over. I mean it. It was over."

Lorie stood looking, gloating like she'd won a Pulitzer Prize.

"You! You, get out!" Christian screamed.

Lorie continued laughing. Laiyah Rose cried louder.

"I said, get your things and get out!" he yelled again.

"You heard him. Get out of our house!" Luna screamed.

"With pleasure," Lorie snapped back.

"And don't you ever, ever, ever come back!" Luna cried.

Chapter 20

How Will I Know

"Never be sad for what is over, just be glad it was once yours." Unknown

Luna, Pepper, and Eliana met at Pepper's house the day after Luna's blowup with Lorie.

"I can't believe she would do something like this," Luna cried. "Then again, I can. Why did I think she had changed? And why did Christian sleep with her? Oh, God, I feel like such an idiot, allowing her into my home, around my kids, my friends, my man, and she was after him the whole time."

"He said it happened years ago, Luna," Pepper said. "Neither of them knew they shared a common link—you."

"That's what they say," said Eliana. "At this point, I wouldn't know who or what to believe."

"Exactly," said Luna. "Christian swears up and down that it happened early in our marriage. Like that's supposed to make it better. They supposedly met at some event, and she got wasted. Of course, him being—quote, a gentleman, he made sure she got home safely. Why he had to be the one? Who knows. Anyway, he said what they all say—one thing led to another, and they ended up sleeping together that night and several more after that until he found out she was my sister and broke it off."

133

"So what? That's supposed to give him brownie points or something?" Eliana retorted. "These men kill me."

Pepper looked at Eliana sideways, like she was trying to tell her to tone down her cynicism.

"I'm sorry, Luna. I'm not the one to be empathetic right now. Just because I'm going through my own crap with Khalil doesn't mean I should take it out on Christian and make him seem like a bad guy. I'm sorry," Eliana said again. "Your situation is different."

Luna showed her palm. "Don't apologize. You're right. Everything you've said is right. But do I want to say that our marriage is over? It may sound crazy, but I don't want to do that. At least, that's not what I'm thinking at the moment. Like you said, Pepper, it happened a long time ago. And look what he's dealing with concerning me?"

"What's he dealing with? I don't understand," said Eliana.

"Me neither," Pepper said.

"He's raising Laiyah Rose as his own, knowing fully well how she was conceived. And, look at me. I'm asking him to help me find out who raped me when every day he's reminded of it when he looks at her. But does he blame me? No. He still treats me with so much love and well, I love Christian."

"What you're talking about are two very different things," Eliana said. "You were raped. Christian went out and had an affair—with your sister. That was a choice."

"Yeah, that's right," said Pepper. "And why wouldn't he still love you? It wasn't your fault what happened to you. You didn't think a child would come out of something so horrific."

Luna wiped away tears. "Right. I'm just saying I think I'm more upset with Lorie than I am with Christian when I should be done with both of them! It's just so unfair. Everything that's happening now. Everything that's happened already. I don't know how much more of this I can stand."

Pepper and Eliana gathered around Luna, embracing her, reassuring her that everything would be all right.

"Come on, let's take a break from talking about our problems. Let's go check on the kids."

"Looks like they're having a good time," said Pepper, turning her focus toward the child monitor that gave her a clear view of her boys' playroom.

Eliana chuckled when she saw Dax following Khaliyah everywhere she went and trying to hug her.

They made the kids' lunches and set them up in Pepper's backyard since the weather had become cooler. This was a welcome relief from the overwhelming heat and the heavy bouts of thunderstorms. Memphis weather was all over the place.

The ladies ate salad and pizza while they talked about *The Pulpit Ladies* meeting.

"Fancy did a great job as a guest speaker," said Eliana.

"She sure did. Let's invite her back in the future."

"Sure, maybe closer to our women's month."

"That's a good suggestion," said Eliana.

"Do you have anyone in mind for the next meeting?" Pepper asked.

"I was thinking about First Lady Loretta from World Ministries. She's always in attendance, and I've heard her speak several times. She is fierce. I know she will give the ladies a positive, inspiring message," Eliana suggested.

"I say extend the invitation," said Luna.

"Do you have anyone else in mind? I'm open to other suggestions."

"I say we stick to your suggestion," Luna said, still sounding sad.

"Me too," Pepper agreed.

"Then I'll contact her."

Pepper's phone rang. "Hello," she said, smiling at Eliana and Luna. "It's Ryan. I'll be right back," she mouthed. She rose from her chair and went inside the house.

"Did I catch you at a bad time?" Ryan asked.

"My girlfriends are here, but I can talk for a minute."

"Good. I won't hold you. I wanted to call rather than text this time. I thought maybe if I called, I might have a chance to convince you to have lunch with me. I know you said you weren't ready to date. Neither am I. We could look at it as a therapy session," he chuckled. "We can catch up on what's happening in each of our lives, and I promise I won't bite."

Pepper laughed at his remark. His voice was so enchanting, so soothing. "Okay."

"Did you just say okay?" Ryan asked, sounding surprised.

"Uh, yes. When?"

"Uh, what about Friday, say twelve-thirty?"

136

"Twelve-thirty Friday is good."

"Text me your address."

"Okay."

"Any place in particular you'd like to go?"

"What about barbeque..."

"Sweet," he said, chuckling over the phone. "I can always eat me some good Memphis barbeque."

Pepper giggled. "Barbeque it is. I know a spot that serves the best rib tips and barbeque spaghetti. The spaghetti has hunks of juicy barbeque all through. It's to die for." She said, smacking her lips.

"Dang, girl, after a description like that, I cannot wait. So Friday at twelve-thirty it is. I'll let you get back to your company. Remember to text me your address."

"I will. See you Friday," Pepper said, turning in time to see Eliana and Luna with their heads poked inside the patio door.

Eliana and Luna started clapping and squealing with delight after she ended the call.

She turned around, folded her arms, and tilted her head. "Y'all were eavesdropping?"

"Yep, we sure were," Eliana said, looking at Luna and laughing.

"Y'all are so crazy."

"So you're going to have lunch with him?" Luna said first.

"Uh, yep. How could I tell him no again after you talked about how wrong I did him? I can't believe he called me back," Pepper said.

"That means he must like you," said Luna.

"We're just going to talk and catch up with each other outside the walls of Stateside."

"Good for you. And whatever you want to call it is fine by me," said Eliana.

"Don't read anything into it," Pepper half-smiled. "It's just lunch."

"That's a start," Luna said, smiling.

Chapter 21

From The Bottom Of My Heart

"One lie is enough to question all the truth."
S. Ansari

Christian greeted Luna as she pulled into the garage. Without a word, he opened her door and then the back door and started unbuckling Dax from his car seat.

"Hey, there, big boy," he said, ruffling Dax's hair as the toddler climbed down out of the car.

"Hi, Daddy," he barely said, taking off into the house.

"Hi," Luna mumbled, waiting until Christian moved so she could get Laiyah Rose.

"I've got her," he said, reaching across Dax's car seat and getting Laiyah Rose out of hers.

Once inside, they worked together to get the kids ready for bed. Christian read Dax one of his favorite stories. In Laiyah Rose's room, Luna sang to her little girl while breastfeeding her. Laiyah Rose's eyes rolled into her head as her suckling slowed, and she fell asleep.

They met in their bedroom. Luna sighed with exhaustion. It had been a long day.

"Did you eat?" he asked, breaking the dull silence.

"Yes, the kids and I spent most of the day at Pepper's house. We had plenty. Thanks for asking," she said dryly. "I brought some leftovers home in case you didn't eat or you're still hungry."

"I ate a meager lunch. Court all day kept me busy. I definitely could eat something. I started to stop somewhere, but I was too tired."

"Well, that's what's on the counter—leftovers. Give me a minute to get out of these clothes, and I'll warm it up for you." Luna began unbuttoning her waist-length crop top.

"We need to talk, and not about leftovers," Christian said without forewarning.

Luna took her robe off the door hook and put it on. "I guess we do," she said, "but then again, what is there to talk about, Christian? You already admitted to sleeping with her. God, I can't even say her name." Luna frowned and tightened her robe.

She left the bedroom and went to the kitchen, putting food in the microwave.

Christian walked up and forced her to face him. "Listen, Luna. Please, I'm sorry. I know that doesn't mean much now, but it's all I know to say."

Luna turned her head, but Christian refused to release her. "Please, I need you to hear what I'm saying, Luna. I love you. I love what we have together. I love what we're building together. I don't want anyone else. I made a mistake; I know that. I knew it back then. I wanted to confess—tell you what I did, but I couldn't. I didn't want to hurt you, Luna. And now look what happened? You don't know how much I prayed that this day would never come. But it did, and maybe it's good that it came out. I hated hiding it from you."

"I hear everything you're saying. And you're probably serious."

"I am, Luna. I am very serious. Every word I said I meant."

"I just can't ignore what you did. I keep telling myself it happened years ago, but what if that's a lie, too? She was in our home for almost two weeks last year. And what about this time? Did you make love to her in our house, Christian?"

"No, Luna, for Chrissakes, no! You know I would never—"

"Just stop it! I do not know what you would never do!" she yelled and raised a hand. "I didn't think you would ever cheat on me, but you did. The more I think about it, I remember how badly you wanted her to leave. You were never comfortable with her in our home. Now I understand why."

Luna forced herself from his grasp. "I need some time to think, Christian. I don't want to hate Lorie, and I don't want to hate you," she began crying.

Christian reached to pull her to himself again, but she moved back just as the microwave dinged.

"Your food's ready," she said and hurried out of the kitchen.

Luna checked on the kids again before she hopped in the shower. Maybe the hot jets of water would calm her down. Being around her friends earlier helped, but no one was around now. She was alone.

Her parents had called several times over the past two days since she told them what happened. She didn't like the idea of them learning that Christian had been unfaithful, but she wanted them to understand what Lorie had done.

They were furious when she told them. Much to her surprise, her parents weren't totally against Christian. They seemed to put more of the blame on Lorie rather than their son-in-law.

Christian was sitting on the edge of the bed when she came out of the bathroom.

"Luna, don't shut me out. Talk to me."

"I told you, I don't know what to say. Look," she said, wrapping a bath towel around her hair. "Do me a favor."

"Anything," he replied.

"Will you sleep in the guest room?"

Christian's head dropped. When he looked up at her, he mouthed, "Sure. If that's what you want."

"It's what I want."

Christian grabbed a few items before he left. "I love you," he said, looking back as he stood in the doorway and disappeared down the hall.

Luna knelt beside the bed, clasped her hands, and began to pray. When she was done asking God to guide her mind and help her to make the right decision about her marriage, she got in bed.

She reached for her phone on the nightstand but stopped and picked up the Bible instead, which she kept open on the 23rd Psalm.

After she read the passage, she rested the Bible on her chest and closed her eyes, praying once more for God to give her peace.

Her phone rang. When she reached for it and saw who it was, she felt like her blood pressure shot up twenty points. How dare Lorie call her.

Right away, she did what she thought she had already done—BLOCKED her.

†

Laiyah Rose woke her up earlier than usual. On the monitor, she saw her bouncing up and down in her crib and making a fuss.

Next, she looked at Dax's monitor. He was still sleeping. "Good," she said, dragging herself down the hall toward Laiyah Rose's room. She passed by the guest room. The door was slightly ajar. She stopped and peeked inside. The bed was made, and the room was empty.

"He must already be gone," she said to herself. She inhaled the faint scent of coffee.

"Hey there, sweet girl," she said lovingly as she entered Laiyah Rose's bedroom. "You slept good, didn't you," she smiled. "Yes, you did. Is that why you're awake and happy so early?"

She picked up a bouncy Laiyah Rose and went to the kitchen to see if Christian was there. He wasn't.

"Daddy's gone," she told Laiyah Rose. Next, she bathed her before feeding her. When Dax woke up an hour later, she got him fed and dressed as well.

The remainder of her day was typical, except for the number of calls she received from Pepper, Eliana, and her parents. All were concerned about her, and she was grateful to have such loving and thoughtful support.

"Ma, I don't know what I'm going to do," she said on one of the calls. "It may sound stupid, but I don't want a divorce. At least I don't think

I do," she said, her voice denoting an amount of uncertainty.

"I'm going to give you my advice. Whether you accept it or not is up to you. But cheating is as old as old can be. I'm sure you know this; maybe you didn't think about it, but in the Bible, the men had concubines, which only meant they had many women. Today, the law of the land says one man to one woman. Of course, in countries like some parts of Africa and other nations, polygamy is acceptable. But as Christians today, we don't practice that."

"Are you saying it was okay for Christian to cheat on me?"

"Of course not!" her mother exclaimed. "I'm not saying that at all. What I am saying is that you have to determine if you want to save your marriage or let it go. You have a way out because adultery is the one act that God honors divorce. But I'm telling you this—if you run because a man has cheated, you'll never stop running."

Luna listened intently. "I don't want a divorce. He's stuck by me. Maybe this is a test to see if I'll stick by him. Ma, I'm so confused," Luna cried.

"Pray on it. I'm praying, and your daddy's praying, too. God will show you what to do. One thing I know is that I believe Christian to be a good man. And Lorie, well, your sister can be a slick one. I'm not making excuses for your husband, but a Jezebel will stop at nothing to destroy everything around her. I hoped Lorie had changed, but it seems that isn't the case. I won't stop believing that God will give her a change of heart, but until He does, I think you need to keep your distance."

"Thanks, Ma."

"Have you heard anything else about the DNA test?" her mother asked.

"No, Christian met with the prosecuting DA the same day Lorie came with all this mess. Did I tell you they're also going to pull my rape test kit and check the DNA and other collected evidence against him on that too?"

"No, but that's great news. I know all this brings up painful memories, but you need this closure, honey."

"Yes, you're right. I sure do."

"And the sooner, the better. You need to know if this is the monster who hurt you. I think it will help bring you and Christian closer. Just knowing may help him accept Laiyah Rose."

"He's trying, and from my viewpoint, I'd say he's getting better with her every day. That's all I can ask."

"Good. Sometimes, it takes a little more time for folks than others, Luna. We are not all the same. Just trust God to lead you the right way. Your daddy and I talked yesterday about how much strength it takes to sustain a marriage. You have to decide if your love for Christian is the kind of love that will hide a multitude of sins. Or is it the kind that fades away with the morning light?"

"So you're saying that's what I need to figure out?"

"That's exactly what I'm saying. Is something that occurred years ago worth ending everything? Baby, in every disagreement in your marriage, remember there is no winner or loser. You are united under God to be partners in every aspect of your marriage. If he wins, you win. When you win, he wins. The important thing to remember is that you should always work together to find a solution. I didn't say it would be easy. God knows me and your daddy have had our challenges."

"But, Ma, I've never seen or heard you and Daddy argue."

"Believe me, we have, and we still have our moments, but we decided early in our marriage that we would not let our children see us arguing or being mean to each other. I heard this fellow say marriage is not fifty-fifty. Divorce is fifty-fifty. He said marriage has to be one hundred-one hundred. You don't divide everything you have. You give everything you've got. I couldn't have said it better myself," Luna's mother said, chuckling lightly into the phone.

"I love you and Daddy so much, Ma. Thank you for praying for me and Christian. Thank you for your godly advice."

"Honey, I want the best for you and for Lorie, too. I love that child. Love her with all my heart, and I'm praying for God to do something new in her."

"Have you heard from her since this happened?" Luna asked.

"Yes, she called the other day, sounding like the world's weight was on her shoulders. And it probably is."

"That's probably because she said she's in deep financial trouble. That's got to be hard. From what she told me, she could face the possibility of prison, and she's losing her business. I feel bad for my sister, even after what she's done to me."

"Your sister needs help. The kind of help that can only come from God. Keep praying for her. Don't stop."

"Ok, Ma. I will. Well, I'm going to get off this phone. I need to start dinner."

"I'm glad to hear you're still doing what a wife should do," her mother said.

"Well, not everything," Luna said, pausing.

"Even with that, you know what the Word says about withholding from your husband. Marriage endures not just because of joyful moments, but rather due to how challenges are managed."

"I know, Ma. But talking about cooking, I don't cook just for him. Me and the kids have to eat too, you know."

Her momma laughed. "I know that's right, baby."

Chapter 22

For Once In My Life

"If life can remove someone you never dreamed of losing, it can replace them with someone you never dreamt of having." Unknown

"Thanks for lunch," Pepper said, sitting in front of her house in Ryan's car.

"Thank you for having lunch with me. You were just as I pictured you'd be. Funny, daring, and spicy," he said, laughing.

"Oh, now you're resulting in name-calling all because I like spicy food?" she giggled, punching him playfully on his shoulder.

"Well, you did ask the server if they had anything spicy enough to make your nose run. I've never heard anybody ask that." He teased.

"There's a first time for everything," Pepper said, laughing.

This was the first time since Xavier's death that she'd gone out with a man. She didn't expect she'd be in this space again, not so soon after she buried her husband. Then again, her friends and her mother had to remind her of how long it had been since he died and that it was acceptable to live life again. She'd promised herself that she would. Now that she had the opportunity, she had to take it.

"I hope we can do this again," Ryan said.

"Uh, sure," she said shyly.

"Maybe next time we'll have dinner, and if there's a movie worth seeing, we can check it out."

"Sounds good. I liked walking along the river and Mud Island. That was nice. I didn't know they had that restaurant over there. I mean, I knew they had built a structure, and there was supposed to be a restaurant or museum at Tom Lee Park, but I never knew it opened. When the pandemic came, so many things shut down, and a lot of stuff was put to a halt. I honestly forgot all about it. But it was nice. Real nice," she said, smiling at Ryan.

"Good, I'm glad you liked it."

She opened the car door and looked at Ryan again. He was so handsome. "Uh, thanks again. Talk to you later," she hurriedly got out, as if she was afraid she couldn't control the emotions beginning to spin around in her head and heart. She ran up to her door, rushed inside, and exhaled deeply when she closed the door.

"You did it," she said aloud. "You did it, Pepper McCoy."

She called Rolonda and told her everything that had happened.

"I am so happy you went. I told you that you would enjoy yourself. It's one step at a time, Pepper. You've got this, girl. So, tell me, when are you going out again?"

"Uh, first of all," she frowned into the phone, "it was not a date, so there is no going out again...until now!" she said and burst into laughter. "Girl, we're going out next week. This time maybe dinner and a movie. I don't know how to feel, Rolonda. I mean, you know Eliana and Luna have been pushing me to do this, too. I know you all are my friends, and you want what's best for me. But it's still a little awkward, especially given the fact that this guy gives me all sorts of weird feelings on the inside. Know what I mean?"

"Yes, it means you're alive, Pepper. You still have so much life to live and so much love to give to more than just Zavion and Davion. You deserve for Mr. Right to find you. I'm not saying it's this Ryan fellow, but who knows? Or, it could be someone you haven't met yet."

"Rolonda, thanks for being my friend. I love you, girl."

"I love you, too, Pepper. Now, let me get out of here and go pick up my kids. I want to beat the school traffic. But remember what we talked about. Live your life. Love ya." She chuckled.

"Love you, too. I'll call you tomorrow. Buh-bye," they said, ending the call.

†

On the other side of town, Eliana pulled into her designated First Lady parking space at Holy Rock. She was dropping Khaliyah off for PARENTS' DAY OUT. Programs like this endeared her to Holy Rock, which offered many programs and outreach ministries for the community.

PARENTS' DAY OUT provided up to four hours of childcare in a safe Christian setting. For a small hourly fee, it gave parents a short respite to run errands without child interruption, catch a second wind, hang out with their spouses or friends, or simply do nothing.

After she dropped Khaliyah off, she made a beeline to midtown for her first meeting with the divorce attorney.

With each step taking her closer to the attorney's office, Eliana felt herself trembling. This was not a good feeling, not a good feeling at all. But Khalil had left her with no choice. Enough was enough, and he only had himself to blame.

"Mrs. McCoy, I'm Attorney Robinson, Arnetta Robinson," she said, extending her hand toward Eliana.

Eliana accepted the handshake. "Nice to meet you," she said with a nervous smile.

"Come this way," the attorney said, walking ahead of Eliana and stopping only to point to an open door leading to her office. A mahogany desk and bookshelves gave a sense of authority and warmth. The walls were adorned with framed degrees, certificates, and interesting pieces of art. Photographs and potted plants added a personal touch. Two gray cloth-covered chairs were in front of her desk.

"Please, have a seat. We've spoken over the phone, but I'm glad to meet you in person. I know it isn't the most pleasant of circumstances. Divorce rarely is, but on the brighter side, I'm here to ensure you are treated fairly and get everything you and your child deserve."

Eliana nodded. "Thank you."

"No need to be nervous, Mrs. McCoy, " the attorney said, seemingly picking up on Eliana's uneasiness. "You can be assured everything we discuss remains confidential. So tell me why you're here. When we talked over the phone, you mentioned adultery."

"Yes," Eliana nodded again.

"You or your husband?"

"Excuse me?" Eliana said.

"I asked if it was you or your husband who stepped outside your marriage."

"My, uh, husband," she said shamefully. "I don't know how much you know about my husband, but he's a prominent minister in Memphis."

"Yes, I've heard of Pastor McCoy. As a matter of fact, I've attended service at Holy Rock before at the invitation of some friends. I have a church home already. But if I didn't, I would probably give Holy Rock a chance. So, Pastor McCoy has a mistress, huh?" she said, cutting through the small talk and getting to the reason for Eliana's visit. "Let me hear everything."

After an hour-and-a-half-long meeting, toward the end, when the attorney divulged that property records showed the house they lived in was the property of Holy Rock, Eliana was told she might have to move.

"Move?"

"Yes, I'm afraid so. Unless your husband or the church agree that you and your daughter can remain living there. But keep in mind that he must continue to reside there as well. As your attorney, I would advise you not to accept that offer. If you do, he has the upper hand and could request the trustees of the church to remove you whenever he wanted since you would no longer be the first lady."

"I see," Eliana said, nodding and thinking about what she'd just been told. "I'm not surprised about the house being in the church's name. What I *am* surprised by is I didn't think about the possibility of me having to move."

"Are you in a position to do that?"

Eliana looked at the attorney initially like she didn't understand what the woman was saying. "Oh, uh, yes, I could do that. It's finding a place. I don't know how long that will take, but I guess I'll start looking immediately."

"Good. Many women can't afford to move or pick up and start over. I'm looking at this financial printout you brought. You're blessed to have some money set aside. You're in a good space."

"Thank you. I've always been a saver. Some people call me frugal," Eliana smiled. "And I plan on getting a job. I've already had a couple of interviews."

"I will, of course, ask that you be awarded spousal support in addition to child support. You said you would have no problems with the two of you sharing custody. Is that right?"

"Yes. Khalil may not be a good husband, but he's a wonderful father. He loves his daughter. I don't worry about her being taken care of, so yes, joint custody will be fine."

"I must inform you that joint custody will affect the amount of child support you receive. You'll receive far less. If you receive any amount at all."

"I can understand that. Attorney Robinson, I want to be clear. I'm not out to screw my husband over. I only want what's fair for me and my daughter. Like I said, I do plan on getting a job and providing for the two of us."

"Certainly," the attorney said. "Any expenses besides child support, such as extracurricular activities for the child or childcare, will be a shared expense."

"Sure, I understand."

"Well, unless you have other questions or concerns, I will get this order written up, and we can file with the court the first of next week. Oh, we're also going to request that he pay all your lawyer fees plus half downpayment assistance on a place for you and your daughter."

"Thank you. Thank you so much," Eliana said, rising from her chair and reaching across the desk to shake the attorney's hand.

"I'll give you a call as soon as we file. Meanwhile, I suggest you start looking for a place for you and your daughter."

†

"Why are you doing this?" Khalil argued when he came home that night. He behaved like someone who didn't know why his wife would want a divorce. So what if he cheated? People cheat every day. That doesn't always call for a divorce. Maybe if she turned it up in the bedroom, he wouldn't have to run to Detria's bed.

"Really, Khalil?" she argued back. "You really have to ask that? Hah, you're a real piece of work.

"I'm going to fight it," he warned.

"Don't you even think about it because I swear, Khalil, if you try to stop this, I'll spread your business all over this city. If I have to stand in front of Holy Rock and tell everybody what you've been doing, I'll do it. It's not like half the congregation doesn't know already that their pastor is a whore!"

"You would do that? You hate me that much that you would try to ruin me, Eliana?"

"Don't play this game with me, Khalil. And yes, I sure would do it. In a heartbeat. Because of your choices, my daughter and I have to find somewhere else to live."

"You can stay here, Eliana. You don't have to go anywhere."

"Oh, but we do have to go, Khalil. After the divorce, I won't be allowed to live here. I won't be First Lady anymore," she said, fighting back tears.

"Don't do this. Please, Eliana."

"The thing is, Khalil, I *didn't* do this. You did," she cried, storming up the hall.

Chapter 23

Yester-Me, Yester-You, Yesterday

"And suddenly, you know: it's time to start
something new and trust the magic of beginnings."
Unknown

"What time is your meeting?" Victoria asked Fancy.

"This afternoon at five."

"Nervous?"

"Not really. Why would I be? He's a client, Vicky. That's it."

"I know, but that doesn't mean he isn't a hunk of fineness," she laughed.

"Well, I certainly can't deny that," Fancy engaged, laughing as well. "I'll call you when I get back."

"Yep, talk to you later."

Pulling up to the entrance of her client's palatial looking home sent a wave of chills running up and down her spine.

"Come in," Noah said, greeting her at the door before she could knock.

"Good afternoon, Mr. Alexander."

He looked at her with raised eyebrows.

"Uh, I mean, Noah," she corrected, almost tumbling to the ground but caught herself.

"Let me take those," he said quickly, stepping up to remove her armful of materials and leading her into his home.

Inside the family room, they sat and discussed his ideas, matching them with the materials and designs Fancy had shared at their last meeting.

"Can I get you something to drink? Eat?" Noah offered after Fancy had been at his home for over an hour.

"Water is fine. I'll grab something when I leave here. I want to get everything finalized, if possible. Once I do that, I can notify the contractors."

"Okay, that we'll do," he said, giving her his full attention.

He got bottled water from the fridge. "Here you go."

"Thank you."

"Are we almost done?" he asked after another half hour passed of them discussing design plans.

"Yes, if you're sure you want to stick with the original designs and color palettes rather than the ones I brought today."

"I like them all, but your original plans are what I like most."

"Great, then I say we're done, Mr. uh...Noah," she said, smiling while she gathered her materials.

He helped her, and they walked toward the door.

"You know all that decision-making has made me hungry," he said, stopping momentarily and rubbing his flat abs. "You said you would get something to eat after you left here, right?"

"Yes, I'm probably going to swing by a drive-thru and pick up something quick."

"Why don't you join me for dinner?"

"Thank you, but I can't."

"You can't, or you won't?" His eyes caught and held hers.

Her gaze dropped as her cheeks flushed a deep crimson, clearly a sign of her embarrassment.

"I wouldn't want to impose. I don't mind picking up something. Really, I don't," she insisted.

"At least let me feed you after I've kept you waiting for me to return for two weeks. Not to mention, this afternoon, I've kept you here all this time. So, please, I won't take no for an answer. You choose where we dine." His smile flashed, and his eyes sparkled.

Fancy couldn't hold back her smile any longer. "Okay," she said, "you got me. I'll follow in my car."

"No, you don't have to do that. I'll bring you back to get your car, or better still, you can leave your car in my garage overnight. I'll take you home after dinner and bring it to you first thing tomorrow."

"No, please, but thanks. I'd rather drive."

"Have it your way," he chuckled.

At the restaurant, Fancy found conversation with Noah surprisingly effortless. His natural charm kept her laughing and made her feel completely at ease, as if they had known each other for years.

"So, if you don't mind me asking, are you married? Guess I should have asked that before inviting you to dinner. I wouldn't want Mr. McCoy to come looking for me." He wiped his mouth with his cloth napkin and took a swallow of his soda.

"No. Divorced. I have two sons." Her countenance suddenly changed when she told him she had two sons.

"You okay?" he asked as if he picked up on the change.

"Yes, it's just that, well, my youngest son passed."

"Oh, I'm sorry," he said, reaching across the booth, taking hold of her hand, and kneading it lightly.

"Thank you. Uh, what about you?" she said, easing her hand from his, "is there a Mrs. Alexander at home in Connecticut?"

He smiled. His teeth glistened like snowflakes. "Nope, there's no Mrs. Alexander. I have a daughter. She's studying abroad. I've been divorced from her mother since she was ten."

"Oh, I see. Studying abroad, huh?"

"Yes, in France. She wants to own a bakery and serve French-inspired croissants, pastries, and sandwiches. I have no doubt she'll do it. She's smart, if I must say so myself," he said, blushing.

"Just from what I've seen getting to know you, I have no doubt she is."

"Thanks. She promises me that when she finishes her education and opens her restaurant, she's going to settle down, meet Mr. Perfect, and give me a bunch of grandchildren." He exploded in laughter.

"Let me tell you, grandchildren are a treasure. They bring a whole new perspective to life. I have three of them. I wouldn't trade them for anything in the world." Fancy beamed.

"Would you like a glass of wine?" he asked, beckoning for the server.

"As much as I want to say yes, I have to say no. Actually, I should end the evening. I'm exhausted, and drinking even one glass of wine would probably get me pulled over for driving while sleeping," she said, chuckling along with Noah.

"We wouldn't want that to happen. Although, if it did, you better believe I'd be the first to bail you out," he said.

Why is this man so dang fine? she thought, captivated by his deep voice. It was one of the things that first drew her to Hezekiah when they met. Even back then, as a young teen, his voice was as deep as the singer Barry White's. The girls loved to hear him talk. Now, here she was, being wined and dined by an upgraded version of her ex-husband.

"So, you were a First Lady. That's what they call women married to preachers, right?"

"Yes, that's right. My ex was recently released from prison. That's a whole other story. He has a church but hasn't resumed his senior pastor role. His brother holds that position until, or if, he returns to the pulpit."

"Are you still affiliated with that church, if that's not being too nosy," Noah said.

"No, you're good. To answer your question, yes, my oldest son is a pastor. I'm a member of his church, but I also attend my ex-husband's church occasionally, mainly because of my relationship with my brother-in-law. He's an excellent Bible teacher. I learn a lot under his leadership. But I am loyal to my son's church.

I'm a ministry consultant there, so I'm required to be actively involved. And what about you? Are you a religious man? Part of any church?"

"I *am* a Christian, but I must admit I do not attend church very often because of my demanding career. But I was raised in the church by my grandparents. Both are deceased now."

"I see. Well, when all this is over, maybe you can squeeze in a Sunday or two to attend Holy Rock at my invitation." She smiled.

"I'm sure that could be arranged. Are you and your ex on good terms?" Noah inquired.

"I guess you could say that. There was a time when I couldn't stand to be around him or in the same space as him, but God changed my heart. I had to learn to forgive. It hasn't been easy, especially after the death of our son, but I'm healing—slowly."

"I'm sorry. I didn't mean to bring up unpleasant memories. I just want to learn more about you."

Fancy looked up at him. "More about me? Why?"

"Because I like you, Fancy. I want to get to know you. Is that okay with you?"

Fancy released a slow smile. "I guess."

"I mean, shouldn't a man know the woman who's seen the most intimate spaces in his home?" he joked.

"I wouldn't say all that, but yes, I guess I am learning a lot about your likes and dislikes when it comes to home décor, that is," she said, her voice shakier than she would have liked.

"So you're learning my tastes, and what I'm learning about you is that you like challenges."

"And you know this because?" Fancy asked.

"Because I can't be the easiest client. I have this big home renovation project. I've hired you to help me bring it all together, but it's hard as heck for you to communicate with me, considering the time I spend traveling. For instance, I don't always answer your texts when you need me to. I don't answer phone calls ninety-eight percent of the time because I'm either in a meeting, on another line, on a virtual call, or in the middle of traveling. Either way, I'm not available like a normal person who's renovating a home. When I do come home, I'm still busy. It never seems to let up." Flustered, he let out a long, audible breath.

"See, that's where I come in," Fancy assured him, detecting his aggravation. "I guarantee when I'm done unraveling what's going on in that artistic home renovation design mind of yours, Noah Alexander, your home will be like paradise. You'll never want to leave."

"Ahh, is that so?"

"Yes, that is so," Fancy giggled.

"I like that. I like that a lot."

"There's not a challenge I haven't conquered yet," she said boldly while trying to suppress another giggle.

"Okay, since you said it like that, I say we challenge each other to learn all we can about the other on a more personal level. If you accept the challenge, it means we will have to spend more time hanging out like this. We won't have much time while you're at the house dealing with the renovations, so dinner and some other fun stuff will have to be included on the agenda.

What do you say? Do you accept the challenge, Fancy McCoy?"

Fancy blushed and picked up her soda. "Noah Alexander, challenge accepted."

Chapter 24

Bridge Over Troubled Water

"If you accept the pain, it cannot hurt you."
Hugh Jackman

Eliana strolled out of Grace Temple feeling invigorated for the first time in years. She had been offered the position of church administrator with a decent salary and benefits.

"I got the job," she texted Pepper and Luna on the way to her car.

Her next stop was the apartment she'd applied for online. Now that she had a full-time job starting in two weeks, she felt extra good about being approved for the three-bed, two-bath townhome.

"We'll be in touch hopefully within the next forty-eight hours," the leasing agent explained.

"Thank you. I look forward to hearing from you. Can you tell me what you think my chances of being approved are? I like this place, and I'd love to live here."

"Right now, I can tell you everything on your application looks good. Thanks for bringing this last bit of information about your finances. Now all I need is to get my manager to sign off on your income qualifications, being you just started your job," the friendly gentleman told her. "But I feel pretty sure our property manager will approve it. This is a new complex. I think you'll fit in quite well. We'll be in touch. You have a good rest of your day."

He walked her to the door. Before she left the parking lot, Luna and Pepper texted her "congratulations" on the job offer.

Twenty minutes later, she was strolling into Holy Rock.

"Hello, Sista Mavis," Eliana said, throwing up a hand when she entered the church and saw her sitting at her desk. "How are you today?"

"Blessed and highly favored, First Lady. How are you?"

"I'm good," Eliana said in return. "He in his office?"

"No, I don't think he's back yet. He said he was going over to the childcare center to pick up Khaliyah. He said you were on your way."

"Thanks. I'll be in my office. If you see him when he comes back, will you let him know I'm here," she said.

"Sure will. You take care. It's good seeing you," Sista Mavis said, watching as Eliana disappeared around the corner.

Eliana had no doubt Sista Mavis knew all the tea about her and Khalil's marriage being on the rocks. The woman had an uncanny way of finding out what was going on at Holy Rock at any given time. If you wanted to know something about somebody at Holy Rock, Sista Mavis was the one who had all the tea. She didn't exactly 'spill the tea' except to her close friends, which just so happened to be quite a large circle.

Eliana entered her office and looked around. It had been weeks since she'd set foot in it. She didn't know why she didn't make more use of it. It offered her the amount of privacy she needed at times, but then again, she could get that at home, too. If she told herself the honest truth, she didn't need or want this office anymore. She didn't care whether she wore the title of First Lady of Holy Rock anymore. She was tired and frustrated fighting for her marriage and a relationship that only *she* wanted. Khalil's words were empty to her now, falling on deaf ears. All he wanted was to save his reputation, but that ship had sailed, and she was on it.

Without prior thought, she got up and walked down the hall to the storage area.

"Oh, hi, Omar," she said, opening the door.

"Hi, Sista Eliana," he said, his Spanish accent adding a melodic cadence to the pronunciation of her name.

Omar and Khalil had been best friends for years, but the two could not have been more different. Omar was a walk by the straight and narrow kind of guy. Whenever Eliana saw Omar's wife, she always seemed happy. Their children seemed ideal. Khalil told her that Omar had talked to him about having a successful marriage like his. It wasn't anything Khalil hadn't heard from Omar before, but like all the prior times, Khalil was still doing what Khalil wanted to do, and being faithful wasn't one of them.

"Omar, I came to get some packing boxes. For now, I think two will do. But not too big. I want the ones I can carry in my arms. Do you know the ones I'm talking about?"

"Yes," he said, smiling.

"Do we have anything that size?"

"Yeah, let me get those for you," Omar said, grabbing two boxes from the back of the space.

"Thanks."

"Do you need anything else?" Omar asked.

She was sure Khalil had told him about the latest drama in their marriage, but being the friend and gentleman Omar was, he did not bring it up.

"No, I think these are enough, at least for now."

"Okay, well, I'll be here for another ten or fifteen minutes," he said. "Let me know if you need more."

"Okay, thanks. It was good seeing you, Omar."

"Same here," he said. "Take it easy, Sista Eliana."

Upon returning to her office, she started gathering pictures, certificates, her college degree, and other knickknacks that would easily fit into the boxes.

"Mommy, hi, Mommy," Khaliyah said, bursting into Eliana's office.

"Hi, sweetheart," Eliana kneeled and gathered her daughter into her arms for a big squeeze. "Did you have fun while Mommy was gone?" she asked and then looked up at Khalil as he stood inside the door.

"Yes," Khaliyah said, looking back at her daddy.

"So you're really doing this, huh?" Khalil said, his voice almost cold and his eyes detecting a level of anger. Was it hurt? She couldn't tell at the moment and wasn't about to try.

"What are you talking about now, Khalil?"

"This is what I'm talking about, Eliana," he said, closing the door behind him as he walked into her office. "You could have told me, given me a heads up," he said, pulling out a brown envelope from his inside suit pocket and passing it to her.

She took the envelope. He had been served. She didn't realize it would be done so quickly.

"And for them to serve me at church? Couldn't you have done this in a more respectable fashion?" He stood motionless, his complexion darkening as a deep frown crept across his forehead.

"Respectable? I know you did *not* just go there. Please tell me you didn't just say that." She was about to snap but quickly held her tongue when she saw Khaliyah standing between them on her tablet.

Instead, Eliana opened the envelope. She had mixed emotions when she saw the first line, McCoy vs McCoy. She didn't know how she would feel when this moment actually arrived. Part of her said she was doing the only thing she could do in such a matter. The other part of her was heartbroken to know that the man she loved was not the man she would spend the rest of her life with. She didn't know if she wanted to cry or smile, so she did neither. Instead, her facial expression remained blank as she folded the paper, placed it back into the envelope, and passed it back to Khalil.

"What do you want me to say? I mean, this is what you wanted," she reminded him. "If you didn't, you would have changed. But this is not the time or place to talk about it. Not in front of our daughter. I suggest you read those papers thoroughly if you haven't already and sign them as soon as possible. There is no reason to delay this for longer than we need to. Come on, Khaliyah." She looked down and took hold of the little girl's hand. "I'll come back another day and finish packing up my office," she said, closing the boxes and leaving them on her desk. "Tell Daddy you'll see him later.

"Bye, Daddy."

"Bye, princess," he said, smiling and bending down to kiss her. "I should be home by eight. We'll talk more about this tonight."

"Whatever, Khalil."

†

Later the same evening, after putting her to bed, Eliana poured herself a glass of wine and went to her bedroom, where she started sorting clothes and shoes she would take with her and those she would donate to Holy Rock's Homeless Ministry.

Humming a spiritual song, she took a sip of the refreshing wine and came out of the closet with an armful of clothes draped across her arm.

After laying them on the bed and placing the glass on the night table, she sighed and looked around somberly. Her sense of loss suddenly manifested itself. She stifled a scream by placing a hand over her mouth.

Plopping down in the bedroom corner chair, rocking back and forth, she was mad. She felt betrayed and used. Khalil only saw her as a mother to his daughter and the trophy First Lady of his prestigious church.

She gulped the remaining wine and was about to throw the glass across the room.

"Whoa," Khalil said, suddenly appearing in the room. "What are you doing?"

"None of your business," she said.

"Look, this isn't the way, Eliana. Drinking?" he said, his voice mounting in anger. "What is wrong with you? And you think you deserve joint custody? At first, I agreed, but seeing you like this, I have doubts."

Eliana rose from the chair and stood in front of him, almost closing the space between them.

"Don't...you...dare...Don't you even think about it," she lashed out. "You can go out and screw whatever whore you want to when you want to, but you want to talk to me about a glass of wine. Negro, please. To hell with you."

"Okay, that was a low blow. I didn't mean it. You deserve to unwind with a glass of wine if that's what you choose."

"I don't need your permission," she snapped back.

"I said, it's all good." He sat on the bed across from her. "I've read the papers. Again, I'm telling you I don't want this, Eliana. I don't want a divorce. I don't want to fight you on this, but I will if I have to," he said, staring at her, his voice straightforward and exact.

"I don't think you want to do that. What I said before, I meant. If you fight me on this, I'll show your congregation who their pastor really is. And not just with words. I have receipts,

Khalil. Way more than you think. Text messages, sext texts, pictures, yeah, don't play me."

"You would stoop that low?" he said, a mixture of disdain and shock that she was willing to ruin him so easily.

"Low?" she broke into laughter. "Are you serious? You know what, Khalil? You're more like your father than you'll probably ever admit. You're selfish and narcissistic. You think the sun rises and shines on you. You see only what you choose to see," she began crying. "I understand now what your mother went through and why she divorced him."

"Don't bring my parents into this. You don't know a thing about their relationship. And this is about you and me," he shot back.

She rose from the chair. "I was offered a job. I start in two weeks. I plan to be moved out of here by then. I'm assuming you'll continue to watch your daughter without us bickering and causing undue stress in her life."

"You think I'm causing stress?" Khalil shook his head and laughed, but Eliana did not see the humor.

"Like I said, please don't fight me on this, Khalil. This time, you won't win."

Chapter 25

How Deep Is Your Love

"Marriage vows are most important in those
moments when they are most difficult to keep."
D. Willis

After returning from the DNA testing, Luna
and Christian stopped and picked up Dax from
the sitter. Now, it was a waiting game for at least
the next 72 hours. Luna was already on pins
and needles.

She thanked God Sanchez remained behind
bars with a ten million dollar bond. That was a
huge relief for Luna, knowing he was no longer
roaming around disguising himself as a
philanthropist and an all-around good guy but
who was, in actuality, a demon who had hurt
and assaulted her and only God knows how
many other women. And how many of them, like
Luna, might he have left a child inside? Oh,
God, it was too much for Luna to think about.

"I'm ordering takeout," Christian said as he
brought both kids inside the house. "How does
Chinese sound?"

Luna shrugged, "I don't care."

He put Laiyah Rose on the floor in the family
room. Dax ran ahead, went straight to his toy
trucks and cars, and began playing.

"Luna, I know you're worried and frightened,
but honey, everything is going to be fine, you'll

see," Christian reassured her. "The rape kit has been submitted; the DNA test has been done. We have to be patient and let them do their job. If it turns out this Sanchez fellow did this, thank God he's already behind bars, and rest assured, Luna, he's going to get what he deserves."

"I hope so," she murmured, her voice trailing off as she turned and made her way to the family room.

She started picking up toys. "I'm going to bathe Laiyah Rose. You get Dax," she said, knowing Dax still preferred his father's attention over hers. He only chose her when he wanted her love and kisses after he scraped a knee or if he couldn't get what he wanted from Christian. There were other times when he wanted to be babied that he would climb in her lap and cuddle against her breast, sucking his thumb, while Luna would softly sing until he fell asleep. She treasured those special moments because they didn't come often.

Dax was a peculiar child. She saw his growth from a withdrawn, shy, frightened little boy to the happy, daddy-loving, loved-his-trucks and cars boy he was today.

Luna understood she was blessed with two beautiful babies. It wasn't easy to think about how Laiyah Rose was brought into their lives, but here she was, and Luna loved her more than life itself.

She picked up Laiyah Rose from off the floor. "Come on here, heavy girl," she said, kissing her. "Don't you think it's about time you start walking? You are getting too big for Mommy to carry around all day," kissing her again on the cheek while Laiyah Rose squirmed in her arms.

"I think she's going to be walking in the next month or two," Christian said, walking up to them and kissing Laiyah Rose on the forehead. "Isn't that right," he said, smiling.

Moments like this Luna felt like she was living in an ideal world. She had so many blessings. It warmed her heart when she saw Christian display affection toward Laiyah Rose. Sometimes, she failed to give him credit for being more than a good man but a good husband and father. Then again, she couldn't forget—he slept with her sister—and not just one time. Would she ever get over that?

"You heard what Daddy said, Laiyah Rose? He said you're going to be walking in a month. Is Daddy right?" she said, shaking away those tormenting thoughts.

Laiyah Rose jumped and bounced happily in Luna's arms, gurgling and laughing.

Dax stood at Christian's leg, looking at his little sister and making funny faces at her.

Out of nowhere, Laiyah Rose leaned over and reached for Christian. "Da-Da," she said. "Da-Da," she kept saying.

Christian's hand flew up to his mouth. "Oh, my gosh, did you hear that? She said Da-Da," he exclaimed, reaching for the baby, kissing her fat cheeks, and swinging her in the air.

"Say it again, Laiyah Rose. Say Da-Da," he laughed.

Luna laughed and clapped her hands, "Christian, she hasn't even said Momma yet. I'm jealous." She pretended to cry and then started laughing again.

At the end of the night, after both kids were asleep, Christian entered their bedroom and sat beside Luna on the side of the bed.

He began rubbing her thigh as she lay underneath the covers. The television was on, but in typical Luna fashion, it was on MUTE.

At his touch, she felt tingling in the pit of her stomach; her heart seemed to jolt, and her pulse pounded.

"Luna," he whispered, "I love you." He laid his head on her belly and wrapped his arm across her.

Her emotions took over. She placed a loving hand on top of his head. "I love you, too."

At that moment, she knew what she had decided. Yes, he had cheated. Yes, it was horrible—hurtful and painful. Yes, the fact that it was with her sister made the wound run that much deeper. But she loved this man. And she believed he loved her. He had stuck by her through the most painful time, and it wasn't over. Yes, this time, love would win.

Christian looked up as Luna willed him to her with the touch of her hands on his back.

His stare was bold as he eased himself on top of his wife, their eyes glued to each other as he moved upward. Pushing the covering back with his leg, her body was his for the taking. His touch was soft and caressing yet demanding and urgent. Their eyes locked as their breathing grew in unison. Her cheeks colored, and a quiver of delight surged through her veins.

"I promise I'll never hurt you again," he said afterward as she lay curled inside his arms and tenderly kissed the top of her head.

"I know," she replied, "I know," and then closed her eyes to sleep.

Chapter 26

Let Me Love You

> "If you carry the bricks from your past relationship,
> you will end up building the same house."
> Kush 'N Wizdom

Fancy gathered an armful of supplies, more color swatches, and a pushcart full of other things to take to Noah's house. The contractors had started, and renovations were in full swing. She couldn't have been happier with how things were progressing.

As she was backing out of the garage, she spotted Hezekiah going to his car.

"Hey, good morning," he said, waving a hand and walking towards her.

"Hi," she said, stopping.

"I haven't seen you lately," he paused as if expecting her to explain her whereabouts. Those days were over. "I haven't seen the grandkids over here either."

He was right. She hadn't seen him in at least two, maybe three weeks. She hadn't been to New Holy Rock, and most mornings when she left, he was either still at his place or already gone.

"Yeah, I know. I've been busy. I picked up a new client. It takes up a lot of my time," she said with a broad smile filling her slender face.

"Good for you. I know the grandkids miss you."

"Yeah, my weekends have been full, too. I have to work around my client's schedule, which sometimes calls for working weekends, except Sundays. You know I don't work for anybody on the Lord's day," she said, chuckling.

"I know that's right. Well, have a good one. I'm on my way to New Holy Rock."

"Ok, you have a good one, too," she said and backed out of her driveway, disappearing up the street.

After several stops, she pulled up to Noah's house an hour later. Some of the crew were arriving at the same time.

Noah met her at the door, removed the supplies from her arms, and she followed him into the massive family room.

"I know you aren't going to like hearing this, but I have to leave."

"You have to what?" Fancy said, a surprised look appearing on her face.

"I have to catch a flight at five in the morning. Something came up at our hub in Arizona. If all goes well, I hope to be back by the end of the week."

Fancy sighed heavily. "It's Friday, Noah. You mean the end of next week, don't you?"

"Well, yes," he said.

"Look, you explained in the beginning, before we started this project, that you might have to go in and out of town, but I want you to know we'll lose valuable time. I can't promise that we'll get this done within our timeline. That's a week's worth of lost time," she sighed again. "I'll let the contractors know." She turned and proceeded to walk away.

"Fancy, wait."

"Yes?" she said.

"I didn't mean that I want you to halt the renovations." He approached her and pressed a set of keys into her hand.

"What's this?" she asked, her face matching the tone of her voice—serious.

"The keys to my house. This one unlocks the guest house, and this is the main house key. Feel free to stay in the guest house if you need to stay over. I would offer you to stay in the house, but of course, you have your crew working everywhere," he said, laughing and looking around as the contractors went about busily working.

Fancy shook her head. "No, I, uh, I can't take the keys to your house. And staying in your guest house is out of the question. I'll wait until you return. Like I said, I'll have to push back our completion date, but so be it." She threw a hand in the air.

"No, listen, I don't want the work to stop. As a matter of fact, I insist that it doesn't. What's wrong? Why can't you take the keys? Are you saying I shouldn't trust you?"

Fancy appeared offended as she reared back in her shoulders. "Of course, you can trust me. You have nothing to be concerned about regarding your privacy or your home's safety. I'm licensed and bonded, so are the contractors I work with," she said.

He chuckled. "Good, then, not another word. You have the keys to come and go as you please. It's all in your hands." He laughed.

Fancy studied the keys and looked at Noah.

"Oh, one more thing," he said.

"What now?" she said, looking amused.

"Have dinner with me this evening."

Fancy smiled and nodded. "That's easy enough; dinner it is."

†

"Thanks again for a wonderful evening," Fancy said when they pulled up to her home.

"How long have you lived in Lion's Gate?" Noah asked.

"A few years. I moved here after my divorce."

"I see. This is a nice community. I wanted to build here but decided against it after I couldn't secure the amount of land I wanted."

"There aren't many large lots left," Fancy said. "People have bought them up. Some people built two houses on their property."

"I haven't been in Memphis long, but where I live now suits my taste, I'd say."

"Good, you have a beautiful home. And it's so large."

"Yeah, I like my space," he said, chuckling.

"Uh, would you like to come inside for a nightcap? I don't have any brown liquor, but I do have wine, sodas, and water," she quipped."

"A cold glass of water sounds refreshing." He laughed.

"Okay, follow me," she said.

He followed her up the walkway and into her house.

"Hmmm, nice," Noah complimented. "Very nice."

"Thanks, I like it. It suits my needs," Fancy said, taking him on a quick tour.

"That's a nice casita," he said, looking through the kitchen window.

"Oh," Fancy said, "I need to tell you about that," she made him a glass of ice water and passed it to him.

"Tell me what?"

"I rent the casita. I have a tenant."

"Oh, cool," Noah said.

"The tenant happens to be my ex." She stared at Noah as if waiting for him to explode or say something about why she would have her ex-husband living on her property, but he did not say any such thing.

"Well, does he pay his rent on time, if you don't mind my asking?"

"Like clockwork," she said, pouring herself a glass of lemonade. "You sure you don't want some of this?"

"No, water's fine."

"So what do you have to say?" Fancy asked.

"Say? Say about what?"

"About my ex-husband living in my casita?"

"As long as he pays his rent, I say good for you." He chuckled.

They continued making small talk in the family room until Noah stood up and told her he was going to leave.

"Again, thanks for a beautiful night," Fancy told him. "I'm praying for safe travels for you. And you don't have a thing to worry about. I'm going to make sure everything goes as scheduled."

181

They stood at her front door, face to face. Momentary silence filtered between them as their eyes connected. Fancy felt her body beginning to get excited, and a warm feeling came over her.

Noah cautiously leaned in and brushed her lips with his. He pulled away, his eyes still lingering on Fancy's. He kissed her again. Again, brushing his lips against hers like a feather, only this time he didn't pull away. He allowed the feathery-like kiss to turn into one filled with passion and desire.

A moan escaped through her lips as her body reacted to his touch. Slowly and carefully, he allowed his hands to roam her curves until Fancy pushed back.

"Uh, you should go," she said, knowing her face was probably beet red, but at that moment, she didn't care. Her resolve was almost gone. If he didn't leave now, she couldn't promise that she would be able to abstain. She suddenly thought about Hezekiah. At that moment, her mind began playing crazy tricks on her, or were they tricks?

"I can't do this," she said. "Never mix business with—"

Noah pulled her into his arms again and kissed her before she could protest further. This time, it was him who pulled away.

"Goodnight, Fancy." He opened the door and walked out just as Hezekiah was getting into his car.

Hezekiah paused and then got into his ride before backing out of the driveway and speeding off.

"Was that your ex?" he turned and asked Fancy.

"Yes," she said.

"I don't think he liked what he saw."

"He'll be fine," she said. "Remember, he's my tenant, nothing more, Noah."

Noah got into his car with a smile plastered on his face.

Fancy watched him until he disappeared up the street before closing her door. Leaning her back against it, she released a long exhale.

"Noah Alexander, wow," she said, smiling as she went to her bedroom.

She took a long, relaxing bath and replayed the evening. His kisses set her afire, making her long for the intimate touch of a man. But she told herself she had to be careful. No more letting a man feed her a bunch of crap. She was done with men like that, men like Hezekiah and Winston. No more.

She poured herself a fresh glass of lemonade when a knock at the kitchen door startled her.

She looked through the window. When she saw Hezekiah, she quickly opened the door.

"Hey, what's going on? Are you okay?" she asked.

"Yes, I'm good. I was making sure you were okay."

"Yes, why wouldn't I be?"

"Well, I haven't seen that guy before. You can never tell about folks these days. He somebody from Holy Rock?" he asked, as if genuinely concerned about her safety. But Fancy knew Hezekiah like the back of her hand. This was no show of concern for her safety. This man was jealous. She almost laughed in his face once she understood his reason for showing up at her door. Car or no car outside, he wanted to make sure no one was sharing her bed.

"Not that I have to explain anything to you, Hezekiah, but I know him. He's a client. If you have to know, we had dinner, and he brought me home."

"Dinner with a client? Since when did you start mixing business with pleasure? That's never been your M-O."

"Change happens, Hezekiah. And who said it wasn't business? But anyway, thanks for your concern. Now, if you don't mind, I'm calling it a night."

"When are you going to get the grandkids again?" he asked, seemingly ignoring what she had just said.

"Maybe tomorrow."

"Okay, let me know when they get here," he said, looking hopeful.

"Yeah, sure. Goodnight, Hezekiah," she said, yawning.

"Goodnight, Fancy."

Unlike with Noah, when Hezekiah left, she didn't watch until he disappeared. She turned out the kitchen light and went to her room, her mind filled with thoughts of Noah.

Chapter 27

Positivity

"Every wall is a door." Ralph Waldo Emerson

Eliana took a deep breath before getting out of her car. The weather couldn't have been more perfect for her first day at her new job. "God, be with me, help me do a good job," she prayed.

She retrieved the boxes she'd packed when she left her office at Holy Rock. Balancing her keys and purse in one hand, she carefully lifted both boxes and headed for the entrance to Grace Temple.

She hadn't thought about how she would open the door once she made it up the ten steps leading to the entrance. After struggling and almost dropping both boxes, she made it up the steps, only to see a ramp she could have used instead.

"Don't start," she said to herself, shaking her head. She used her backside to push the glass door open. "Whew," she murmured.

Not able to see quite in front of her, she stumbled, and the top box fell out of her arms.

"Dang it," she mouthed under her breath, placing the other box, purse, and keys on the floor to regroup.

"Let me help you with that," she heard a low and smooth voice say.

She looked up to find him watching her. "Uh, thank you," she said, fiddling with the spilled items.

When she looked at him, it took several seconds for her eyes to adjust. The beginning of a smile tipped the corners of his mouth, and he began putting the spilled items back into the box and then picked up both boxes.

"You must be Sista McCoy?" he said. "Our new church administrator?"

"Yes, that's me," Eliana said, engaging his smile and calming tone.

"Nice to meet you. Do you know where your office is?"

"I think I remember," she said, smiling.

"Okay, let's go. Follow me, Mrs. McCoy," he said, refraining from saying *sista* this time.

He opened the door to her office and stood to the side, allowing Eliana to enter ahead of him.

"Thank you. Oh, this is nice," she said, shaking her head as she looked around. It was a simple space, smaller than her previous office at Holy Rock. It was furnished with what looked like a prefab cherry peninsula u-shaped workstation with a hutch. There was a small window with a view of the side parking lot and neighborhood houses across the street.

He entered the office and placed the boxes on top of the desk.

"Thanks for your help," she said again, this time extending her hand toward him for a handshake.

She didn't want to stare, but he was handsome. The remnants of perhaps having acne as a teen, she guessed, made his look even more appealing. His complexion was not very dark or light, but she would describe it as peanut butter brown, with a black mustache and a small beard.

"Uh, I don't think I introduced myself," he said, breaking her stare. "I'm the youth pastor, Mason Roberts. I wasn't here when you were introduced to the staff last week. The youth were on their last summer outing before school."

"Oh, yeah, where?" she said, instantly sparking her interest.

"Gatlinburg, the Great Smoky Mountains."

"Oh, I bet they liked that," she said, a broad smile appearing as she began to relax.

"Been there?" he asked.

"Yes, but not enough," she said. "I love it up there. It's so peaceful and tranquil. I feel like I'm right there beside God. I haven't been in quite a long time, though." Her voice dropped.

"Well, you're part of Grace Temple now. Our youth engage in a number of programs and ministries. I know it's nothing like where you previously worked. I saw your resume," he said. The staff had to review it before you were called for an interview."

"Yes, I know. They told me."

"Anyone who knows anything about Memphis churches knows that Holy Rock is rocking," he said, laughing. "Seriously, I heard you guys have over two hundred active ministries that benefit the community and the city. Man, that's amazing," Mason said, his excitement evident. "Our church is nowhere near the size of Holy Rock, but God is increasing every day."

"Yes, God has blessed Holy Rock considerably, and He is also blessing this place. I'm grateful to be part of your ministry," she said, nodding.

"I take it your last name being McCoy, that you are some kin to the pastor of Holy Rock? Sister? Sister-in-law? Cousin?" he said, smiling.

"More like First Lady," she said. "Soon to be Former first lady," she added.

"Oh, I'm sorry."

"Don't be," Eliana said. "All things work..."

"Gotcha," he said. "Well, Mrs. McCoy."

"Please, you can call me Eliana."

"I will unless we are among congregants, of course."

"Oh, that's understood," she said. "I've been in ministry long enough to know the little rules and all the innuendos one is expected to know and follow."

"Good for you. Look, my office is three doors down. If you need anything, feel free to come by," he said, showing his pearly whites.

"Definitely. Thanks, Mason. I'm going to do some unpacking."

"Okay, sounds like a plan."

After spending the next hour unpacking and decorating as much as she could, she left for the main conference room. There, she was going to meet with the senior pastor, assistant pastor, and their administrative assistant.

Eliana smoothed down her black straight skirt and followed up by tugging slightly on the fitted waist-length jacket. The light cream shirt she wore underneath had a bow at the neck, and buttons trailed the front, complementing the fashionable business suit.

Her black and cream cap-toe pumps clicked across the polished tiles of Grace Temple as she boldly strolled through the church corridors, familiarizing herself with the sanctity of the place. She loved being inside churches, especially when they were void of members, and it was just like it was now—quiet, peaceful, like the presence of God was right there.

Before reaching the conference room, she paused at the entrance to the sanctuary and felt an irresistible pull. She went inside and was immediately enveloped in a deep sense of calm. The soft glow of light filtered through the stained glass, casting colorful patterns across rows of empty pews. In the center of the small sanctuary, she spread her arms wide with her palms facing upward and closed her eyes. A deep sense of peace washed over her when she began to pray, and for that fleeting moment, the heartache and pain she had endured seemed to fade away.

†

Saturday mid-morning, Eliana stood by the bay window in the living room of her three-bedroom, two-bath townhome, watching as the delivery crew carefully unloaded furniture. The modern pieces she had selected looked even better than she had imagined as they were carried inside. The bedroom furniture for Khaliyah was perfect.

Shortly after the movers left, Luna and Pepper arrived. The three women wandered through the townhome, admiring the fresh setup.

"This place is gorgeous," Pepper said, her voice full of admiration as she glanced around.

"Absolutely," Luna agreed, nodding her approval. "The furniture is perfect. You've got great taste."

Eliana smiled warmly. "Thanks, I'm glad you like it."

"Yes, this is nice," Pepper said, running her hand over the back of the sleek new sofa.

Eliana's smile widened, and her expression had a mix of pride and relief.

"Fancy is decorating Khaliyah's room, right?" Pepper asked.

"Yes, thank God for a grandma who is an interior designer," Eliana laughed.

"Hey, speaking of Khaliyah, where is she? Wait, I don't know why I even asked that question. Fancy has the boys, so I know she has Khaliyah, too."

"Yep, she does. She's coming over later this afternoon to look at the room with the furniture inside so she can know exactly how she's going to transform it into a princess castle. I know Khaliyah will love whatever she comes up with," Eliana beamed as they stood inside the little girl's room.

"You know she has some skills," Pepper said.

"I'm surprised she has the time. She's been busy lately working for some big-time FEDEX executive. He's supposed to have a huge mansion way out past Collierville somewhere," Eliana told the ladies.

"I know it's been keeping her busy because she hasn't asked for the boys to come over for their Saturday night sleepover in a while. That is until tonight. I'm not saying there's anything wrong with that; it's just unusual. I'm glad her business is expanding, though."

"Of course," said Eliana. "I want nothing but good for Fancy. She's a good person."

"Yeah, she is," said Pepper.

"I don't know as much about her as the two of you, but I can say my interactions with her have always been positive. She offered prayers for me while I was going through what happened, and I enjoyed her when she spoke at the last Pulpit Ladies luncheon," Luna said.

"She was very inspirational," said Pepper. "I know it took a lot of strength, spiritual and mental, for her to stand before a roomful of people and bare her soul about her hurts and grief and how God carried her through all those times. It was powerful." Pepper wiped a tear before it fell.

"Yes, it was," Luna said. "Hearing her speak has helped me with what I'm going through. I've been so nervous about getting these results. I know it's in God's hands, but I want all of this to be over with so that me, Christian, and our babies can move on with our lives."

"It'll happen," said Eliana, walking up to Luna and side-hugging her.

"How long is it supposed to take for the results to come back?" Pepper asked.

"We could hear something as soon as today. But it's more than likely going to be tomorrow or the day after."

"Well, just hang in there. It'll all be over soon," Eliana said.

Chapter 28

Tell Your Heart

"Never trust your fears. They don't know your strength." Unknown

Luna woke up yawning and stretching. She smiled and turned over to snuggle under Christian. His side was empty. She eased up in the bed, wiped her eyes, and looked around the room. Their bathroom door was open.

"Christian," she called. No answer. Then, the tempting aroma of freshly brewed coffee came underneath her nose, and she smiled. She looked at the monitors. The kids weren't in their beds.

She got up and strode to the bathroom. Memories of last night in her husband's arms made her tingle again. Their lovemaking had been magical.

When she finished grooming herself, she followed the aroma. In the kitchen, she saw Laiyah Rose in her walker, and Dax was drinking juice at his table in between sucking on his binkie.

"Hi, Mommy," he said as she entered the kitchen.

"Good morning, sleepy head," Christian said, walking up to her and planting a wallop of a kiss on her lips.

Dax laughed and bounced up and down in his chair.

"How many pancakes?" Christian asked as she walked over and kissed Dax and then Laiyah Rose.

"Two," she said. "No, make it three. I'm famished and haven't had your pancakes in a long time."

"Three it is for the lady," he said, returning to the stove.

Luna poured a cup of coffee and made it to her liking. "Hmm, this is good," she said, sitting at the island when Christian's phone started ringing.

He flipped the three pancakes before stepping to the side and looking at his screen. His smooth-skinned melanin face showed a slight questioning frown.

"Hello, Christian Black. How may I help you?"

Christian listened, and Luna watched as intently as she saw his facial expression.

"Yes. Okay, eleven-thirty, we'll be there. Thanks, see you then." Christian laid the phone on the counter and turned to face Luna.

"Court?" Luna asked before he could say anything.

"No," Christian said. "They want us at police headquarters at eleven-thirty for the results of the rape kit and Laiyah Rose's DNA test."

"Thank you, God," Luna said, looking upward and raising a hand of praise.

"That's the system for you. Let's you know when they want things to get done, they can do it," Christian surmised.

Luna sipped some of her coffee before placing it on the counter and getting up. She walked over and leaned down to Dax's level as he remained at his superhero table.

She smiled when she saw Christian's attempt to make Dax a Mickey Mouse-shaped pancake.

"Let me help you with that," she said when he picked up the syrup container.

"No," Dax said and jerked away.

"Ok, okay," Luna said and backed off, then focused on Laiyah Rose, who was content sucking on a piece of cinnamon-buttered toast.

"You okay," Christian asked, walking up to her.

"Yeah. I couldn't help thinking of all we've been through since everything happened, you know? And today, in a matter of a couple of hours, we might finally have closure. If DNA proves Sanchez did this, I will be so relieved, Christian. But...but," she stuttered, "what if it isn't him? Oh, God, then what?"

"Shhh," Christian said, pulling her into his arms and holding her close. "No matter how it turns out, we're a family. Nothing or no one can ever change that."

When Luna and Christian arrived at the police station, they were led to an interrogation room. They were met by the lead detective and another officer, a black female who appeared near retirement age.

An hour or so later, Luna and Christian left for home. Luna, visibly upset, got inside the car and broke down. Her sobs rang out, and as people passed, they looked curiously.

"He did it. He did this to me!" she bellowed. "Oh, God. I hate him, Christian. I know I shouldn't say it, but I do. What kind of crazed monster is he?" She pounded a fist against the dashboard repeatedly.

"It's alright, sweetheart. We know it's him for sure now. You don't have to look over your shoulder anymore. You're safe. Thank you, God," said Christian, placing his arm around her. "He's behind bars, and he's going to stay behind bars for a very long time. He's going to be punished for what he did to you and all those other women." He kissed the side of her face. "Now, we can move forward with our lives. You, me, Dax, and Laiyah Rose," he said, holding her in the crook of his arm.

Luna looked up. "I love you, Christian," she whispered, her voice breaking with each word. She sat up and wiped her tears with the back of her hand.

"I didn't know how I would feel when I learned who did this. I thought I would be ecstatic, jumping up and down with joy, but that's not how I feel, Christian. I'm angry. I'm pissed. To think, he was walking around in the same building as me. He was someone people looked up to. Someone who was supposed to be this...this huge figure who gave to charities, and people patted him on the back for his achievements," she ranted. "But," she pointed a finger in the air, "behind closed doors, he was a real live monster. Evil. Demonic. I hate him!"

"Whatever you're feeling is justified, sweetheart. But remember, he can't hurt you, or anyone else, anymore." Christian grabbed hold of her hand and drove off.

Luna rested her head against the headrest.

Christian turned on the radio.

A slow-forming smile enveloped her, and she exhaled in peace when she heard the woman sing, *"All my life, you have been faithful... "* Luna closed her eyes and sang along.

†

At home, Luna and Christian sat in the family room, talking. Luna was calmer and more positive than when the detective told them the results.

DNA proved not only was he the one who sexually assaulted her, but he was also Laiyah Rose's biological father. When all this information had a chance to die down, she wondered if Christian would now be able to fully accept Laiyah Rose as his daughter. She prayed that he would. If his words and actions today were an indication, then she believed with all of her heart he would grow to love Laiyah Rose as much as he loved Dax.

"Here you go," he said, passing her a wine glass filled with sparkling white grape juice.

"Thank you."

"Come on, let's toast," he suggested.

"Okay." She raised her glass. "Here's to releasing the past," she said.

"And moving toward what lies ahead," Christian finished. "Cheers."

They sipped their beverages but stopped when they saw the words "BREAKING NEWS" scroll across the mounted 65-inch television.

Christian grabbed the remote off the arm of the sofa and turned up the volume just in time to hear reporter Jeremy Parker.

"Rex Sanchez, a 59-year-old former tech executive and philanthropist, is facing a growing list of sexual assault charges. Initially accused of first-degree and second-degree aggravated rape and kidnapping involving the abduction of five women in the mid-south region over thirty-six months, Sanchez's charges have now expanded. We learned that authorities have now linked Sanchez to the abduction and sexual assault nineteen months ago of 35-year-old pharmaceutical executive Luna Black, wife of prominent criminal defense attorney Christian Black. The connection was established through DNA, adding to the mounting case against Sanchez. This is Jeremy Parker, News Channel—"

Christian turned the volume back down and locked eyes with Luna.

"It's over," she mouthed. "It really is over."

Chapter 29

Too Much, Too Little, Too Late

"Sometimes, if you wait too long, it's too late."
Susan Strohmeyer

Fancy and Hezekiah returned home with the grandkids after spending a fun-filled afternoon at the zoo. The weather couldn't have been more perfect, as if fall had arrived early.

"Come on, kids, settle down," Hezekiah said. "It's time to eat."

While Hezekiah made sure the kids washed their hands and were seated, Fancy made them plates of spaghetti.

"Today was fun," he said, walking up and standing next to her, pouring glasses of berry lemonade for each kid. "Thanks for letting me tag along."

"I'm glad you could come," Fancy said as he helped her carry plates to the grandkids.

Returning to the stove, she began fixing another plate. "How many slices of garlic toast do you want?" Fancy asked.

"Two for now. You remembered?" Hezekiah said, taking a seat at the dining room table.

"Uh, why wouldn't I? As long as I've known you, you will not eat spaghetti and meatballs without slaw and garlic toast." She sat the plate in front of him.

"Thank you," he said. "Is it good?" he turned and asked the grandkids.

"Yes," they squealed.

Fancy made her plate and joined Hezekiah at the table.

"This is good," said Hezekiah. "I miss meals like this."

Fancy smiled as she twirled her spaghetti around the fork before placing it on a piece of garlic toast and adding a dollop of coleslaw on top.

Hezekiah laughed. "I can't believe you still do that."

"I don't know why not. It's the only way to eat spaghetti." She stabbed a meatball, sliced it in half with her fork, and then put it into her mouth.

Hezekiah shook his head, turned up his glass of iced tea, and gulped it until over half of it was gone.

"Slow down," Fancy said. "You're eating and drinking like you just got out of prison," she teased.

"I can't help it. It's so good, man," his tone suddenly serious. His words were carefully chosen. "I miss your cooking. I miss hanging around you. I miss the trips we used to go on together. I miss making love with you. I miss you, Fancy," his face serious, his voice yearning.

Fancy's phone rang. She glanced at the screen and smiled. "Just a second," she said, holding up a finger and rising from the table. Walking away, she greeted the caller with a big grin.

"Hi," she said.

"Did I catch you at a bad time?" he asked.

Hezekiah leaned back in his chair. She was on video chat. When she disappeared from the kitchen, he went to the grandkids. They started asking for the ice cream cone they were promised for dessert.

"Before you can have dessert, you know what you have to do. Finish your food, and pick up those noodles from off the table and floor. Y'all have made a mess," Hezekiah lightly scolded.

Moments later, Fancy reappeared at the kitchen's entrance.

"Oh, that was my ex," Hezekiah heard her tell the person on the call.

"So seven o'clock is good?" he heard the man ask.

"Yes, that's perfect. The grandkids will be leaving shortly, so seven's good. See you then," she said, blushing into the screen.

"Can't wait," the caller replied, and the chat ended.

"A date?" Hezekiah asked.

"Huh?" she said, looking confused, but then she realized his question. "And that is your business? Why?"

"Whoa, back off, your highness. I didn't mean to incite World War Three," he said, hands raised in surrender.

"Don't start again, Hezekiah. Are you going to help me get the kids ready? Khalil is supposed to be picking them up. He's keeping Khaliyah tonight."

"Keeping Khaliyah tonight?" Hezekiah questioned. "What does that mean? Eliana off to a Pulpit Ladies meeting or something?"

200

"Oh, I suppose you haven't heard."

"Heard what?" Hezekiah said while making ice cream cones.

"Khalil and Eliana are separated. She filed for divorce, and she's moved into her own place. Even went and got a job. I think it's at Grace Temple, if I'm not mistaken. I believe that's what she told me. I've had so much on my mind lately. But yeah, he has the same problem as you—letting the little head outthink the big head. I don't know what it is about Detria Graham, and I don't know who holds the most power between her and Rianna Jamison. What I do know is that they definitely know how to sink their wicked hooks into you and your son. What a shame."

"I didn't know they were divorcing," Hezekiah said. "Man, I hate to hear that." He shook his head in dismay.

He chose not to address what she said about Detria and Rianna. After all, everything she said was the truth. There was nothing for him to get bent out of shape about.

"Grace Temple, huh? I wonder what she's going to be doing there?" He carried two ice cream cones to where the grandkids eagerly awaited.

Fancy came behind him with the remaining cone.

"I don't know much of anything about the folks over there. Do you?" Fancy asked, their concern swiftly shifting from who she had been video chatting with on the phone to their son and his family.

"Not a lot. I've heard him preach once. From what I *do* know, he's a fairly young minister. He's been at Grace Temple for less than three years."

"Does he have a First Lady?"

"I don't think so," said Hezekiah.

"If he does, I don't think she's attended any of *The Pulpit Ladies* luncheons. Not that she has to. I'm just saying I don't recall that name or church signing up."

The phone rang again. "Yes, let him through," she said. "That was the guard gate. Khalil is on the way."

It was not surprising, but certainly not an everyday occurrence, that the father and son exchanged pleasantries and engaged in small talk, often about religion, sports, or the grandkids.

Pastor's death seemed to have been the glue that was slowly bringing the family together again. To see Hezekiah and Khalil laughing and talking was an answered prayer.

She heard Hezekiah bring up Khalil's divorce. Fancy gathered the grandkids and led them into the living room so the men could talk without interference.

Watching them embrace as Khalil left with the kids was a tender moment for Fancy.

"I told him if he wanted to talk, I was available," Hezekiah said proudly.

"Good. I was glad to see the two of you talking without blowing up at each other. It takes a lot to let go of past hurts. But the two of you have started gluing the broken pieces back together. It may never fully be the same, and just like a mirror, you can fix it, but you will always be able to see the cracks. But think about this—those cracks signify healing is taking place."

"Thanks," Hezekiah said, returning to the kitchen. "I'll help you with the dishes before I leave," he said.

"Okay, thanks."

"So, you didn't answer my question. Are you going on a date?"

"I *did* answer, but let me put it this way, and I hope I don't come off as condescending, but some things speak for themselves."

Chapter 30

Since You've Been Gone

"And be not conformed to this world: but be ye
transformed by the renewing of your mind...."
The Bible-Romans 12:2 KJV

Pepper listened intently as Khalil delivered
his second sermon of the day to a packed
sanctuary. His voice resonated with conviction
as he seamlessly blended preaching with
singing—something the congregation loved.

The First Lady hadn't been seen at Holy Rock
since Khalil was served divorce papers the
month before.

Fancy was seated on her usual pew. Sista
Mavis sat on one side of her, and Pepper and
Victoria sat on the other.

This was Pepper's third Sunday in a row
attending service. She wasn't ready to return to
New Holy Rock because she didn't want to face
memories of Xavier. She would always see him
there, a place where he ultimately did not want
to be. That was why it had been hard for her.
Knowing that even in church, he was wearing a
mask was a hurtful realization. But the tug to
return to worship drew her to accept an
invitation from Fancy to attend Holy Rock,
which was nothing out of the ordinary, seeing
that when she met Xavier, they both attended
Holy Rock. When he decided to join his father's

church, New Holy Rock became their church home—until his death.

At the end of service, Pepper took Zavion and Davion to Corn Dog Delights, one of their favorite places to eat. Sundays were the most time she spent with them because her days had been hectic since she decided to start a nonprofit. Organizing a nonprofit from scratch without prior knowledge and still having to take the boys to karate lessons, soccer practice, and swimming lessons was quite a challenge. They were always on the go. But the 501c3 paperwork had been filed.

Pepper had already started planning to hold an official ceremony to announce the opening. She located a space for lease in one of the buildings in the same neighborhood where she lived. It was on a good transit line for people who may not have traditional transportation. She wanted to be accessible to everyone who needed the services that would be offered at *The Xavier McCoy Healing Together Foundation.*

Ryan and Rolonda were her right-hand people. Eliana and Luna helped whenever they could, even though they were experiencing their own trials and tests of faith. Yet, they were a team, and Pepper was grateful for their support and friendship. They helped to ensure every *I* was dotted and every *T* crossed.

It wasn't easy mixing starting a nonprofit with single motherhood, but she knew in her spirit that she was supposed to do this. Not just to keep the memory of Xavier alive but to help others who may have gone to a dark place after losing a loved one, especially a child or spouse.

She watched the boys devour their corndogs and waffle fries in the shape of alphabets. Times like this she missed Xavier the most. He would love seeing the boys grow up and be such little gentlemen. He would take pride in taking them to school every morning and picking them up every evening. She smiled at them and then pulled herself back to reality.

"You guys ready?" she asked, knowing they would say no.

"No," Davion said.

"I want ice cream cake," Zavion said, referring to Corn Dog Delights' signature dessert. It was cheesecake and ice cream, and Pepper agreed it was delicious.

"Okay, since you ate most of your food, I say we get some yummy-for-our-tummies dessert," Pepper exclaimed, and she and the boys broke out laughing.

†

On the opposite end of the city, Eliana sat toward the back of the medium-sized sanctuary at New Holy Rock. Since she filed for divorce, she couldn't see herself continuing to attend Holy Rock. Maybe she would at another time, but not now. Things were too fresh, not yet settled. She would not want to sit on her usual pew, the pew reserved specifically for the First Lady. Everyone, or almost everyone at Holy Rock, probably already heard that she and Khalil were separated. That kind of thing spread like wildfire. Not seeing her sitting front and center at any of the services made it evident that

206

First Lady Eliana McCoy was no longer in the building.

"It was good having you today," Stiles told Eliana at the end of service.

"I'm glad I came. I just told Luna how much I enjoyed it. Your message was right on time," Eliana told him.

Stiles smiled and shook her hand. "I'm glad to hear that." He then turned to Luna and hugged her.

"Hello, Sista Luna. God is good, isn't he," he said, holding her hand and placing his other hand on it.

Christian beamed as he stood proudly next to his wife.

"Yes, he is," she said and suddenly started crying. "Oh, my, I'm sorry. I'm just so thankful."

"Don't apologize. You have every reason to be in a constant state of praise. God has shown himself worthy of it once again. Deacon Black knows, and you do too," Stiles said, looking at Luna and then placing a hand on Christian's shoulder, "that I've been in constant prayer for you. God heard us. So, you be blessed."

"Thank you, Pastor Stiles," Luna said, wiping tears with the handkerchief Christian pulled from his suit pocket.

"And Sista Eliana, I hope you visit us again."

"Thank you, Pastor Stiles. I'm sure I will. May God continue to bless you."

Hezekiah walked up, spoke to them, and offered blessings for a good week before telling Stiles he was about to leave.

Shelia E. Bell

†

Outside, in the church parking lot, Eliana and Luna talked.

"It's like a boulder was removed off of us. I'm so happy," Luna cried.

"And I'm happy for you. I'm glad you won't have to worry about that monster ever again."

"Me too. And how are you? We have to catch up, girl. How are you enjoying your new home? I bet Khaliyah adores her room."

"Yes, she loves it, and I love it too. It's hard, though; I miss Khalil, but oh well. I still love it."

"Good for you. And what about the job?"

"Eazy peazy," Eliana said, laughing. "It's quiet around there. None of the drama like it used to be at Holy Rock. The staff is nice. There are only five of us, that includes me. I attended one of their Sunday services."

"How did you like it?" asked Luna.

Eliana nodded. "I liked it. I can see myself going again. The pastor preaches the Bible. His delivery might be considered a little rough to the older crowd, but I guess he's preaching to a younger congregation of people because they seem to have more people my age in his congregation. Two deacons are older and have been there for some years, but the others are ones the pastor appointed."

"Maybe you'll meet someone there. And before you cuss me out on the church parking lot, I meant maybe you'll meet new people."

Eliana rolled her eyes and shook her head, and they giggled.

"Here comes Christian," Luna said, looking toward the side door of the church.

"You better be glad he saved you," Eliana said, still laughing. "Okay, well, I'm going to get out of here. I think I'll stop at Olive Garden and get me a salad and soup before I head home."

"Be safe. I'll call you or FaceTime later," Luna said.

"Sounds good. Talk to you later."

They hugged, and Eliana left.

Later that evening, after she'd showered and laid out her work clothes for the week, Eliana made a cup of hibiscus tea, said her prayers, and crawled into her bed.

Her phone rang. It was Khalil facetiming her.

"Hi," Eliana said nonchalantly.

"Hi," he said. "Here's your daughter."

"Hi, Mommy," Khaliyah said.

"Hi, sweetie. How are you?"

"Good."

"Did you enjoy church school today?"

"Yes," Khaliyah answered.

"Mommy misses you. I love you. Have a good night."

"Okay."

"You good?" Khalil asked, returning to view.

"Yes."

"I missed seeing you at church today. What's up with that?" he asked, looking irritated.

"I didn't know I was required to attend Holy Rock now that I am no longer First Lady," she said with a bite of sarcasm on her furrowed face. "And you know darn well I haven't been there in weeks, Khalil. Don't play."

"Come on now. I hope you aren't petty like that," he snapped back.

"I don't call it petty, Khalil, and I don't want to get into this with you right now."

"That's the problem, Eliana. You never want to get into anything that might have to do with saving our marriage."

Eliana noticed Khaliyah in the background, listening to every word they exchanged.

"Look, we'll talk. Baby," she said, looking past him at Khaliyah.

Khalil turned and saw her. "Here," he said and gave Khaliyah the phone.

"I'll see you tomorrow," Eliana said. "Say your prayers and be good for Daddy. Goodnight, sweetheart."

The screen went blank.

Chapter 31

Old Folks

"Have enough courage to trust love one more time and always one more time." Maya Angelou

Fancy admitted to Victoria that she was having the time of her life getting to know Noah Alexander.

"Vicky, you should have seen the look on Hezekiah's face when Noah called while he was there."

"Poor Hezekiah, the green-eyed monster has bitten him," Vicky laughed over the phone.

"I'm sorry for him, Vicky, then again, I'm not. I mean, what do I have to be sorry about? Hezekiah and I have been divorced for years. He's had a kid on me, plus he's had a whole other wife, so pooh on him," Fancy said, slightly chuckling. "I look at it like this—Hezekiah is my past. Noah is showing me what my future could be like."

"I heard that. I'm glad my bestie is happy. He's pleased with how the renovations are coming along?"

"Yep," Fancy answered. "I told you he gave me a set of keys to his place a couple of weeks ago so I could go in and out of the house when he's away. That way, the contractors don't have to stop every time he's not there, which is mostly all the time."

211

"Yes, you told me, and I'm still amazed with that move. A key to the man's castle? And you say you ain't putting it out?" Vicky laughed.

"No, nothing's happened. You know I would have told you if it had. Every time we've spent time together, he's been the perfect gentleman. Of course, there's the one time I told you about when we kissed, and things got heated, but nothing came of it."

"Not because you didn't want it to," Vicky teased. "When you told me how that man put it on you, girl, I thought you were going to forget you used to be a first lady. You were ready to forget all about morals."

"You ain't lyin'," Fancy said, cracking up on the phone. "Thank goodness he stopped, or I would have probably started acting like a teenager instead of a fifty-two-year-old."

"Okay, so how do you see things progressing between y'all?" Vicky asked, her tone turning serious.

"I don't know, Vicky. I like him, but well, that's all I can say. I told myself not to focus too much on what might happen and just live for the moment. And for the moment, I'm having a good time, a very good time."

"You know I can relate. I'm enjoying spending time with Wyatt. Did I tell you he asked me to go to Butte with him for Thanksgiving?"

"What? That sounds serious, Vicky. What did you tell him?"

"I told him I'd think about it."

"Think about it? What's there to think about? You're the one who's always talking about how we're not getting any younger, so we should have fun and excitement. Now listen to you."

"I know, I know, and I'll probably tell him yes, but it's weird."

"Weird? How?" Fancy asked.

"I've never had a man want to take me to meet his family other than my ex-husband."

"Vicky, listen to yourself. You're trying to talk yourself out of it. I don't think Wyatt will get you to Montana and feed you to the wild animals or anything. On the other hand, maybe his family will," Fancy broke into laughter.

"Don't make me think about crazy stuff, Fancy."

"You know I'm messing with you. Tell the man you're going. I want to know how their stuffing tastes." Fancy laughed.

"Okay, I made up my mind. I'm going. I can't miss eating Thanksgiving with a bunch of Montana folks!"

"Look, let me go. I need to get ready. Noah's picking me up in an hour," Fancy said.

"Okay, have fun. We'll talk later," Victoria said, and they ended the call.

†

Fancy and Noah dined at a casual dining spot in midtown.

"Everything is progressing quite nicely," he told Fancy.

"Thank you, Noah. But remember what I told you—tomorrow is the absolute last day you're allowed inside until the final renovations are completed. Until then, you can stay in your guesthouse or wherever you choose, just as long as it isn't the main house."

Noah frowned and tilted his head.

"What's that look? You promised, Noah."

"I know, I know," he said, picking up his napkin and wiping his mouth. "How long will this be?" he asked, smiling.

"Ten days. You can stay away for ten days, I know. You do it all the time with your schedule, sometimes longer."

"Traveling for work is a vast difference. There's rarely a moment of rest. It's always one meeting to the next. One city to the next. So when I'm in Memphis, I want to relax since I've made this my home base, at least for the next three to five years. That's why I bought the place, don't get me wrong; I'm not complaining. I know perfection takes time," he said, smiling at Fancy, reaching for her hand, and kneading it in his. "Look at you."

Fancy blushed.

When they left the restaurant and reached Fancy's house, they sat in her driveway like two high school lovers, talking more about the renovations until the car suddenly grew silent as his mouth claimed hers. It was a light, lingering kiss.

"Uh, would you like to come inside for a glass of wine?" she asked, her breath slightly heavy.

"Yeah, sure."

Inside, they sat in the family room.

"What type of music do you like?" he asked, sipping his wine.

"I have some R&B on my playlist, or we can listen to something you like."

"R&B is fine. That's my kind of music, especially music like we listened to when we were coming up."

She connected her Bluetooth and started playing the music. "If Only For One Night," by Luther came on.

"That's what I'm talking about," Noah said.

"Yeah, that's my song; I love Luther," she said, putting the glass to her lips.

"Come on, dance with me," he said, tugging her hand and leading her to the middle of the floor.

She buried her head in his chest as Luther crooned, *"Let me hold you tight, if only for one night..."*

Noah began caressing the middle of her back. Fancy squeezed him tighter as they grooved and moved to the sensuous melodies of Luther singing, *"It would be so nice..."*

They were so into the song that their feelings and emotions soon began to take over. His kisses deepened, and her sounds of satisfaction increased.

"Should I stop?" he said hungrily as his eyes raked over her and his mouth devoured her lips. "Tell me if you want me to stop," he growled.

"No, don't...don't stop," she whispered.

As the song neared an end, he pulled her to him, slightly raising her off her feet when several hard knocks were heard at her back door.

Fancy's eyes widened as they popped apart like someone had set a firecracker between them.

The knock grew louder and harder.

"Excuse me, Noah," she said, walking off, her anger growing at knowing it could be no one other than Hezekiah.

She yanked open the door. "What do you want, Hezekiah?"

He looked over her head and into the house. "Are you okay?" he asked.

"Why wouldn't I be?" she said, folding her arms and standing back in her legs.

"I saw that car outside. I've never known you to have company this late. I was concerned."

"I'm a grown woman, Hezekiah. I don't need you or anybody looking after me like I'm a child. Now, if you'll excuse me, I'm busy."

"Look, Fancy—"

"Is everything all right?" Noah asked, appearing in the kitchen and standing behind Fancy.

"Yes," Fancy replied, her voice a mixture of anger and amusement at the lengths Hezekiah would go to keep her life on lockdown like she was a prisoner. The thought quickly rushed through her head about Winston. Here, Hezekiah was about to act a fool that Noah was at her home, but the same Hezekiah went behind her back and paid another man to seduce her.

"Noah, this is uh, Hezekiah McCoy, my ex-husband and my tenant. Hezekiah, this is Noah Alexander."

"What's up?" Noah nodded, keeping a straight face and extending his hand.

"What's up," Hezekiah mumbled and shook his hand briefly.

"Hezekiah, uh, I'm fine. You can leave now," Fancy told him after the speedy intro.

"I'm sorry. I didn't mean to disturb you. I just wanted to make sure you were good. Goodnight," he said and walked back to the casita.

"Now, where were we before being so rudely interrupted?" Noah asked, wrapping an arm around her waist and leading Fancy back into the family room, obviously unbothered by Hezekiah's untimely interruption.

†

Fancy and Noah exited the house the following morning, giggling as they walked to his car. Coincidentally, Hezekiah happened to be getting inside his car at the same time.

Fancy glanced at Hezekiah, shifted her eyes, and then looked at Noah as he opened her car door, and she got inside.

Hezekiah backed out of the driveway, followed by Noah.

As they drove, Noah held her hand.

"Last night was remarkable," he said, leaning over at the traffic light and kissing the side of her face.

"Yeah, it was," she agreed, looking at him with eyes filled with leftover desire.

"I want you to know that I like you. I really, really like you, Fancy. Making love with you last night meant something, is all I'm saying."

"I'm...I'm glad to hear you say that 'cause I like you a lot, too, Noah, and I want you to know that I don't sleep around with random executives from FedEx," she said, breaking into a light chuckle.

Noah laughed out loud as he pulled from the light. "That's good news, my darling. You had me worried there for a minute," he joked. "Now, where would you like to grab breakfast? I'm starving."

"Cora's Diner, the best diner food in the city," Fancy replied rapidly.

"Cora's it is," Noah said as they drove along the highway.

Chapter 32

Face It – It's Over

"Don't waste time on revenge. The people who hurt
you will eventually face their own karma."
Positive Oasis

Luna rushed to the backyard where
Christian and the kids were playing. Saturdays
were one of the days they found peace and quiet
at home with the kids before Christian faced
another full week of court and clients.

The trial for Sanchez was set to start in three
weeks. Luna wasn't looking forward to attending,
but she also wasn't planning to miss a single
day. She wouldn't rest until she knew justice
had been served for her and the other victims.

They hadn't heard from Lorie since Luna put
her out and told her not to come back. Part of
her hated to treat her sister that way, but Lorie
had no respect or regard for her, so why would
she have any toward her?

Luna wouldn't openly admit it, but she still
missed her. It had only been two years since
they patched up their relationship, and then, in
true Lorie style, she went and ruined it with her
confession of sleeping with Christian.

"Christian," Luna screamed, running through the
house, frantic from the call she'd just received.

"Christian!" she called again as she raced to
the backyard.

Christian popped his head out of the custom treehouse he had built for Dax, holding Laiyah Rose, who was starting to get into everything.

"Hey, what's up?" he asked, concerned.

"Christian," she cried, "It's Lorie. Oh, God, Christian. Come down."

Christian led Dax by the hand while holding on to Laiyah Rose. They carefully came down the steps of the treehouse.

"What happened? What's she done now?" Christian fumed, hearing Lorie's name.

"Baby, Daddy just called. Lorie was in a bad accident this morning. He says she was drunk and hit a pole."

"Is she okay?" he asked, putting Laiyah Rose on the floor of the lanai and letting her crawl.

Luna cried, "No, she....she fractured her back. She might not ever walk again."

"Oh, my God. Where did this happen? In Virginia?" Christian asked.

"No, in Bluffton. Daddy said she showed up at their door three days ago. Momma told him not to tell me because she didn't want to upset me. He said she was talking about how sorry she was for being such a horrible daughter and that she was going to change her ways. He said she left out the night before, saying she was meeting a friend at some restaurant, and that was the last they heard from her until the police showed up at their door this morning."

"What do you want to do? Do you want to go see her?" he asked, concern filtering through his voice.

Luna stopped crying and wiped her face with a cloth towel she picked up from the lounge table. "I don't know. Should I?"

"I'll leave that up to you. Just know that whatever you want to do, I'm all for it. I'll support you, get you there, whatever we need to do."

"I...I want to talk to Ma and Dad again before I decide. Oh, God, Christian, I hope she's going to be okay. I know she's done terrible things, but she's my sister. I hope she won't be paralyzed for the rest of her life. That would be terrible."

"Yeah, it would, but she also could have lost her life."

"You're right," Luna said, sniffing and wiping her nose.

"Was anyone else hurt?"

Luna shook her head before answering and, with sad eyes, said, "No, what a blessing. She could have killed herself and other people, too. Thank God no other cars were involved," Luna lamented, sauntering up to him and resting in his arms. "This is awful," she cried. "Just awful."

"I know, sweetheart. You've been going through one upset after the next, but you got to hold on, baby. Hold on to your faith. Like you always remind me— God is in control. And Lorie will be all right, whatever the outcome. It's all in His hands. I'm just sorry I've added to your stress. I'm so sorry," Christian cried, embracing his wife. "Please, please forgive me, baby. Please. I love you so much."

"And I love you, Christian," Luna said as they cried in each other's arms.

Chapter 33

The Keys of Life

"Sometimes, the bad things that happen in our lives put us on the path to the most wonderful things that will ever happen to us." Nicole Reed

"Did you hear about Luna's sister?" Eliana asked as she and Pepper chatted on the phone.

"Yes, Luna called and told me last night. That was terrible. She's really upset, and I can't blame her. She said her sister may never walk again."

"Yeah, I know. Isn't that sad? Life can change in the blink of an eye," Eliana said sadly.

"Sure can. That's another reason for me starting this nonprofit. I want to make a difference in people's lives while I still can. I have the resources, although they came as a result of Xavier's suicide, but I'm grateful for the idea and for naming it in his honor. I hope he would be happy to see the good I'm trying to do to keep his memory alive."

"He would be. And as for the nonprofit, I already know it will be successful, Pepper. You've come a long way. I was worried about you for a long time. But girl, am I glad to see the old Pepper coming back," Eliana told her.

"Me too, but I hope I'm a new and improved version," Pepper chuckled. "I also know that without God, family, and, of course, friends like you, Rolonda, and Luna, I would still be in a very dark place."

"Yes, and I thank him that you're not."

"Speaking of me getting back into the swing of things, I can't wait until the boys start Pre-K. Let the countdown begin," she laughed.

"Time is sure passing fast. Tell me, what's up with you and Ryan?"

"You ask that question like Ryan and I are a couple. We're not. We're friends." Pepper smiled.

"Yeah, but you know it's more than that. You like the guy. He likes you. You're both adults. Nothing is holding you back from getting closer, Pepper."

"I didn't say there was. I'm just saying we haven't talked about anything serious like that. He has his own self-healing to do. The man lost his family, Eliana. As for me, I don't need added drama in my life, especially now. How many times do I have to say to you, Rolonda, and Luna, I'm not ready."

"Okay, don't get your panties all in a wad. I'm just saying, don't close yourself off from possibilities."

"And are you calling the kettle black? You need to be following your own advice."

"I'm still married, though, and until my divorce is final, I cannot operate in these streets like I'm single. And, I have to agree with you— I'm not ready either," admitted Eliana.

"Let's drop that subject for now, or else we'll be on this phone until tomorrow at this same time."

"Okay, and I still have a lot of work to get done in preparation for my grand opening. Can you believe it's less than a month away?""

"No, but I do know it'll be here before we know it," Eliana said.

"Right. I'm getting ready to take the boys to PARENTS' DAY OUT for a few hours and then come back home and get on this computer. There are a ton of things I still have on my checklist. I can get a lot of it done when the house is empty. Know what I mean?"

"Girl, yes. Speaking of work, let me get off this phone, too. I've been running financial reports. They take most of the morning, which is why I could talk for as long as I have."

"Okay, hey, before I let you go, let me ask, do you still like working there?" Pepper asked.

"Yes, I mean, it's still new, and I had to get used to getting up every morning and going to a nine-to-five again, but I like it. It pays a decent salary. The staff is pretty cool, and I'm learning their church software and how they operate things. It's a smaller church so there isn't half as much for me to do like when I used to work at Holy Rock."

"That's good. I know it can't be easy going through a divorce, returning to work, and add being a single mom to that, but hey, I'm here for you."

"I know," Eliana said, "and thanks. Okay, we'll talk later. Call or text if you hear anything else from Luna."

"I will. You do the same. Buh-bye."

Chapter 34

Hear Me Out

"A promise means everything, but once it is broken, sorry means nothing." Unknown

Eliana pulled into Khalil's driveway. Seeing an unfamiliar car parked in the curve of the driveway, she let the car idle while she called him. If he had company, she didn't want to intrude. All she needed was for him to bring Khaliyah outside, and they could be on their way.

Her stomach ached with a dull, uneasy pain, another reason for her to get home as quickly as possible. She didn't know if it was bundled nerves, stress, a stomach virus, or something she ate. Maybe it was a combination of them all. Nevertheless, she needed to hurry.

"Hello," he answered.

"I'm outside. Will you bring Khaliyah to the car?"

"Sure," he said and cleared the call. Within minutes, she saw one side of the black eight-foot double entry doors open, and her pride and joy appeared bouncing out.

Eliana's chest tightened as waves of emotion washed over her, leaving her breathless. Little Khaliyah, despite her world being torn apart, was a blessing, and Eliana was grateful. Some children exhibited emotional trauma or behavioral issues when their parents went through a divorce, but so far, Khaliyah seemed to be adjusting just fine.

One of the things she admired and loved about Khalil was that he didn't let anything keep him from his daughter. Khaliyah always came first, or maybe she never came first. *What was she thinking?* That was one of the problems and the reasons for the divorce. Khalil wasn't so perfect. He was always on the go and rarely at home. The more she thought about it, the more her opinion of him changed. How could a man be a good husband and father when he was always laid up with Detria Graham or at Holy Rock doing only God knows what? She reminded herself of all the reasons she needed to go through with this divorce.

"She just ate some pasta and green beans," he told her.

"Good, that's one less thing I have to do when I get home," she said, grabbing her stomach and wincing.

"You good?" Khalil asked, showing concern.

"Yeah, it's just a stomach ache. I want to get home so I can take something and get some relief."

"If you want to come inside and use the bathroom, you know this place is still yours and Khaliyah's home. I'm sure there's something in the medicine cabinet you can take."

"Thanks, but that's where you're wrong." She spoke calmly, no smile. "This may still be yours and Khaliyah's home, but it is no longer mine. By the way, did you receive your letter about the hearing? Unless you protest something, we can have all of this over in no time. That way, both of us can move on with our lives."

Khalil looked like someone who had been struck in the face. "I got them, and I read them," he said. "What do you want me to say?"

She winced again and looked over her shoulder. Khaliyah was falling asleep in her car seat. "I don't want you to say anything," she frowned. "I was just asking if you got the papers. Goodbye, Khalil."

"Yeah, well, I'm not looking forward to court or this divorce, Eliana."

"I need to go," she said, glancing in the back seat again and holding her tummy. Khaliyah was sound asleep, her head now hung over to the side.

Eliana rolled her eyes and drove off. Looking in her rearview mirror as she pulled out of his driveway, she saw her past growing smaller and smaller until, like a vapor, it was gone.

†

As evening approached, her upset tummy passed, especially after she drank a can of ginger ale and nibbled on some saltine crackers.

Khaliyah was asleep, so she spent time getting reacquainted with social media.

She rarely used social media, but since she was about to be a single woman, she thought it wouldn't hurt to see what other women like her were doing. To say she was shocked and, at times, offended by some of the stuff she saw would be an understatement.

Her phone rang. It was Pepper. "Hey, girl."

"Hey, how's it going?" Pepper asked.

"Good. Thank God it's Friday. I'm tired," Eliana said, yawning. "I was about to crawl up in this bed and put on a movie until I fell asleep."

"I was just checking to see if Khalil got the papers about the hearing."

"Yes, I meant to call and tell you, but my stomach was hurting something awful. All I could do when I pulled into my driveway was get to the bathroom. I guess I forgot after that."

"You okay?"

"I guess. For a minute, it was coming out of both ends, girl. But now I'm starting to feel better. Could be a stomach virus or stress."

"Well, the last thing you need to be doing is stressing. If you're having second thoughts about the divorce, then call it off, Eliana. You don't owe anyone an explanation about the decisions you make."

"I know, and thanks for reminding me. If I thought there was any way other than divorce, I would consider it, but I told y'all I'm past that," Eliana cried. "But yeah, he got them. You know he wasn't happy about it, but, oh well."

"Have y'all talked about counseling? I mean, a faith-based counselor who will give you Godly and wise advice? Anything before y'all call it quits. Especially since you say you still love him."

"I thought about it, and Khalil mentioned counseling once, maybe twice, but I told him I wasn't interested."

Pepper sounded surprised as she exclaimed, "You never told me that he suggested you go to counseling."

"I didn't tell you because I knew we were beyond counseling at that point, Pepper. That text his slut sent me was the icing on the cake. After that, there's nothing a counselor can tell me or advise me to do other than what I'm doing now, and that's divorce his cheating behind."

"Have you talked to Fancy? What is she saying? You never said how she felt about it."

"She hasn't said a whole lot. Of course, she doesn't like it, and she hates to see the marriage come to this, but she certainly understands why I'm doing what I'm doing."

"She told you that?"

"Yep, those were her words. You know Fancy. One thing she's going to do is be real."

"You're right about that," Pepper said.

"She promised to still be there for Khaliyah as much as she can, although she reminded me that her design business has been keeping her busy."

"I know. My mother introduced her to this big-shot FedEx executive who bought a huge house in the suburbs. According to what my mother said, he hired Fancy to run the whole renovation project," Pepper shared. "That's why she hasn't been keeping the kids as much as she used to on the weekends. I was surprised when she called about keeping the boys last weekend."

"I was glad she got Khaliyah, too," Eliana laughed. "Any word from Luna?" asked Eliana.

"I texted her earlier and asked her how Lorie was doing?"

"What'd she say?"

"She said nothing had changed. She said, "'She still has no movement or feeling from the chest down, and she's saying very little,'" Pepper read from her phone. "'She's still in ICU. No visitors, only immediate family.'"

"Oh my gosh, that is so sad," Eliana said, shocked.

Her doorbell rang, followed by a knock. "Pepper, wait, don't hang up. Someone's at my door. I don't know who this could be. It's nine-thirty at night," she complained, going to the door, tightening her thin lavender robe as she went.

Looking through the peephole, she was taken aback when she saw the person on the other side.

"Pepper, it's Khalil."

What? Khalil?"

"Yeah, I'll call you later. Let me see what he wants."

"Okay, call me back."

She opened the door. "What do you want? Did Khaliyah forget something? Is something wrong?"

"No, can I come in?" he asked. His eyes were bloodshot, and the strong stench of weed wreaked from his clothes and attacked her nostrils.

"When did you start smoking weed again, or did you ever stop?" she said, sarcasm dripping with every word as she inched back, allowing him to enter.

"I needed something to relax me. It was just a joint. But look, we need to talk."

"Talk about what, Khalil?" Eliana sighed.

"This divorce. Being apart from you and my daughter is driving me nuts," Khalil said, rubbing his head nervously back and forth. "I want you to call it off."

"Call it off? Call it off and do what, Khalil? Go back to the way things were? I don't think so."

"I told you Detria is out of my life. She did that because it was her way of trying to get next to you, and she did. Believe me, she won't do anything like that again."

Eliana folded her arms and stormed up the hall, with Khalil following her into the kitchen.

She poured a glass of juice and stood opposite Khalil on the other side of the counter.

"Yeah, you got one thing right, Khalil—her text sure did get next to me," Eliana bit back. "So much so that it woke my dumb behind up, made me see you for who you really are," she said, frowning and taking a swallow of the juice. "Look, if this is what you came to talk about, then you should leave. I'm tired. I don't have time for this. And I don't like you thinking you can pop up over here whenever you get ready."

"Tell me you don't love me," Khalil said, walking up to her.

Eliana darted from the kitchen, but Khalil stopped her and turned her to face him. "Say it, Eliana. Tell me you don't love me," he demanded, his breath hot and heavy as he drew her close.

231

Eliana could feel her heart racing, not from fear but from missing his touch, his closeness, his hands on her body. Having him next to her, giving her no means to escape, she twisted and moaned.

"Get back, Khalil," she weakly protested, pushing him away.

Khalil would not relent. He answered by hungrily and savagely attacking her lips. With animalistic groans, he explored underneath her robe, massaging her secret places until her cries of passion revealed her desire for him.

"I said, stop, Khalil," pushing him off her with all her strength. "You need to leave. Now!"

"I'm not leaving. I can't. I want you to be certain you never want me to touch you again," he said, coming up to her again. He walked her back toward the kitchen island. Her protests meant nothing as he lifted her buttocks onto the counter while Eliana fought against him, pounding him. Her cries went unanswered as he sunk himself into her.

"Get out!" she said, pointing to the front door and pushing him aside with another thrust, giving her seconds to jump off the island counter. "Get out right now, Khalil McCoy, or I swear I'll call the police!"

His look sent a shimmer through her as he deeply exhaled. His body was relieved, and his tension was gone. He said nothing, but that piercing look said what words failed to say. He fastened his belt and pants and stormed up the hallway and out the door, leaving Eliana in tears.

Chapter 35

Coat Of Many Colors

"Sometimes you have to walk away from what you
want to find what you deserve." Pinterest

October

"I am *soo* glad the boys have started school,"
Pepper told Eliana as they walked out of Holy
Rock Academy together. "They love it. What
about, Khaliyah? How does she like daycare?"

"She likes it, but remember, she's used to
going to the childcare center anyway. The
difference is this is a more structured program,
and she's going five days a week instead of the
three half days, but she still likes it."

"Good. I know I'm probably enjoying it more
than they are." Pepper laughed.

"Do you have everything finalized for the
grand opening?" Eliana asked.

"Just about. I have a few last-minute details
to iron out, but other than that, everything is
set. I can proudly say that the official grand
opening of *The Xavier McCoy Healing Together
Foundation* is almost here. A week from
Saturday, to be exact.

"I'm so excited for you," said Eliana as they
arrived at their cars parked across from each
other. "Is there anything else I need to do? Do
you need me to print more flyers?"

"No, we have plenty. The volunteers are going to start distributing them this week."

"That's great." Eliana opened her car door and stood inside. "Hey, have you talked to Luna since the trial started?"

"Other than the group texts she sends, no."

Pepper stood at her car door as well. "Yeah, I haven't tried calling her because I know she has a full plate. With going to the trial every day, what happened to her sister, and the kids to deal with, I've been giving her space."

"Yeah, I agree," said Eliana. "After being in court all day, listening to all that horrific stuff that pervert did to her and all those other women, it's hard on her. She said she's mentally drained when she makes it home in the afternoons."

"She told me it should be over sometime in the next week or so. I hope so, for her sake. Enough is enough. That trial has been going on since September. She deserves to be able to move on with her life. And with her sister's accident added to it, I know she's at her wit's end," Pepper said, shaking her head.

"I just hope they send his behind away for life," said Eliana. "He doesn't deserve to see the light of day ever again."

"I agree," said Pepper.

"Well, look, I've got to go. I don't want to get caught in traffic and be late for work."

"Okay, have a good day," Pepper said.

After leaving Holy Rock, Pepper stopped at the grocery store and did her weekly shopping.

Once home, she did some light housecleaning. When she was done, she got dressed. Rolonda arrived, and the ladies went to get mani-pedis, something she hadn't indulged in in a very long time.

"So, what's going on with you and Ryan? Have you seen him anymore?" Rolonda asked, sitting in the Pedi chair next to Pepper.

"We went to a movie the other night when he was in Memphis. They don't make good movies like they used to, but I still had a good time. We also went to tour the building where I'm going to house my nonprofit."

"Oh, cool. I can't wait to see it," said Rolonda.

"I'll show it to you the next time we get together. It's perfect, Rolonda. Wait, I'll text you the pictures."

Moments later, Rolonda's text notifier started dinging. "Oh, I like this," she said, scrolling from one image to the next as they came on her phone.

"Yeah, it's a godsend."

"Okay, so getting back to Mr. Ryan, when's the next time you're going to see him?"

"He lives in Jackson, Rolonda. It's not like it's a hop, skip and jump."

"Oh, but it is because it sure seems like he's hanging around more often."

"Look, he's a nice guy. He understands what I'm going through losing Xavier because he's going through the same thing, probably worse. Either way, I feel comfortable talking to him," she admitted. "Mentally, he's helped me a lot."

"Sounds like things are picking up between you two."

"Don't start, Rolonda."

"What are you talking about? I only said things are picking up between the two of you. And they are. You said you talk to the man every day."

"I didn't say I talk to him every day," Pepper paused. "And even if I did, so what? Can't a guy and a girl be friends? Dang," Pepper said, irritated.

"Chile, don't bite my head off. You don't have to try to convince me," Rolonda laughed. "I haven't heard you say you *don't* like him, so I take that to mean that you *do* like him. Am I wrong for assuming that?"

"No, I wouldn't say that you're wrong. I'm just saying I like him as a friend. That's it."

"Who said anything about anything else?" Rolonda replied. "I'm just glad you're giving the man a chance," Rolonda said, and they burst into laughter.

"I have to admit that I am starting to feel better, mentally," Pepper said as they left the nail shop and headed to the retail outlet for shopping and lunch. "I mean, I still miss Xavier, but I don't think about him every single day like I used to."

"You mean since you met Ryan, don't you?" Rolonda stated.

"No, I mean since leaving Stateside. I also think starting the nonprofit is helping. I'm already thinking about programs to add to the ones we already plan to offer."

"That sounds like a great idea, Pepper. You're really into this, aren't you?"

"Yeah, I guess I am. I mentioned some of my ideas to Ryan. He thinks they're great. I'm still working on a mission statement. He's helping me."

"Oh, good. Sounds like you and Ryan have it together. Whatever you need me to do, give me a shout."

"Okay, I'll let you know. I already know I could use your software skills. You know you are the queen of knowing how to use the latest software and social media."

"I can't help it if your girl lives to be an influencer with millions of followers."

Rolonda and Pepper laughed.

"Seriously, whatever you need me to do, just holler at your girl."

"You know I will," said Pepper.

Chapter 36

Here I Am

"We don't meet people by accident. They are meant to cross our path for a reason." Unknown

Eliana arrived at work, logged onto her computer, and went to the church breakroom stocked with a variety of snacks. She made a cup of coffee, grabbed a couple of Danish, and returned to her office.

"Good morning," Mason said, sticking his head in her office.

"Good morning, Mason. Have a good one."

"Thanks, love. You too. Talk to you later," he said and headed toward his office.

While she read her emails, she drank her coffee and devoured the first Danish.

Moments later, she felt her stomach twisting into knots, and her face flushed. She got up from her chair and raced past Mason's office to the bathroom.

Within seconds of opening the door to one of the stalls, all she could taste were remnants of the Danish and coffee mixture. She couldn't hold it down even if she wanted to. She made it just in time for the vomit to land in the toilet.

"Oh my gosh! What was that?" she asked herself, holding her belly and going to the sink to splash cold water over her face. She looked up in the mirror and gasped at her reflection.

She was pale as a ghost, and her eyes were sunken and bloodshot. She remained in the bathroom until the bout of sickness passed, and she could return to her office.

For the remainder of the morning, she didn't feel her best. She couldn't tell if she was coming down with a stomach virus, the flu, or COVID. Then she remembered feeling the same way the month before, but that only lasted for 24 hours, and then she was back to normal. Maybe that's what was going on again today. She would see a doctor if this continued.

When lunchtime rolled around, Eliana didn't want to think about food. Though she enjoyed her job, today, she couldn't wait for the work day to end so she could pick up Khaliyah, go home, and get in her bed.

"You okay?" Mason asked, stepping into her office. "You've been quiet all day."

"I feel like I may be coming down with something, but I'll be okay," she said, shrugging it off. "What's up? What do you need?"

"Just checking to see if you finished running the weekly reports. I was going to add them to mine and get them printed for tomorrow's meeting."

"I still have a couple more to run, and then I'll be done. I'll let you know when I finish."

"Thanks, but hey, if you don't feel any better, you should get out of here, go home, and take care of yourself," he suggested.

"Thanks, Mason. I'm good."

"I can run the other reports for you."

"No, I'm almost finished. I'll probably take your suggestion and leave early when I get done.

I can do the rest of my work from home, at least most of it."

"Well, I hope you feel better," he said, leaving her office.

She made it to the end of the day but didn't feel any better.

"Hey, can you keep Khaliyah tonight? I don't feel good, so I'm going home to take something and hopefully feel better."

"Sure," Khalil said. "No problem. Do you need me to come over and take care of you?" he asked, sounding like he was really sincere.

"No, I'll be fine. I just need a little rest. Let Khaliyah FaceTime me tonight before she goes to bed." Maybe he was genuine, but Eliana wasn't entertaining anything he said. She hadn't forgotten about the last time he was at her apartment. He swore up and down that he did nothing wrong, but she didn't see it that way. She didn't care if she was still his wife. When she told him to stop, he should have listened.

"You were complaining once before about your stomach. You might need to get checked out."

"I told you, I'm straight, Khalil. It's just an upset stomach. Something I had no business eating."

"Okay, well, I'll check on you later," he said, and they ended the call.

At work for the remainder of the week, almost every time she ate something, she would have to rush to the bathroom and puke. She continued to feel feverish and weak.

After she didn't feel better by that Friday, Mason suggested, "You should see a doctor."

"I think I will," she said. "I thought I would be better by now, but I'm not," she said, wiping light beads of sweat off her forehead. "Thanks for your concern, Mason. I think I'm going to the minor med at lunch."

"That's a good idea. I'll take you if you don't feel up to driving."

"No, I wouldn't ask you to do that. I don't know how long it'll take. Sometimes, you can get in and out of there; other times, those places are packed."

"I don't mind waiting. Really, I don't. As for work, I'm caught up, and I have my outline done for this week's Youth Night, so I'm all set. Get your things, and we can get out of here. I'll let the front office know we may be gone a couple of hours."

"Thanks, Mason. You're a saint," she said, smiling weakly. "Let me put these papers away, and I'll be ready," she said, wiping her forehead again.

She rose and reached for a stack of papers off the side of her desk. Again, she grabbed her forehead, but this time, she looked at Mason with crossed eyes and fainted.

†

"I can't believe I fainted," Eliana said, sitting beside Mason at the minor med office.

"Well, you did. Scared the heck out of me. I'm glad you didn't hit your head or anything. You fell awfully close to your desk. I thought we were going to have to call an ambulance, but thankfully, Sista Smith had some old-fashioned smelling salt. Woke you right up."

"Is that what that was?" Eliana giggled. "I haven't seen or heard of that since I was a kid."

"I know, right?" Mason added.

"I'm glad you're here," she said, looking at him, her eyes lingering on his briefly before she looked away.

"Me too," he said. He reached over and grabbed her hand, holding it lightly.

She didn't protest. Rather, she welcomed his touch. It made her calm and less frightened.

"Eliana McCoy," the nurse called after they had been sitting in the waiting area for about twenty minutes.

An hour later, Eliana appeared at the checkout counter.

"You said your pharmacy is CVS on Havana? Is that right?" the woman asked Eliana.

"Yes."

The woman paused and focused on the computer. "There, I just sent them a script for two prenatal meds. You can contact them for pickup."

"Thank you," Eliana whispered, turning slightly and seeing Mason standing behind her.

"Are you okay?" he asked on the way to his car.

"Yes, I'm fine," she mumbled.

"A kid? Did you know?"

She stopped and looked at him, her eyes squinched, her tone uneasy. "No, I didn't."

"I guess this will change a lot with your marriage when you tell your husband."

"You mean soon-to-be ex-husband, remember," she snapped as he opened the door, and she got into his car. "And please, Mason, I would appreciate it if we didn't discuss this. I didn't mean for you to even hear what she said."

Eliana looked at him as he started the car.

Mason looked at her, his eyes steady, enchanting, inviting. He was a nice guy, a good man. He was single, loved the Lord, and wasn't gay, so why hadn't some lady at Grace Temple or any of the other churches put their hooks in him? She wondered only momentarily as she returned to her reality, which was that she was pregnant with Khalil's baby.

"You can trust me, Eliana," Mason said, smiling tenderly and reaching over to squeeze her hand. "I won't say a word. Just know that I'm here for you."

"Thanks, I appreciate that. I really do," she smiled back and then looked out her side mirror as tears formed.

When they returned to Grace Temple, she headed straight to her car. "Thanks for everything," she told Mason as he walked beside her.

"I was glad to do it. Look, are you sure you're good to drive home? I'll be glad to take you, and you can pick up your car tomorrow, or I'll get one of the guys here to drive my car, and I'll drive you to your house."

"No, Mason," she said, smiling as she reached her car. "You've been more than kind and helpful." She reached up and hugged him. "Thanks. I'll be fine."

"Okay, then at least text me when you make it home," he said. "Where's your phone? Let me give you my number."

She removed her phone from her purse, unlocked it, and passed it to him. "Here you go," she said, watching as he added his number.

When he was done, he returned her phone. She pushed the CALL button, and his phone started ringing. They smiled.

"Now you have mine," she said.

"Got it," he said, chuckling. "Drive safely. Remember to text me."

"I will," she said, getting into her car and driving away.

Chapter 37

The Greatest Gift Of All

"For whatsoever a man sows, that he will also reap." Galatians 6:7 NKJV

The trial lasted five weeks, and now Rex Sanchez's fate rested in the hands of the jury. Luna called on her church and every prayer warrior she could think of to join her in praying that he would be found guilty and sentenced to life in prison.

The jury had been out less than three hours when Luna and Christian received a call that the jury had reached a verdict. Without giving thought to the plates of food that had just been served, and before they barely had a chance to taste any of it, Christian quickly paid the check, and he and Luna, hand-in-hand, ran the three blocks back to the courthouse.

"Christian," she whispered, breathing heavily, "please let them find him guilty."

Christian replied by squeezing her hand but otherwise said nothing.

Today, Eliana and Pepper were also in the courtroom.

"Will the jury foreman deliver the verdict out loud to the courtroom?" the judge pronounced.

"Yes, your honor," replied the jury foreman. We, the jury, in the case of Rex Sanchez, charged with....do hereby find the defendant."

The courtroom was quiet.

Luna dug her fingernails into her palm and looked without flinching at the jury foreman.

"Do hereby find the defendant—guilty..."

"Ahhh!" a loud gasp escaped Luna's lips. More gasps and praises could be heard all over the courtroom.

"Quiet, quiet! Order in the courtroom," the judge demanded, hitting his gavel against the oak bench.

The courtroom settled as Luna, and her entourage left.

Standing outside the courthouse, Luna was beaming with joy on cloud nine. She quickly FaceTimed her parents to share the news. Their new responsibility—caring for Lorie—was proving to be a significant challenge. Managing her needs required immense time, patience, dedication, and energy. In their late sixties, her parents had been relishing retirement and anticipated frequent visits to see their grandchildren. But now, their plans were on hold, as Lorie's demanding care had become a full-time commitment.

Luna had briefly talked to them about getting more care for Lorie and perhaps placing her in a group home where she could receive proper care, but so far, they had refused. They told Luna it was their obligation to care for their child. Luna wouldn't argue against their wishes but prayed that they would change their minds.

"Oh, honey, we wish we could be there," her mother said, sharing in the excitement.

"I know, Ma, it's okay. I felt your and Dad's spirits and your prayers. I can never thank you enough for those prayers."

Her father popped his head on the screen, chuckling. "Ain't God good, baby."

"Yes, Daddy, he sure is," Luna replied.

"Honey, we are so happy for you. I just wish we could be there to hug you and to see those grandbabies," he said, his voice quivering.

"But now you can enjoy your babies without worrying. Maybe you can bring them to see us since we can't get there right now," her mother said, eyes longing for Luna to say she would.

"I think that can be arranged," Luna said. "Right, babe?" she looked over at Christian.

"Yes, of course," Christian said happily. "We'll start making plans."

"Oh, that's great!" her parents said and started clapping.

Luna and Christian laughed. "Well, Mom and Dad, I'll call you later. I'm standing outside on the courthouse steps, talking all loud. Christian and I are headed to pick up the kids. I'll FaceTime you tonight."

"Okay, darling," her father said.

"Goodbye, sweetheart," said her mom.

"Oh, wait, Mom."

"Yes, baby?" her mother replied.

"Uh, tell Lorie hello."

"I sure will, baby. I sure will."

Luna hadn't spoken to Lorie since the day she revealed about her and Christian. Their relationship remained just as broken. The accident hadn't softened the devastating arrow of betrayal; Luna wasn't sure if anything would

ever fix it, but she knew one thing for certain—
it was right to forgive her sister and let it go. She
believed she had done that, at least in her heart.
But no one said she had to rebuild their
relationship. Luna wasn't ready for that. Not
yet. Still, she believed today was a small step.
Asking their mother to pass along a simple
greeting to Lorie from her had taken more
strength than anyone could possibly understand.
But she did it. And for now, that was enough.
She hoped God would see she was trying.

Once home, Christian and Luna ordered food
and beverages for themselves, the kids, and the
roomful of guests who joined in celebrating
today's victory. Among those in attendance were
Eliana, Pepper, Stiles, and Mya.

"Now, we have to wait on the sentencing
hearing," Luna said.

"That's another blessing," chimed Christian.
"The sentencing hearing can take up to ninety
days, sometimes more, but in this case, you
heard Judge Perro; he's not prolonging it. He
plans to hear it in two weeks. That's another
huge victory!"

"Isn't that like God?" said Stiles. "He's a God
of surprises, a God of suddenlies," he said,
sounding like he was about to break out
preaching.

"Yes, he is," Luna said overjoyed.

"I say we have a toast," said Stiles.

"That's a good idea," said Christian.

They raised their beverages, and Stiles
proclaimed, "To God be the glory."

"To God be the glory," they all repeated and
clicked their glasses.

†

Two weeks later, Luna and Christian returned for the sentencing.

"I do hereby sentence you, Rex Hawthorne Sanchez, to thirty years to life for the abduction and aggravated sexual assault of one Luna Black. With the chance of parole after serving thirty years."

Luna inhaled sharply and exhaled with a liberating *whoosh* sound as if all the air had been suddenly let out of her.

The judge proceeded to deliver the rest of Sanchez's sentence, addressing the remaining crimes against the other victims. By the time he finished, there was no doubt—Sanchez would never again see the light of day as a free man.

It was over.

Luna exhaled, bracing herself for what came next. Would her marriage survive? Could she move forward, like everyone expected? And Christian—would he finally accept Laiyah Rose? The uncertainty of it all weighed heavily on her, but with this behind her, she was ready to face whatever lay ahead, no matter how frightening. Fear lingered, but she placed her trust in God to safeguard her and her little family.

Chapter 38

God Only Knows

"It's the unexpected that changes our lives."
Unknown

Eliana arrived at Holy Rock to pick up Khaliyah. Instead of going inside, she asked Khalil if he or Sista Mavis would bring her to the car. After learning she was pregnant, she came up with excuses for not going inside to pick up her daughter. She even suggested that Holy Rock Academy start a drive-thru pickup lane like many preschool and elementary schools had. She couldn't understand what would be so difficult about that.

Since what happened that night at her apartment, she was torn, trapped in a cycle of confusion and doubt. Did Khalil force himself on her, or was it all in her head? But now, the answer didn't seem to matter because, regardless, she was pregnant with their second child. What should have been a joyful time now felt tainted by the state of their relationship. In a matter of days, she would officially be divorced and a single mother of a three-year-old and another child due in five and a half months.

"You look different," Khalil said when he brought Khaliyah to the car.

"Different?" she said, snappy. "Different, how?"

"I don't know. You just look different," he said. "It's almost like you're glowing." He laughed.

"Oh, well, I don't know what you're seeing because I certainly don't feel like I'm glowing. If anything, I'm exhausted. I just want to get home, get Khaliyah and me some dinner and our baths, and crash."

"If you're that tired, I don't mind her staying over tonight or the rest of the week if that'll help."

"No, I wasn't implying that, Khalil," she said, irritated. "Anyway, I'm here now. Tell your daddy bye," she said dryly.

"Bye, Daddy."

"Bye, princess. I'll call you tonight and read you a bedtime story. Okay?"

"Okay," Khaliyah said happily from the back seat.

"Be good for Mommy," he said, then looked at Eliana again.

"What?" she said.

"Uh, take care of yourself, Eliana."

Eliana responded by driving off.

Later that evening, when she got settled at home, she FaceTimed Luna and Pepper.

"Oh my gosh, pregnant?" exclaimed Luna, throwing a hand over her mouth in astonishment.

"Are you sure?" Pepper asked as the friends video chatted.

"Honestly, I'm still in shock. I can't believe this is happening."

"What about the divorce?" Pepper asked. "The hearing is right around the corner. What are you going to do? Call it off?"

Eliana paced around her bedroom. "The last thing I'm going to do is call it off. I can't let this pregnancy change that. At least, I don't think so," she added.

She swore Mason, Luna, and Pepper to secrecy until she decided what she was going to do. But no way did she want the news of her pregnancy to get back to Khalil. Not yet.

"Are you sure you still want to divorce him?" asked Luna. "Raising two kids on your own will not be easy, Eliana. And honestly, why did you sleep with him if you were so sure things were over between the two of you? I know he's still your husband on paper, but you said you weren't doing the do," Luna said.

"We weren't, but what I didn't tell y'all," she said, looking and sounding ashamed.

"What is it you didn't tell us?" asked Pepper, eyebrows raised.

"Something happened not too long after I moved." Eliana went over the whole story about the night Khalil showed up at her place high, and they had sex.

"What? Are you saying he raped you?" Pepper exclaimed.

"Oh, no, please don't tell me he made you have sex with him when he knew good and well how you felt?" said Luna.

"I know, and I was furious," Eliana replied.

"Why didn't you tell us before now?" Luna asked, frowning.

"Yeah, why didn't you say anything?" Pepper added.

"Because I didn't want you to hate him, and at the same time, I told myself that he didn't rape me. I mean, I can tell y'all the truth. That night, I missed him so much, so when he made advances toward me, I initially told him no, but then I gave in to him. It felt so good to be in his arms again."

"I can understand that," said Luna. "And he's your husband, and you said you still love him."

"Yes, that's right, but still, in the middle of us making out, I told him to stop, that I didn't want to have sex. I didn't want to give him any false hope that we were getting back together, so I told him to leave."

"And?" said Pepper.

"He ignored what I said, and he....that's when, well, that's when he did it anyway. Afterward, when he saw I was serious, he looked at me like the villain and left. The next day, he apologized, but then he said I wanted him just as much as he wanted me. But the thing is, even if I *did* want him to make love to me, I didn't want it like that. Not by force," Eliana cried. "And now look what's happened. I'm pregnant. Oh, gosh, what am I going to do?"

"You have to tell him. You have to tell Khalil, Eliana. He deserves to know that he's going to be a father again," Luna said.

"I can't tell him, not now. If he finds out before the divorce is final, he may fight me on it. Knowing I'm carrying another child can change the whole dynamics of the divorce. I just need to wait a few more days, and it'll all be over. The divorce will be final, and that will be that on that."

"I still wish you would think this through and tell the man," Luna said.

"She has to do what she feels is best," Pepper said. "We may not agree with it, but it's her choice."

"You're right; it *is* my choice, and my choice for now is not to tell Khalil until after we are divorced."

"Alright, have it your way," Luna shrugged. "My lips are sealed," she added, making a zipping motion across her mouth with her finger.

Eliana suddenly burst into tears. "I hate this. I hate everything that's happening to me. Why couldn't I have a good marriage? Why couldn't my husband be faithful? Is it me, y'all?" she looked at Luna and Pepper. "It has to be me."

"No, of course it's not you," cried Pepper. "This is not your fault."

"Pepper's right. Don't cry, Eliana. Please, everything will work out," Luna said, starting to cry as well.

"Luna's right," Pepper said. "This has to work out. You watch what we tell you. God's got you. He's got you in all of this."

Chapter 39

Don't Look Back

"Divorce is the death of a dream you thought was going to last." Trina Read

The day had arrived. Today, she would officially become single again. What a sad day. She had always dreamed of being married forever, until death do them part. But those dreams were no more.

She stood in the mirror and surveyed her figure. Already, her belly was protruding. It seemed that as soon as she learned she was pregnant, she blew up like a balloon. She changed into several outfits before settling on a colorful pantsuit that she hoped hid any baby bulge.

Eliana grew more nervous with each step as she entered the courtroom with Luna and Pepper by her side. Minutes after her arrival, Eliana's attorney arrived.

Following that, the next time the courtroom doors opened, Khalil paraded in, accompanied by his attorney.

Eliana had been able to avoid having Khalil see her in all of her pregnancy glow. With Khaliyah, she barely showed a belly bump until she was in her last trimester. With this pregnancy, however, she was entering her second trimester, and her belly was already protruding.

She whispered a silent prayer that the pantsuit did its job and kept her secret.

Once the hearing started, much to Eliana's surprise, it was over relatively quickly. Khalil didn't protest the order. They were to share joint custody. He would pay Eliana spousal support and child support. They had three modes of transportation. Eliana was awarded the Lexus sedan she usually drove, and Khalil kept his BMW and his Porsche. The assets, including bank accounts, were divided equally, with no objections from either party.

When the hearing ended, they gathered at the back of the courtroom.

Khalil approached. "I guess you got what you wanted."

"Excuse me, Mrs. McCoy, sorry to interrupt," Eliana's lawyer said, stepping beside her, "but I have to be in another courtroom in about ten minutes, so I'm going to get out of here. If you need me, you know how to reach me."

"Yes, sure. Thank you," Eliana said, smiling and shaking her hand.

When the attorney left, Eliana focused her attention back on Khalil.

Pepper and Luna went and stood by the escalators, talking while they waited patiently for her.

"I didn't want any of this, Khalil," Eliana swiftly reminded him.

"Look, I'm not going to keep beating a dead horse," he said. "You want this to all be on me, then so be it! I'll take the full blame, Eliana. But

I'm telling you, I love you. I have never stopped loving you," he said, his eyes filling with tears. "I'm sorry for everything. But let it be known, this divorce is not going to stop me from trying my darndest to get you back." He swiped his eyes to keep the tears from falling. "Anyway, I guess I'm out of here."

With her hands in front of her belly, she turned and started walking toward Luna and Pepper.

"You good?" Pepper asked when they got outside the courthouse.

"Yeah, it's just that I didn't expect it to be over so quickly. I mean, my lawyer told me it would take less than an hour, but dang, it seemed like this took ten minutes tops! I guess I thought there would be a lot more to it. After all, two people are ending their marriage, their lives are forever changed, and it all was dissolved in ten minutes?" Eliana shook her head and swiped tears from her eyes.

"No boohooing," said Pepper.

"That's right," Luna added. "We are going to have lunch, and I mean a big lunch," she expressed with outstretched hands. "And....we are not, I repeat, we are not going to be concerned about counting calories or how much we eat. None of that. So, let's get out of here," she said as the friends looped arms and strolled to Pepper's car.

Twenty-something minutes later, they pulled up at the restaurant.

"Okay, here we go," Luna said. "Let's get this party started. Girls day out!" she said, laughing loudly along with Pepper and Eliana.

Chapter 40

Feelings Don't Lie

"Strength grows in the moments when you think
you can't go on, but you keep going anyway."
The Reset

"Do you have everything?" Eliana asked
Pepper.

"Yes, I think I'm straight. Just nervous is all,"
she said, twisting her hands together.

"It's fine," Eliana reassured her. "You've got
this. Look around. This place looks amazing.
You've done a great job! And look at the turnout!
I'm so proud of you, Pepper."

"Hello, ladies," Ryan said, walking up,
looking suave in a charcoal gray suit with a
black knit shirt underneath. "You all look
lovely," he complimented.

"Thank you," each of them said.

"Eliana, I wanted to let you know the caterers
have arrived. I already showed them to the
kitchen. The volunteers are at their assigned
posts, and the band has set up. So, I think we're
ready to do this." Ryan clasped his hands.

"Thanks, Ryan," Pepper said with a broad
smile. "I couldn't have done this without your
help." She turned to Eliana. "And yours too—
don't think for a second I'd leave you out," she
added, her tone leaving no room for doubt.

Eliana smiled and flippantly threw up a hand. "No need, I know that." She glanced over Pepper's shoulder. "Hey, look, there goes Luna and Christian. If you'll excuse me, I'm going to holler at her. It was nice seeing you again, Ryan."

"You too," he acknowledged.

"Ok, I'm going to get started in a few minutes," Pepper said.

"Whenever you're ready," Eliana said and walked away.

†

"Thank you all for joining us at the grand opening of *The Xavier McCoy Healing Together Foundation*, where our mission is to offer compassionate support and healing to spouses who have lost loved ones due to suicide and other heartbreaking tragedies and accidents. We are committed to helping them find strength and hope again.

Many of you may know that two years ago, my husband, Xavier McCoy, whom this nonprofit is named after, chose to be his own judge, jury, and executioner by taking his own life. He left me and his two small boys with broken hearts that are still in the healing process." Pepper cleared her throat, scanned the room, and continued talking. "In honor of him, this nonprofit will strive to offer solace, compassion, and resources to help spouses and families find strength and healing together.

"Xavier always believed in the power of community and the importance of supporting one another through life's darkest moments. It is in this same spirit that we hope to embody through the services we will offer. In such a short time, we have already begun to see the impact our efforts have made through the stories of those we've been able to support— stories of resilience, hope, and new beginnings. We aim to continue this work, reaching out to those in need and ensuring that no one has to face their journey through grief alone.

"Before I take my seat, I'd like to acknowledge those who have helped me to stand here today in this capacity. First, I thank God for my mother." She locked eyes with Victoria, sitting at one of the tables with Fancy and some others. "Without her by my side, I don't know how I would have coped. I thank God for my friends. Rolonda, Luna, Eliana," she stretched a hand and looked toward them, "you have been my lifeboat. Those perilous times when I thought I would drown, you reached down and pulled me up. To all the volunteers who helped me plan this entire thing, I can't thank you enough."

She looked behind her briefly at Ryan before saying, "And a special thanks to you, Ryan. Ryan, you understood my pain, the heartache I felt losing my life partner. And even though my pain runs deep, so deep, I can't imagine what you are experiencing, having tragically lost your wife and children. Thank you for being my strength when I wanted to forget this whole nonprofit idea, but you wouldn't let me. You reminded me it was needed and that it was what Xavier would want me to do. I'm so glad I listened," she said, wiping fresh tears from her eyes.

"Thank you, and God bless you all," Pepper said, bursting with a feeling of pride and a sense of accomplishment.

The packed room burst into applause. Ryan nodded and smiled.

"Thank you all," she said again. "May every person who comes through these doors for help be blessed. May they find healing. May they find acceptance, love, and understanding. Thank you all for coming."

The room erupted in applause again as Pepper returned to the head table. People began rising from their seats, one by one at first and then all at once, until almost everyone who was able was on their feet, giving her a standing ovation. The sound of clapping hands filled the space, echoing off the walls, while smiles and nods of approval spread across the crowd.

Pepper's face flushed with pride and gratitude, her heart swelling with joy, and she beamed back at the audience.

†

"I hope you're proud of yourself," Ryan told her as they stood at the back of the room surveying the people and the vibe of the space. The program had ended. Most people were leaving, but some others continued mingling.

"I am. I'm very proud," she stated. "Everything was perfect, Ryan."

"I agree. It ran like a well-oiled machine," he said, chuckling. "We had almost 300 people in attendance and more than enough food and drink to serve them all—"

"That was a blessing, but the big blessing is we raised over ten thousand dollars, Ryan. I didn't know people would be so generous with their giving. Did you?"

"No, actually, I didn't. I felt like starting this nonprofit was a good idea you came up with, but like you, I was shocked to see how much people supported you by giving their money. That should let you know that what you're doing is important, Pepper. Folks need a place like this, a refuge, where they can vent and share their grief and pain, a place where they can find healing and hope, together," Ryan said, turning to her and looking into her eyes. "I know it's helped me a lot."

Pepper looked away shyly and then back at him. "I said it before, I'll say it again; I couldn't have pulled this off without you." She smiled.

"So what now?" Ryan asked as he watched volunteers begin the cleanup process, and the space was emptied of people.

"I don't follow you," Pepper said, eyebrows raised. "The center will start helping people immediately if that's what you mean."

"That's not what I'm talking about, Pepper."

"Okay?" Pepper said awkwardly.

"I'm talking about you. You and me," Ryan said. "I don't want this to be the end of us. I mean our friendship."

"How could you think something like that? I value our friendship. I value your help, Ryan. I know you have a life outside of this place, but I want you to be part of what we will be doing here as much as possible. Look, I was going to present this to you later this week, but I guess I should ask you now," she said.

"Ask me what?" he said.

"I'd like you to consider taking on the role of my assistant director. I know it might seem like a lot to ask, but the pay is quite attractive—we've secured a substantial grant from the city that covers salaries and positions for the next two years. Please give it some thought," she said, talking fast, her gaze steady on him. "And before you say no, I understand you already have a full-time job and that you don't live here, but you won't have to commute from Jackson to Memphis very often. There will be a lot of things you can do remotely. And you could start out working part-time, sorta like you're doing now; only you'll get paid."

"Wow, that sounds amazing. But you're right. I need to think about it. I mean, like you said, I do have a job, you know."

"Yes, I know, but I also remember you telling me you were burnt out on that job and that you would love to do something like this full-time. At the time, I didn't know how or even if I would secure operating funds or have a budget, but God came through big time, Ryan. This could be your answered prayer to do something you love, something in honor of your family," she said, her voice sadly lowering.

They looked at each other in silence.

"What?" she said, breaking the awkwardness.

"Working for you? I don't know, Pepper. That might be kinda hard."

"Hard? Why?"

"What I mean is I don't want to mess up anything."

"Mess up? What's there to mess up, Ryan? We've gotten along this whole time you've been working with me on this. Even before we started working on this, we got along at Stateside, so I don't get it." She looked confused.

Ryan took her into his arms, devouring her mouth, releasing every bit of emotion he had penned up inside.

"That's why," he said when he released her.

"Oh, I see," she said, her words soft, her eyes revealing, and her heart racing.

"Any objections?" Ryan said, his voice tempting, seductive.

"None," she finally spoke.

Chapter 41

Loyal

"The best relationship is not the one being shared in good times, but rather the one who has the staying power through rough times." Jingersam

Getting accustomed to being a divorcee was harder than Eliana anticipated. Every day, when she arrived home, she was reminded of her new norm. Days when Khaliyah was with her father made those times even harder. She was lonely and alone, and her heart still longed for Khalil.

Her phone rang. Grabbing her belly, she got up from the sofa and retrieved it from the coffee table nearby. She looked at the screen before answering.

"Hello, Mason. What's up," she said, sticking a hand in the side pocket of her jeans and pacing the floor.

"Hi, look, I know this is last minute, but I have two tickets to the Grizzlies game. My partner's kid fell off his bike and may have broken his leg. They're taking him to the ER. So, of course, he can't go now, so he gave them to me."

"Don't you have another friend, homeboy, or whatever who'd like to go?" she asked.

"Nope. And you are a friend, right?"

"Well, yeah, but—"

"And don't you profess to be a diehard Grizzlies fan?"

"Uh, I sure am," she said boastfully while breaking into laughter.

"So, what's your excuse? Do you have your daughter tonight?"

"No, it's her father's week with her."

"Then I'll be there by six," he said.

"Uh, well...okay," she said, unsure why she just agreed to go. Why in the heck did she say yes? She may have been divorced, but it didn't keep her from feeling like she would be cheating on Khalil. Now she could understand how Pepper felt when she said she felt like she would be dishonoring Xavier if she started seeing another man. *But Xavier's dead, so Pepper gets a legitimate pass. Khalil is very much alive. And though he cheated on you, the same doesn't apply to you,* she thought.

She called Luna. No answer. Next, she called Pepper.

"Hey, girl, what's up?" Pepper said, answering right away.

"I'm in a dilemma," Eliana explained, filling Pepper in on what had transpired.

"Girl, if you don't get in that closet and find yourself something cute but comfortable, you got to do comfortable," Pepper laughed, "and go to the game with that man, I'll come over there personally and drag your behind to the FedEx Forum. I keep telling you, like you, Rolonda, and Luna tell me—live your life. We can't sit up inside every day being depressed and sad about what happened in the past. I'm telling you what I need to be telling myself. What I'm saying is you're a smart, beautiful, funny, and kind person, Eliana. You deserve to laugh again, even fall in love again. And I'm not trying to put you and Minister Mason together. Although I think it would be kinda nice," Pepper said, chuckling. "But seriously, come on, now," Pepper pleaded, "get out and have fun. And it's a Grizzlies game, too? For free? Child, you better get out of that house."

"Okay, enough with the making me feel guilty lecture," Eliana chuckled into the phone. "I'll go. I haven't been to a Grizzlies game since last season."

"Well, get off this phone and find you something to wear. Oh, and be sure to wear shoes that won't hurt your feet. You don't know if y'all sitting on the floor or in the nosebleed section," Pepper said, laughing.

"Bye, girl," Eliana said, laughing along.

†

The halls of Grace Temple buzzed with the sound of young people. Some raced up and down the halls, not running but walking fast, knowing running in the hallways at church was not allowed. Others hung around talking to each other, and some were propped against the walls with their heads in their phones or tablets.

Eliana smiled, almost giggled, as she went along. Seeing young kids like this reminded her of her youth when she attended Youth Night. It was one of the most fun times of her life.

This evening was her first time attending Youth Night at Grace Temple. She came at

Mason's invitation. Since attending the Grizzlies game, they had been to dinner twice and had lunch together at church on several occasions. She was loosening up to enjoying being around him. With him, she didn't have to hide her pregnancy concerns, and he was someone easy to talk to.

Tonight, at Youth Night, he delivered a message to the youth, and afterward, they served hotdogs, burgers, and pizza.

"So, did you enjoy it?" Mason asked, walking her to her car.

"Yes, I loved it. Thanks for inviting me."

"We're always in need of more volunteers," he said as they approached her car.

"I might consider if that's what you're saying," she said, smiling. "But—"

"That's exactly what I'm saying," he cut her off. "How about it? Becoming part of the Youth Ministry?"

"I was about to say I might consider it if I was a member here, but I'm not, Mason. I work here. That's it."

"Oh, that can easily be fixed. All you have to do is join our church family." His smile turned into laughter. "Right?"

"Uh, I hadn't thought about that. I'm still officially a member of Holy Rock. Although, I haven't attended since my divorce. You know, I feel awkward now that me and Khalil are divorced. I don't feel like I belong there."

"First of all, you belong wherever the word of God is being shared. Second, God is at Grace Temple just as well as he's at Holy Rock, so there you have it, you can join!" He raised both hands and laughed again.

"You are so silly," she said as he opened her car door, and they stood underneath the sparkling church lights.

"Think about it. Until then, you're invited to come every Thursday night as my personal volunteer. How about that?"

Eliana's face turned serious. "Look, Mason, I better not. I mean, I'm not looking for, well, I don't want to—"

"I understand; there's no need to explain. You're fresh off a divorce, pregnant, and have a lot on your plate, which is why I'm offering you my friendship. That's it, nothing more, Eliana. I just want to be there for you through whatever you're going through."

"But why? Why do you want to be here for me, Mason? I don't understand. You said it yourself—I'm a divorced mother with a small child and another one on the way," she said, looking briefly at her belly. "You're a single man, a very eligible bachelor, and no kids." She giggled and then turned serious again. "You can have any woman in the church or outside the church. Why me?"

Mason laughed. "Did you say I could have any—" He stopped midsentence, threw a hand aside, and kept talking, "Never mind, I'm not going there. But look, seriously, Eliana, I've made it no secret that I like you. I like you a lot. So now, I've put it out there, but I also respect you too much to make you feel uncomfortable or give you a reason not to want to be around me. I don't want things to be awkward between us just because I'm telling you this. And like I said, I'm not asking for a relationship. I just want us to be friends. Until, or *if* you decide you want something more. That's it."

"Friends?" she said.

"Friends," he repeated.

As if in deep contemplation, Eliana was silent for several seconds before saying, "I think I'd like that, Mason. I'd like that a lot."

Chapter 42

Lovin' You On My Mind

"I don't need to be someone's whole life; I just want someone who sees me as their favorite part."
Pinterest

Fancy and Noah walked along the streets at the 901 Festival, taking in the array of vendors, food trucks, and performances. "This event grows bigger each year," Fancy said.

"This is my first time attending. I hadn't heard of it," Noah replied. "Before I purchased a home here, I flew in and out of the city, and I didn't venture out, especially to anything like this."

"Well, all that's changing. I'm going to be personally responsible for showing you around Memphis. True, there's a lot of crime that takes place here, and I hate that. But there's also a lot of good here, too. A lot to see and do. That's what we're going to concentrate on. The good. How about that?"

"I like the sound of that," Noah said, taking hold of her hand and stopping at one of the hundreds of booths lined up and down Tiger Lane.

"The house should be ready in a few days."

"I can't wait. Unfortunately, I have to fly out again the day after tomorrow. I should be back before then, but I can't say for sure. I have to travel to Dubai. Hopefully, if everything pans out, I shouldn't be away more than a few days, but sometimes I've been there for as long as a month. This shouldn't be the case this time. At least I don't expect it to be."

"I hope it's not. I wouldn't want you to wait that long before seeing what we've done to the house," she said, smiling as she looked at several potted plants being sold at one of the vendor booths.

"You like plants, huh?" Noah asked.

"Certain ones. I have to be careful with what I have around Sebastian. You know, make sure it isn't poisonous for him. I want this one," she told the vendor, pointing at a beautiful, healthy-looking succulent.

"Fourteen ninety-nine," the seller stated. "Cash or card?"

"Card. Oh, wait," she said, opening her wallet, "I think I might have enough cash—"

Before she could pull out her money or card, Noah whisked out his wallet, opened it, and gave the woman a twenty. "Keep the change," he told her.

"Thank you, sir," the vendor said.

"And thank you, Noah," Fancy blushed, looking at her plant and smiling.

"Anything to see that smile," he said, squeezing her hand again.

They walked around the festival enjoying the entertainment, tasting various foods, and buying items like the plant he bought for her until Fancy said, "This has been fun. I'm so glad you came."

"So am I. This is quite an event. Where do you want to go from here?" he asked. "It's still early," he stated, eyeing his expensive timepiece. "Would you like something to eat?"

"No," she said, shaking her head, "I've eaten enough already to fill me up for the rest of the day." She chuckled and patted her stomach.

"Awe, we barely ate. And you are not going to convince me that an ear of Mexican corn equals a meal."

"Uh, excuse you, I ate more than that. Remember those corndogs?"

"Are you kidding me?" he teased. "Those were mini-corndogs, and you only had two. Come on now, if you and I are going to continue to enjoy each other's company, then there's something we have to learn to agree on."

"And what is that?" she quipped, looking at him as they strode toward the festival exit.

Holding onto her hand, he stopped momentarily and looked at her. "You have to learn not to be so modest or shy when you're with me. I like to have fun and go on adventures, and you should know by now that I also love to eat. Can you hang? Because I'm telling you now that turkey leg was not enough to put a dent in my appetite," he said, flashing that enchanting smile.

She looked at him in astonishment. "Oh, okay. Let me prove I can hang, starting right now."

"Oh, let's see what you got," Noah remarked. "Here's my suggestion. After we leave here, what do you say we go to this spot I just learned about? Me and some of the other executives recently had a business luncheon there. It's called Capitol Grill. Have you been there? Their "surf and turf" is *fye*."

"No, I haven't, but I'm willing to try it."

"Okay, Capitol Grill it is."

†

"Fancy, I have a confession," Noah said as they sat in a booth at the restaurant.

"A confession?" she remarked as she sipped on a virgin lemon drop martini.

"Yes, a confession. I like you. I like spending time with you."

"Uh, I like spending time with you too, Noah." She smiled.

"Good. I just want to be clear that I'm not one to waste my time or anyone else's time. What I mean by that is I'm serious when I say I want to get to know you. I know I travel a lot; that's the nature of my job, so I would understand if you say you don't want to get involved."

Fancy covered her laughter. "What? You said what? How can you say I don't want to get involved? For chrissakes, Noah, we're sleeping together, something I don't take lightly. It means I like you a lot, too, a whole lot."

He reached across the booth and grabbed her hands. "That's music to my ears. I promise not to hurt you, Fancy. We're both too old to play games. I want someone I can enjoy being around, spending time with, laugh with. That's what you bring to my life."

Fancy nodded and smiled. "That's what I'm looking for, too."

"Okay, then look no further."

She smiled again. "Noah, are you asking me to be your girlfriend?" she laughed. "Like the boys used to do back in the day?"

Noah broke into laughter. "I guess that's exactly what I'm asking."

"Then let's make it official," she laughed. "We need a pen and paper. You have to write it down and put the two check boxes on the paper."

"Hey, you don't have to tell me. I wrote enough of these in my day," he kept chuckling. "Excuse me, may I use your pen for a second?" he asked their server as he passed.

"Yes, here you go. When you're finished, leave it on the table. I'll get it," the server said.

On the white paper napkin, Noah wrote, "Will you be my girlfriend?" Then, he drew two boxes. Next to one box, he wrote YES, and next to the other box, he wrote NO. When he was finished, he passed it to Fancy.

"Umm," she teased, looking at the napkin with a playful smirk. "O M G, what should I say?" flippantly, throwing a hand to her face. She paused before checking one of the boxes and passing it back to Noah.

He broke into a wide grin when he saw the box she checked. "Yes!" he exclaimed, pumping his fist in the air and bursting into laughter. Next, he rose slightly, leaned over, and kissed her.

When their lips parted, Fancy blushed. She looked around the restaurant nervously, expecting to see all eyes on them. She laid a hand over her chest.

"Thank God, no one is paying us any attention," she exhaled. "We're not school kids, you know," she said, sounding embarrassed. "And I know how church folk can be. Somebody sees me out here kissing a strange man, and the whole church would have my name in their mouth," she whispered. "And not in a good way."

He reached for her hand again. "Look, you're right, we're not school kids. But I also believe there is nothing wrong with showing some affection when the girl of my dreams just said she'd be my girlfriend."

They laughed. Fancy said, "I guess I'll give you a pass—this time—I mean, since you *are* now officially my boyfriend."

Chapter 43

Friendship

"Sometimes the greatest relationships are the ones you never expected to be in. The ones that sweep you off your feet and challenge every view you've ever had." Unknown

"Hey, you're home from church already?" Victoria asked. "You must have gone to first service?"

Fancy stood at the counter, making a sandwich, looking at Victoria with a weird expression plastered across her face.

"What's wrong with you? I know you hear me talking, and you most definitely see me. Why do you look like that?" Victoria pressured.

"I didn't go to church," Fancy mumbled.

"What?"

"I said I didn't go to church today," Fancy repeated.

"You didn't? What's wrong with you? Are you sick?" Victoria asked, her voice full of concern as she gazed intently at Fancy.

"Uh, no, I'm not sick."

"Talk up. Dang, what's wrong with you? I can't believe you missed church if you say you aren't sick. That's not like you. What's up?"

"I just got home," she whispered, looking around her house as if expecting to find someone eavesdropping.

"Did you say you just got home?" Victoria's hand flew up to her mouth. She started jumping up and down and turning around. "Girl, no, you didn't miss church for the....O M G, girl," Victoria squealed.

"Stop, Vicky. I feel so ashamed," Fancy said, laying her sandwich on a paper plate and pacing across the shiny tiled kitchen floor.

Victoria laughed louder, hand over mouth, and bent over. "I am so proud of you," she said.

"Proud of me? How can you say you're proud of me? Oh, my, I can't believe I missed church for—for—"

"Say it, girl. You know what you missed it for," she laughed. "How long have you been home? Did Hezekiah see you when you got home?"

"No, he was already gone. Not that it matters. He knows the deal."

"I heard that," Victoria said. "I am so happy for you."

"Please, stop, Victoria. I barely know anything about the man, and here I am, sleeping with him. What is wrong with me?"

"Nothing is wrong with you," she said, frowning at Fancy. "Stop that crazy talk. It's about time you laugh again. I know you don't like to talk about Micah, but after what happened to him, God rest his soul, you deserve to have fun, Fancy."

"I don't want to talk about Micah or think about him. It hurts me all over again when I think about how his life was taken, all by some stupid, crazy, jealous female. It's a shame. But who knows, maybe Noah has a crazy woman somewhere. The man travels all over the world. There's no telling how many women he has."

"You need to stop it," Victoria chastised her friend. Pointing her finger at the phone and shaking it, she continued trying to hammer some sense into her. "So you missed church today. Who's going to spank you? Not Hezekiah. Not Khalil. Not Stiles. No one. Absolutely no one, Fancy McCoy," she said, looking directly into the phone at Fancy. "Not even God. Now, if you really think you did something wrong against God, then you know the deal—ask for forgiveness and move on."

"You're right," Fancy raised a hand in surrender. Walking back to the counter, she picked up her sandwich and took another bite.

"I know I'm right. The man said he wants to spend more time with you. He said he was serious and that he was too old to be playing games. From what I've heard about him, he's a good guy. He threw himself into his work after his wife died. He has a little money, too, and from what he's doing to that house, he isn't cheap. Didn't you say he's paying you and the contractors fairly?"

"Oh, yes, he is," Fancy admitted. "Actually, more than fair."

"Okay, then stop beating up on yourself. That's all I'm saying," Victoria said. "And if you're so bent out of shape about not going to church, you have plenty more opportunities to show your face, whether at Holy Rock's mid-week service or New Holy Rock. Your choice."

"Okay, Vicky. You can stop the lecturing. I hear you, and I'm good."

"Praise the Lord," Victoria said, raising a hand as if praising God. "Now, tell me all the juicy details, and why didn't you bring your fast tail home last night."

Victoria laughed until Fancy couldn't help it. She burst into laughter too and said, "Well, first we—"

Two and a half hours later, Fancy and Victoria were ending their video chat.

"Remember, we're meeting Mya tomorrow at six," Fancy reminded Victoria. "The wedding will be here before you know it, and you and I have a long list of things we still have to do as far as planning the reception. I want it to be a grand reception, something memorable, something Mya will remember forever," Fancy said.

"Oh, dang, I'm glad you said something. I have it on my phone, but I hadn't thought about it until now. You want me to pick you up?"

"Uh, yeah, that'll be fine. But if it's a problem, I don't mind driving."

"Nah, I'll swing by after work. Are we still meeting at Juniper's?"

"Yes," replied Fancy.

"Good. I'll see you tomorrow. Get some rest. I bet you need it," Vicky said, laughing.

"Girl, bye," said Fancy, ending the chat.

Chapter 44

Should Have Known

"You hang out with trash, and you start to smell like garbage." Unknown

"That traffic was brutal, of all days," complained Victoria. "Usually, I can make it to your house from work in about fifteen minutes. Today, it took double that amount of time."

"I heard there was a bad accident on I-240," Fancy said, "It has traffic backed up for miles. Plus, it's getting close to the holiday season, so the more traffic there will be on these streets. But we should still make it on time since we're going in the opposite direction."

"I know. It's just frustrating. There's always something happening on that interstate. I'm going to start going through the city. Sometimes it's easier and saves time," Victoria huffed.

"I don't blame you," quipped Fancy as they proceeded to the restaurant.

"I think that's Mya's car," Fancy said, pointing to a white Honda sedan a few spaces from where Victoria parked.

"Yeah, that might be her," Victoria said as they walked toward the restaurant.

Stepping inside the casual dining spot known for its comfort food, the hostess approached.

"Would you like a table or booth? It's a lovely evening. If you'd like, you can dine on our patio. With the clear weather, there's a splendid view of the lake."

Fancy and Victoria looked at each other. "If you don't mind, can we wait? We're expecting another person. We'd actually like to see if she's already here."

"Oh, sure. Let's check in the waiting area. Maybe she's in there," the hostess said politely.

"There she is," Victoria said, walking toward Mya. "Thanks," she said, turning to the hostess.

Mya walked up, and the three of them hugged. "We're ready to be seated," said Mya, addressing the hostess. "Would you like to sit on the patio?" she asked Fancy and Victoria.

"That's fine with me," replied Fancy.

"Me too," said Victoria.

"Follow me," the hostess said.

Fancy's feet froze in place, and she stood still like a statue when she spotted Hezekiah sitting at a corner booth near the patio entrance.

Victoria stopped when she saw him, too. He wasn't alone. The woman with him was recognizable, even more so when she locked eyes with Fancy, smirked, rolled her eyes, and then refocused on Hezekiah.

"Come on, Fancy," Victoria said between clenched teeth, tugging Fancy's elbow and pulling her toward the patio.

"No, wait, wait just a second. I promise that's all it'll take," she said to Victoria.

Mya looked on, quiet, seeing Hezekiah but not seeming to understand why Fancy appeared suddenly upset.

"Don't cause a scene," Victoria mouthed.

Fancy jerked from Victoria's grasp and walked toward the couple. She tapped Hezekiah on the shoulder.

"Hi, Hezekiah," she said with a fake smile. "And you wanted to give me a hard time? Why?"

Hezekiah opened his mouth to speak while the woman wore the biggest look of satisfaction on her face.

"Don't," Fancy said, showing her palm in anger. "You always said if I don't see it with my own eyes, then I shouldn't believe it. Well, I see this little thing you have going on here with my own eyes, Hezekiah. And I see some things never change."

"This is not what it looks like," he said, turning around and fully facing her while Rianna sipped on a mixed cocktail, slick smiling like a Cheshire cat.

"Hezekiah, sweetheart, don't bother trying to explain. There's a reason she's your ex," Rianna chimed in, her tone dripping with sarcasm as she reached out and affectionately stroked his forearm.

Hezekiah pulled away. Rising, he began looking around from the corners of his eyes as if to see if anyone was taking notice of the growing fiasco.

Victoria rolled her eyes, and Mya stood to the side, looking timid and lost. She'd never seen this type of interaction between Pastor Hezekiah and Fancy. She hadn't been privy to what had transpired in their relationship to cause them to divorce.

"Don't get up, Hezekiah. I only wanted to say hello. You go right ahead and continue enjoying your—trash." Fancy turned around swiftly. "Shall we, ladies?" she said and followed the startled-looking hostess to their seats.

Minutes after they were seated, Fancy saw Hezekiah leaving with Rianna following alongside him.

"Don't mind him, Fancy," Victoria cautioned. "You've moved on. Right?"

"It's not that. It's just the fact he had the audacity to want to go off on me when he saw me with Noah. But all the time, he's still messing with that heffa. Girl, I should have known he hadn't changed. He's still the same lying, cheating, good for nothing—ugh."

"Let it go, sis," Victoria said, reaching beside her and squeezing Fancy's hand.

"She's right, let it go," Mya added.

"That heffa just makes me so dang sick," Fancy said angrily. "And he's so stupid for messing back with her after all she's done to him."

"Yeah, she's the one responsible for sending him to prison," said Victoria. "How stupid can he be?"

"I know, and he's still dealing with her? But you know what? Good for him. They're two peas in a pod. Let them be. Now, let's talk about this wedding reception," Fancy said, smiling big and shifting her attention to Mya. "Let's hear what you've got."

†

Fancy had been home for just over an hour when a loud, persistent knocking at her front door, accompanied by the relentless ringing of the doorbell, startled her as she emerged from the shower. Barely drying off and quickly wrapping herself in a robe, she bundled her hair in a towel and hurried toward the front of the house.

If the guard shack called, having been in the shower, she didn't hear it. And who would they have let come inside the gate to see her without notifying her first? She would have to have a word with them.

"Who is it?" she yelled as she approached the door. The doorbell buzzed again, followed by more knocking. She peeped through the window.

"What the heck?" she said, opening the door and seeing Hezekiah standing on the other side, nostrils flared like a bull.

"What's wrong with you beating on my door and ringing my doorbell like a crazy man?"

"Look, I just want to make it clear. I do not have anything going on with Rianna. I had just finished a meeting with a church member when she came into the restaurant," he began explaining. "He had just left when she walked up and sat at my booth. When you came up, I was telling her to stay the hell away from me, to leave me alone. I swear Rianna means nothing to me," he barked, "and you should know that."

"What? You said I should know that? Are you serious? Hezekiah, you must have forgotten," Fancy said, tightening her robe as the water began to penetrate it and reveal her curves, "I am no longer your wife. I do not care what you do or who you do it with. But," she giggled while raising a finger, "I must say I *am* a tad bit surprised that you would go back to fooling with the likes of Rianna. Surely, you can do better, Hezekiah," she said sarcastically. "Anyway, goodnight." She prepared to close the door, but Hezekiah stopped it with his hand.

"Wait, Fancy. I need you to believe me. I swear, it was purely coincidental that she showed up at the same restaurant. Look, let me in so we can talk this out."

"Talk? There is nothing to talk out. I'm good. So, if you don't mind, I have a very long day tomorrow. I really need to get some rest. Goodnight, Hezekiah. Oh, and let's get another thing straight. Don't ever come to me again about what I'm doing or who I'm doing it with."

She closed the door, leaving him on the other side, looking like he'd lost his best friend. Maybe he had.

Chapter 45

Caught Up

"Love is friendship that has caught on fire."
Ann Landers

The nonprofit had taken off ever since its opening. People were coming in to receive services ranging from grief counseling to mental health classes. With Ryan as her assistant director, they spent numerous hours together.

"One evening, after a long day, she and Ryan were alone at the center, tidying up and ensuring everything was in place for a community festival they planned.

"I'm exhausted," Pepper said, yawning and leaning back in her office chair. "Are you ready to get out of here?"

Ryan yawned shortly after, covering his mouth and stretching. "I am. Let's go," he said and drove her home.

"Let me walk you to your door," he told her when he pulled into her driveway.

"No, that's okay, Ryan."

"That's what a gentleman does," he said, flashing that million-dollar smile she couldn't resist. "Oh, and didn't you say you wanted to give me the box of handouts for tomorrow?"

"Oh, yeah, that's right. Come on," she said. He followed her inside.

"Can I get you something? Water, tea, juice?" she said, walking deeper into the house.

"No, I'm good," he said, remaining in place.

"I'll be right back."

Moments later, she returned with a stack of rack cards inside a small box.

"I didn't know we still had this many left," he said. "I thought the street team would have passed out more."

"They did. These are different. They tell about the programs we offer. Those other ones were for the last event. We can have these available tomorrow for anyone who wants to learn more about the foundation."

"I like them," he said and walked toward the door. "You get some rest. I got to get going. I have an hour's drive ahead of me."

"Yeah, I hate that you have to make that drive," she yawned again. "But I've enjoyed every minute of today. We got a lot done, and the meeting with those investors was the icing on the cake. I'm just so happy, Ryan. I'm so thankful for how everything is working out. I know Xavier," she said, her voice lowering, "I know he would be proud." Tears began falling along her cheeks.

Ryan stepped up and gently wiped her tears away with the swoop of his thumb.

She looked at him, and their eyes connected.

He continued wiping her tears as they fell. "Shh, don't cry," he whispered. "Please, don't cry."

He closed the gap between them, and this time, with an urgency he couldn't seem to contain, he used his one free hand to hold her head and pull her to him. His mouth covered hers, and her breath grew short as it caught in her throat.

Her light moan revealed her need and desire for him. The box fell from his other hand and the contents went flying across the hardwoods, but it didn't stop them.

He picked her up, and in his arms, he continued kissing her as he stepped over the flyers and carried her up the hallway toward her bedroom.

Pepper tried to deny the pulsating knot that had formed in her stomach but failed. Her heart shuddered, and shivers of delight ran through her as his large hands held her face tightly.

Twisting in his arms and arching her back, she looked at him with pure unadulterated longing.

"Are you sure?" he said, his voice gentle, seductive.

"Yes," Pepper whispered. "Yes, but wait." She looked at her hand and slowly removed her wedding ring, placing it on the nearby table.

He looked at her as if photographing her with his eyes before sending spirals of ecstasy coursing through her from his touch.

Her thoughts raced as her body awakened, and her willpower to resist slipped away. The last time she felt like this was with Xavier. For a brief moment, she remembered their time together, but Ryan quickly pulled her back to the present. Feeling the warmth of his skin against hers made her forget the past, forget the pain, and focus on what mattered now—this moment with him.

†

Holding her in his arms afterward, he kissed the top of her head. "You good?" he asked.

"Yes," she replied softly. "This is," she paused, "the first time I've been with a man since my husband died."

"Is that right?"

She nodded, snuggling closer underneath the safety of his arms.

"You may not believe me, but you're the first woman I've made love to since I lost my wife."

Pepper eased from underneath his arm, propped herself on one elbow, and looked at him strangely. "Are you serious? You don't have to say that just because I said it."

He looked deep into her eyes. "I wouldn't lie about something so, well, I wouldn't lie on the memory of my wife," he said, his voice suddenly sullen, shaking.

"I'm sorry," she said. "I believe you. I know we have a lot in common. Both of us lost our spouses, even though in two entirely different ways, but it hurts just the same. Forgive me?"

He pulled her into him, and his lips seized hers as she opened her mouth, welcoming him with a small whimper.

"You're forgiven," he said hungrily, sinking into her again.

Chapter 46

Confessions

"You have to be at your strongest when you are feeling at your weakest." Kush 'N Wizdom

In the days leading up to her and the kids' trip to see her parents, Luna mentally tried to prepare herself. She had been to Bluffton only once since she and Christian had the kids. Her parents visited them in Memphis, usually at least three times a year. That all had to change now that they were Lorie's full-time caregivers. Making sure she was properly cared for 24/7 was something Luna did not want her parents to experience, but they were adamant about doing it.

"We trust in the good Lord," her father told Luna when she learned they would be Lorie's caregivers. "God won't put no more on us than we can stand."

Luna hoped that was the case because she did not want her parents burdened by their new calling in life, taking care of Lorie.

As for Luna, with her abductor behind prison bars, she had begun to emotionally relax. When she looked at Laiyah Rose, she rarely, if ever, thought of how her beautiful little girl was conceived. All she could see in her child was love, unconditional love.

"Hey, I've been meaning to ask you how things are at home since that monster's conviction?" Eliana asked as the two friends chatted.

"It may be in my head, but ever since they locked that lunatic away, it seems like Christian has made a hundred-and-eighty-degree turnaround when it comes to Laiyah Rose. He plays with her more often, and he's taken her out with him and Dax to the park, something he used to never do. It's something I've been praying for."

"Yeah, I know you have. I'm glad to hear he's trying. That can make all the difference in the world," Eliana said. "And maybe he's more interactive with her because she's getting older. She's trying to walk, and he doesn't feel like he has to be so delicate with her. You know, things like that."

"That's true, too, but whatever it is, I'm glad to see them bonding."

"And you and him? How are the two of you if you don't think I'm being too nosey."

"Nosey? You? Girl, never. I prayed about that too, and it took a lot of talking to God and my two besties," she laughed over the phone. "Without you and Pepper, I think I would have done something awful to that man. I mean, knowing he slept with my sister broke me, Eliana. You know it did, and you, of all people, know exactly how I feel."

"Knowing Khalil was sleeping with someone else was the worst period of my life, so yeah, I understand. But unlike me, what happened with them happened a long time ago. It was early in your marriage. I know it doesn't lessen the pain of betrayal, but it's not like he was sleeping with her in your face, up in your house, or anything like that."

"No, he didn't. At least, he says he didn't sleep with her when she came here, but I can't be sure. What I *can* be sure of is that I'm doing my best to let it go, to forgive and forget. After her accident, I tried to change my way of thinking about it. I also realized that my husband is really a good man. He's loved me through some of my most difficult times. Who am I not to forgive him or my sister?"

"Are you going to be back in time for the last Pulpit Ladies luncheon? It's the last one of the quarter," Eliana said, changing the subject.

"I plan to. It's a week from Friday, right?"

"Yes," replied Eliana.

"Ok. I'll be back by then."

"Sounds good. Well, I'm going to let you go. I know you probably have a ton of things you still have to do before you leave."

"I do. But hold up. What's the latest on you and Khalil? When are you going to tell him, Eliana? Come on, the man deserves to know you're carrying his child."

"Why, Luna?"

"What do you mean why?"

"I mean, why does he deserve to know? I don't feel like I owe him a thing."

"But you do. He's the father. You didn't make this baby by yourself. Don't punish the child or him because of what he did. At the end of the day, I've never heard you say one negative thing about him when it comes to Khaliyah. As a matter of fact, that's the one thing you said you could never complain about. You said he was a good father. What makes you think he won't welcome this child?"

"I'm not saying he won't welcome this child," she emphasized. "I'm saying I'm not going to go out of my way to tell him. He'll find out soon enough when the baby arrives."

"When the baby arrives? Okay, suit yourself," Luna said, frowning. "When is your next doctor's appointment?"

"Thursday," Eliana said. "I'll send you a picture of the ultrasound. I'm supposed to learn the gender then, too. That is if I want to know."

"Don't you want to know?" Luna asked.

"Yeah, I think so."

"Just please don't forget to send pictures."

"I won't. I promise."

"Dang, I wish I could be there to go with you. Is Pepper going?"

"No, she'll be out of town again doing something for her nonprofit. She's been going nonstop ever since the doors opened."

"I know. I'm so happy for her," Luna said, "and it seems like someone has a crush on her," Luna laughed.

Eliana chuckled. "I think so, too, and I think the feeling is mutual. She may not say it, but I think she likes him, too. You have to admit, Ryan seems like a cool guy. The fact that they share the same tragic heartbreak of losing their spouses I think it's bringing them closer. I just want her to be happy. She's such a sweet person."

"Yeah, she is," Luna agreed. "Look, girl, I'm getting off the phone for real this time. I still have to pack the kids' things. I'll call or text you when we get there."

"Okay, have a safe flight."

Luna was glad to get out of the city, even if it was for only a week, well, eight days. Ever since they moved to Memphis, her life had been like a whirlwind, full of chaos with sprinkles of good times. She was finally settling in and accepting the southern city as home, in spite of all the crime and what had personally happened to her.

Her parents met her and the children at the airport. Just as she knew they would be, they were ecstatic when they saw their grandkids.

When she arrived at their house, it was almost more than she could stand, seeing Lorie in a wheelchair, unable to move or do the simplest things. She had lost considerable weight and looked frail and weak.

Lorie was totally dependent on the care of others. She could no longer use the bathroom alone, feed herself, or do any of those things the old Lorie could do. Seeing her like this was heartbreaking, yet Luna also felt like 'you reap what you sow.' She didn't want to have that attitude, but she couldn't help it. Every time she looked at Lorie, she could see her sister and Christian making love. The sight and thoughts would not go away.

For the week she was there, she tried to connect with Lorie. But Lorie remained in a deep funk. She would barely talk, and she didn't interact with the kids at all. That was one of the biggest surprises because before her accident

Lorie liked being an aunt, but *that* Lorie was no more.

Honestly, Luna felt as though she could understand why Lorie was like she was. She'd gone from being wild and crazy and adventurous to isolated, alone and lonely. She would probably feel the same way if she were in Lorie's situation.

However, she did try to talk to Lorie. "I hope you mean it when you said you forgive me," Lorie had told her one afternoon when they were at the house alone. Their parents had taken the grandkids to the park a few blocks away.

"I forgive you, Lorie. But if you're asking me to forget what you did, that will take some time. Your accident doesn't change what happened between you and Christian," Luna said sadly.

"I know," Lorie struggled to speak. "I just need you to tell me that you don't hate me."'

"You're my sister. I can never hate you." Luna started crying when she saw tears streaming down Lorie's face.

Luna got a paper towel from the kitchen and wiped her sister's eyes and her own.

Chapter 47

No Limits

"We upgraded from 'just friends' to 'just awkward' in the blink of an eye." Unknown

She didn't know why she told Mason about her doctor's appointment. The first two times, she'd gone alone, and one other time, Pepper accompanied her. However, Pepper's free time was cut short because of her nonprofit, and Luna was still in Bluffton.

"I shouldn't have told you," she said, walking with him to his car as they left Grace Temple.

"Oh, but I'm glad you did. I would feel really bad if I found out you went to an appointment like this alone."

"I'm fine. Really, I am Mason."

"Get in the car," he ordered, opening the door for her.

Stubbornly, she got inside.

"I want you to know how much I appreciate you," she said somberly.

"Look, aren't we friends?"

"Yes, of course we are," Eliana replied.

"Well, you said your other friends couldn't go with you today, so here I am," Mason said, chuckling as he drove.

Mason sat beside her in the doctor's office after her ultrasound exam. "Is this Mr. McCoy?"

the doctor asked, seeing a nervous-looking Mason seated next to the exam table.

Eliana giggled and looked at Mason, who smiled. "Uh, no, he's a good friend."

"Oh, I see," the female doctor said, raising her eyebrows in wonderment.

"Well, as I said during the ultrasound, the fetus looks good, healthy, and is definitely growing. It's about the size of a grapefruit."

Eliana giggled. "A grapefruit?"

The doctor nodded.

"And you're sure it's a boy?" Eliana asked, looking at the doctor and then at Mason.

"Yes, but you know, of course, we can be fooled. Nothing is one hundred percent. And we've been fooled time and time again, but from what I saw on the ultrasound, here are some images," she said, passing them to Eliana, "it's a boy. See," she said, pointing at the image again and smiling.

"Wow, that's insane," said Mason, looking at the 3D images.

When he suddenly grabbed her hand, Eliana looked at him but didn't attempt to remove it. In fact, his touch made her feel relaxed and calm and no longer nervous or anxious.

"Congratulations," he said, smiling.

"Well, Mrs. McCoy, I'll see you again next month," the doctor said. "Stop at the front desk and make your appointment. Until then, continue to take your prenatals, get plenty of exercise, but rest when your body calls for it, and eat healthy."

"Thanks, Doctor," Eliana said. "I will, and I'll see you next month."

In his car, Mason congratulated Eliana again. "You good?" he asked, looking tenderly into her eyes, making her a little uneasy, but in a good way.

"Yes, look at these," she said, pulling out the images and showing them again to Mason.

"They look so real. Have you told your ex yet?" he blurted.

"No."

"When do you plan on telling him? You can't hide it much longer, you know. I mean, look—" he looked at her belly. She wore oversized shirts and sweaters now to conceal it. Whenever she picked up Khaliyah, she ensured she was covered and she didn't linger. She would pick up her little girl and get out of there quick, fast, and in a hurry. But like Mason reminded her, this could not go on forever. It was time for her to tell Khalil whether she wanted to or not.

†

Curled on her sofa, Eliana stared at the ultrasound images. "A son, I'm going to have a son," she said aloud, smiling as she thought about it.

"What did the doctor say?" Luna texted, pulling Eliana from her thoughts.

"I am doing good. Told me to keep taking my vitamins and watch my weight."

"you take the ultrasound?" Luna texted.

"Yes, I am having a boy!" She followed up with several smiley emojis.

"O M G! a boy? That is so cool," **Luna** texted.

"I know. Can you believe it? Two kids. Girl, I'm going to have my hands full," **Eliana texted.**

"Send the pics."

"Ok, I sent them."

"Oh, my gosh, look at him!" **texted Luna.** "He's going to be a big boy."

Eliana sent a laughing emoji.

"Girl, tell that man he's having a son. Don't deprive him of knowing that."

"We'll see," **texted Eliana.**

"Look, suit yourself," **Luna texted.** "I'm going to bed. This chick is tired."

"Ok, talk to you later," **Eliana texted.** "Gnite."

Chapter 48

Risk It All

"Love snuck in through the back door of friendship,
surprising us both with its unexpected arrival."
Unknown

The next few days passed swiftly. The
weather was perfect. Fall had arrived; Fancy
loved the sudden change. Humming a song by
CeCe Winans, she gathered her satchel, phone,
and purse before retrieving her cup of coffee
from the Keurig, adding tons of cream and
artificial sweetener, and off she hurried to her
car.

Today was Noah's home reveal. The renovations
were complete. She was excited but nervous. He
was expected to arrive in Memphis in precisely
an hour, and she did not want to be late picking
him up.

She was surprised when he asked her to pick
him up from the airport. Usually, he had a
driver that transported him to and from. She
wasn't complaining; she liked being with him.

She hadn't seen Hezekiah since he knocked
on her door the other night, acting a fool. Let
him act a fool with Rianna because Fancy told
Victoria that she was done after seeing them
together. Not that she wasn't already fed up with
him, but this time, she knew there would be no
turning back, no matter how much her heart

and body missed Hezekiah McCoy. It was time for her to do what Victoria told her time and time again—live life now because tomorrow was not promised to anyone.

In the car, she did one last check. She wanted to make sure she had Noah's house keys. After entrusting her to carry on the renovations in his absence and giving her access to his home, she wanted to be sure to return them today.

When she arrived at the airport, her heart raced when she saw him coming out of the airport, looking handsome as ever. The leisure suit he wore accented his tall physique.

He walked toward the car, and as soon as he got in, he leaned over and kissed her fully, long, passionately.

"Miss me?" he asked.

"Did I ever," she said, laughing, and drove off.

†

Noah paraded through the house, his eyes darting from one corner to the next, his mouth hanging open in disbelief. Each step he took was slow and deliberate as if he were trying to absorb every detail around him, his astonishment evident in every breath he took.

"This cannot be the same house," he said, looking next to him at a blushing Fancy. "Man, I can't believe it."

They explored nearly every room in the sprawling 17-room house. Fancy's decorative touches and redesigns were evident in almost every corner, giving each space a unique flair.

"You like it?" she asked.

"Do I? Are you kidding me? I freaking love it," he said as they arrived at bedroom number seven.

He scooped her up, spinning her in his arms, a laugh escaping her lips. His hands traveled down her back. With her feet dangling inches above the hardwoods, he gently kissed her lips, and then it deepened into something more heated, fiery.

"Does that answer your question, *Miz* McCoy?" he whispered, slowly lowering her until her feet touched the floor.

"Yes... yes... I think it does, Mr. Alexander."

A mischievous glint sparked in his eyes, his grin widening as he looked down at her. "What do you say then? Shall we christen this room?"

"Whatever the client wants, the client gets," Fancy flirted back as they locked lips again.

Chapter 49

It's Gonna Get Better

"I trust in God, my savior, the one who will never
fail." Elevation Worship

Today was First Lady Eliana's final meeting
as President of *The Pulpit Ladies*, the ministry
she founded and loved. Her heart ached with the
bittersweetness of the moment, but she knew it
was the right decision. Divorced and no longer
the First Lady of Holy Rock, it was time to pass
the torch.

As Eliana approached the podium, the room
fell silent, every eye drawn to the woman who
had once been the First Lady of Holy Rock. She
wore a deep navy blue dress that fell gracefully
to just above her knees. With its empire
waistline, the dress cinched just under her
bust, allowing for a flowy shape that concealed
any hint of her growing belly. Over it, she had
chosen a long, tailored cardigan in a complementary
shade, its open front cascading softly down her
sides, adding an extra layer of coverage.

Her carefully styled hair framed her face, and
her poised and confident demeanor commanded
the room's attention, ensuring the focus
remained on her words rather than her
appearance.

Her voice steady, she proceeded, "Good
afternoon, Pulpit Ladies. Being surrounded by

so many incredible women of faith is a blessing. I am sad, however, that this is our last gathering of the year. But God is good."

Many of the ladies in the room clapped and said, "Amen."

"When I knew I would speak today, my heart was drawn to Proverbs thirty-one-ten. A virtuous woman, who can find? For her worth is far above rubies. Let this verse remind you that your worth is not defined by your outward appearance, wealth, status, mistakes, or how many times you have faltered. A virtuous woman is defined by her character, her strength, and her love for God.

"Today, although I am resigning as President of *The Pulpit Ladies*, please know I am not stepping away from this ministry. I am merely stepping aside. I challenge you to carry yourselves with dignity and purpose, remembering that your worth is far above rubies because of who you are in Him.

"Before I take my seat, I'd like to express my deepest gratitude. First, to First Lady Fancy McCoy, who has been more than the best mother-in-law a woman could ask for—she is a friend, a mentor, and an incredible grandmother to my daughter." Eliana looked over her shoulder, nodded toward Fancy, and smiled.

"I want to thank Pepper McCoy, another strong woman, a good friend, and my right hand in making this ministry the success it is today. Thank you, Sista McCoy. You have faced some heavy trials, but you continue to persevere gracefully." Eliana nodded and smiled at Pepper.

Next, she looked at Luna.

"And to Luna Black, who has become like family—thank you for being my friend and an example of a virtuous woman. Your challenges since moving to this city have been what some would describe as insurmountable, yet here you are. A living example of God's grace and mercy towards us. Thank you, Sista Black, for all you do for this ministry."

"So, Pulpit Ladies," Eliana said, raising her voice and hands, "I challenge each of you to reflect on what it means to be virtuous, to let your light shine so brightly that others can't help but see Christ in you. Our worth is far above rubies—not because of what we have but because of who we are in Him. Thank you, and God bless you all."

Eliana stepped back, her heart full, knowing she had given everything she could.

After the meeting, Eliana, Luna, and Pepper lingered long after everyone had left. The fellowship hall was quiet, and the ladies gathered at one of the tables and chatted about today's luncheon, among other things.

"Do you really think she will make a good replacement?" Luna asked, speaking of the lady voted on to take Eliana's place.

"Sure, she will," Eliana said. "I have no doubt she will lead this ministry to do great things."

"Well, I know one thing, I'm still going to miss you. I know we'll still be seeing each other, but with you resigning and leaving Holy Rock, it's like losing a part of me," Pepper said, wiping a tear. "And to think, I was no longer a member here, but this ministry has still been like a lifeline."

"Me too," said Luna. "You don't have any idea how much you've helped me and so many women like me who have experienced trauma. This ministry has been a blessing. And the quarterly luncheons are the icing on the cake," she said, laughing between her tears.

"Stop it, you two. I don't want us to be sitting up here boohooing. Let's get out of here."

The ladies rose from their chairs and embraced each other in a sister group hug.

Epilogue

Because of You

"Cherish those who seek the truth, but beware of those who find it." Voltaire

Eliana paraded through the halls of Holy Rock like she had no cares in the world. The temperature outside was especially pleasant, not the typically brisk weather that fall could bring to the city.

"Is he in his office, Sista Mavis?" she asked, stopping at the front office.

"Yes, First Lady, he's in there."

"Do you know if he's by himself?"

"Yes, he is."

"Thanks." Eliana walked up the hall.

Rapidly tapping on his door, she heard him say, "Come in."

"Hello, Khalil," she immediately said, her face fixed as she stared at him.

He looked at her like he was looking at a stranger.

"Why are you looking at me like that?" she asked, standing by the half-open door.

"I don't know. You look different. But yeah, what's up? You off work early?"

"Yes, the church office closed early."

"You must have forgotten that this is my weekend with Khaliyah. You didn't have to come to pick her up."

"I know that, but I'm here for another reason. We need to talk," she said. "There's something I, something I need to tell you."

"Uh, sounds serious," he said, walking past her and closing the door.

"Have a seat," he said, pointing to the bright red leather office chair and taking a seat himself.

She sat down, carefully holding her coat together.

"What's going on? The divorce is what you wanted. I've abided by your wishes. What is it you want now?"

She sucked in a deep breath and slowly released it, rolling her eyes. "Please, get over yourself, Khalil. If I could get around this, I would, but unfortunately, I have no choice but to tell you."

"Tell me what?"

"I'm pregnant." She allowed her jacket to fall open, exposing the round belly of a woman who was entering her sixth month of pregnancy. "You're going to be a father again."

His mouth fell open, and he sprang from his chair. A haughty, deep, almost guttural laugh erupted from him, slightly scaring her.

"Is this some kind of prank because you can't be serious," he said.

"Does this look like it's a prank, Khalil?" she retorted, standing up, pulling her jacket back, and holding her belly so he could get a full look.

"This is insane," he said, stroking his head back and forth. "When exactly did you plan to share this news, Eliana? I mean, I see you're telling me now, but from the looks of it," Khalil barked, unable to take his eyes off her pregnant belly, "you've known about this for a while. *Soo,* you were pregnant before the divorce was final? Why did you wait until now to tell me?"

"What does it matter, and what did it matter *when* I told you? I'm telling you now," she said, growing irritated.

"Is it mine, Eliana? Is it?"

"What did you just say? Are you serious? You bastard!" she exploded, jumped toward him, and slapped the fire out of him.

Her face twisted with disgust. "You low down, good-for-nothing piece of slime. How dare you ask me if this is your baby." She burst into tears. "Like you don't remember the night you raped me," she said and began pounding her fists against his chest, hitting him in his face, and kicking him repeatedly with all her might.

He grabbed her wrists and held them. "You're crazy. Hah, raped you? Don't even go there," he said, biting his bottom lip. "You know I didn't rape you. You know what that night was all about, so don't even try to go there with me. You were my wife. You wanted me just as much as I wanted you. I didn't force myself on you, and you know it. Jeez, I can't believe you sometimes, Eliana."

"Let me go," she demanded, but Khalil ignored her.

"How far along are you? We've been divorced for almost three months," he snarled. "And you want me to just believe it's mine. I don't know who you could have slept with."

She looked at him with looks that could kill, as some folks would say. "Look, whatever you want to say to make yourself feel better, go for it, Khalil. I don't care anymore," she yelled.

She wrenched herself out of his grasp, fury igniting her every move. With one swift motion, she reached inside her coat pocket, yanked out the ultrasound photo, and slapped it down on his desk. Without a second glance, she spun on her heels and stormed toward the door—she took a few steps into the hallway and then stopped dead in her tracks while continuing to release one insult after another, her voice slicing through the air like a sifting blade. At this point, she didn't care who heard her or saw her.

Outside the front office, Sista Mavis pretended to fiddle with a clipboard, but clearly, she was straining to catch the heated exchange.

"Calm down, you're making a fool of yourself. You're in God's house, Eliana. Show some respect. What you're doing isn't called for. And you call yourself a First Lady," he scolded.

Eliana released a wicked laugh. "God's house? You have some nerve. You know what? You're an even bigger fool than I thought. You're nothing but a pawn in the devil's workshop," she seethed, her voice trembling with utter contempt. "You've humiliated me, embarrassed me, and ran around this church and city chasing after that two-bit slut—and who knows who else! And I'm sick of it. I'm sick of you! You, Khalil McCoy, are a disgrace. And to think you stand in that pulpit week after week and call yourself a man of God. You're a phony." Her words dripped with venom as she bared her soul, her voice growing even louder as her anger took over. "You can go straight to hell, for all I care, 'cause, *babee*, one thing's for sure, and two things are certain—I'm done with you. I just wish I wasn't carrying your baby, but here we are," she spat, her tears falling but her gaze remaining fierce.

Behind her, Sista Mavis's eyes widened, and two other clerical staff stepped out of their cubicles, gawking as they leaned in behind Sista Mavis.

Eliana wasn't finished. Her voice dropped but remained raw with emotion. "Oh, and by the way," her words chillingly calm yet her voice shaking, "if you can't tell from that ultrasound—it's a boy. I pray to God he doesn't turn out like you— or your good-for-nothing pappy." She delivered the words like a final blow, then walked away with her head high, her steps unwavering.

As she passed the front desk, she threw up a hand in a dismissive wave, ensuring her pregnant belly was front and center.

"Have a blessed day, Sista Mavis; all of y'all have a blessed day," she said, her voice cold yet laced with satisfaction, before she strutted out of the building, leaving everyone, including a red-faced Khalil, stunned to silence.

More to come in this sensational family church saga!

Words from the Author

As I continue writing about the lives of the Grahams and McCoys, I'm reminded of how imperfect we all are. We may not share the same struggles or make the same choices as the characters in these stories, but we are all flawed vessels in need of the one and only perfect God.

The beauty of it all is that we can rely on Him no matter what we face. He alone can bring perfection in His time—turning our darkest nights into days, our sorrow into joy, and doing what we believe to be impossible. But it all starts with trust—trust in His plan, in His timing, and in His power. I'll be honest; it's not always easy. However, scripture tells us *not to lean on our own understanding.* I can only speak for myself, but I've found that challenging to do at times. But even when I resist, when I don't understand, or when I try to solve things on my own, God never forsakes me. He may let me wander for a while and do it my way, but He never leaves or abandons me. I am deeply grateful for His unconditional love.

The good thing is that God doesn't discriminate. No matter what you think, I'm telling you He is no respecter of persons. What He does for one, He is well able to do for us all!

In this installment, four women face life-altering challenges—enduring sexual assault, betrayal, grief, divorce, and their mental health.

Each must find the strength to persevere and rise above their trials.

As you read each installment of the "My Son's Wife" series, I sincerely pray that you will find a message of hope even with all the drama these folks encounter.

I hope you remember that no matter how fierce the storms rage or how dark the path may seem to get in your life, with God by your side, you can make it through any trial or adversity you face. Trust Him. Call on Him. Lean into His strength. He will never fail you.

Please continue to read my literary catalog, and I will continue to write "Perfect Stories About Imperfect People Like You....and Me!"

Shelia
God's Amazing Girl

What Readers Say

"Your books are *soo* very intriguing to read while eating a hot bowl of homemade soup and cornbread with a glass of homemade ice-cold lemonade along with a slice of warm rice pudding. I love you, God's Amazing Girl!" *Carolyn Denise Rooks-Herndon*

"Shelia Bell writes characters that keep you hooked with relatable storylines. Not only do I recommend this book, I recommend this entire series. There's no way the Grahams, McCoys, and now the Blacks are letting us off this easy." *Author LaCricia A'ngelle*

"Another phenomenal story by an amazing author. This book was perfectly penned, flowed well, and kept me entertained from beginning to end..." *Charlotte*

"Shelia's mission is to write perfect stories about imperfect people. This book is no exception. The families in this story deal with a number of real-life issues, such as infidelity, suicide, dementia, and even incarceration, just to name a few. Even in the midst of these issues, God is ever-present and all-knowing in their lives, both individually and collectively." *Yvette Lewis (Sisters of Ruth Bookclub)*

Join my mailing list for literary update info at
www.sheliawritesbooks.com

Literary Catalog

My Son's Wife Series

My Son's Wife: The Beginning (Book 1)
My Son's Ex-Wife: Aftershock (Book 2)
My Son's Next Wife (Book 3)
My Sister, My Momma, My Wife (Book 4)
My Wife, My Baby...And Him (Book 5)
The McCoys of Holy Rock (Book 6)
Dem McCoy Boys (Book 7)
My Brother, Father...And Me (Book 8)
My Truth, My Time, My Turn (Book 9)
Dem Folk at Holy Rock (Book 10)
Thicker Than Water (Book 11)
Redeeming Holy Rock (12)
Whom the Son Sets Free(13)

Holy Rock Chronicles Shorts
(My Son's Wife spin-off)

Set #1
Calling Dr. Daniels
The Woman in Apartment 3D
Ruthless Rianna

Set #2
Christian Black, Esq.
If Your Price Is Right
Love Shoulda Brought You Home

Beautiful Ugly 2-book series

Beautiful Ugly
True Beauty

Adverse City Series

The Real Housewives of Adverse City 1
The Real Housewives of Adverse City 2
The Real Housewives of Adverse City 3
The Real Housewives of Adverse City 4

Young Adult Titles

House of Cars
The Life of Payne
The Lollipop Girl

Standalone Novels

Always Now and Forever Love Hurts
Into Each Life
Sinsatiable
What's Blood Got To Do With It?
Only In My Dreams
The House Husband
Cross Road
Forever Ain't Enough

Anthologies

Bended Knees
Weary to Will
Learning to Love Me
Show A Little Love (1)
Show A Little Love (2)

Nonfiction

A Christian's Perspective: Journey Through Grief
How to Live Your Life Like It's Golden

Journals

Journal Your Way Through It
Sister Sister Book Log Journal

www.sheliaebell.net

www.sheliawritesbooks.com

sheliawritesbooks@yahoo.com

www.facebook.com/sheliawritesbooks

@sheliaebell (Twitter & Instagram)

bit.ly/sheliabell

If you enjoyed this book or any of my books, please go to your favorite review site and leave a positive review!

Other links to my books

bit.ly/sheliabell
bit.ly/sheliaebell
bit.ly/sheliabn

www.sheliawritesbooks.com

#iwriteforfilmandtv
#iwritebestsellers
#iwritepageturners
#iamgodsamazinggirl

Perfect Stories About Imperfect People Like You ...and Me!